"I MAY BE FAL... IN LOVE WITH YOU."

As Patrick spoke, his fingers slid down to capture and squeeze hers.

"Oh," Angela said.

"Oh?" He only half laughed. "All she says is 'oh.'" Propping himself up on one elbow, he smiled lopsidedly down at her. "How about something more original."

How about, I'm scared to death? "We haven't known each other that long, Patrick."

We've known each other long enough to make love, he thought, but only said lightly, "Listen, we'll just leave it for now." He stroked the valley between her breasts. "There are other things to talk about...and do. Right?"

"Right," she sighed in relief, feeling his readiness against her thigh.

Later, not caring that it was too soon, or that she heard him, Patrick whispered at her temple, "I do love you, Angela. I really do."

ABOUT THE AUTHOR

Jessica Jeffries is a native Texan now living in Houston with her cardiologist husband. A former pharmacist, she left that career to realize her dream of writing fiction. She has written one American Romance and is already well into her third Superromance.

Books by Jessica Jeffries

HARLEQUIN SUPERROMANCE
71—A CERTAIN SUNRISE
136—MEMORIES TO SHARE

HARLEQUIN AMERICAN ROMANCE
22—ALL IN THE GAME

These books may be available at your local bookseller.

Don't miss any of our special offers. Write to us at the following address for information on our newest releases.

Harlequin Reader Service
P.O. Box 52040, Phoenix, AZ 85072-2040
Canadian address: P.O. Box 2800, Postal Station A,
5170 Yonge St., Willowdale, Ont. M2N 5T5

Jessica Jeffries

MEMORIES TO SHARE

Harlequin Books

TORONTO • NEW YORK • LONDON
AMSTERDAM • PARIS • SYDNEY • HAMBURG
STOCKHOLM • ATHENS • TOKYO • MILAN

Published October 1984

First printing August 1984

ISBN 0-373-70136-5

CHAPTER ONE

THE IMPACT WAS A SNAP of metal against metal, immediately followed by a grating sound along the right rear fender. Her burnt-orange Audi swerved into the left lane and back as Angela Carruthers' foot slammed on the brake. A streak of raw fear sliced through her body—she steered the car toward the freeway shoulder, her hands tight on the wheel.

Frantically she scanned the highway ahead and behind. There was nothing, not a car in sight on this early-December evening. Yet *something* had struck her car. But what? It couldn't have been another car, for she hadn't noticed one on this side of the divided four-lane for the past mile or so. As her car decelerated along the gravel shoulder, Angela glanced at the speedometer; it read thirty-five miles an hour. What had she been doing? Forty-five, fifty at most.

The Audi rolled to a stop, her heart continuing to pound furiously. She closed her eyes, drew in a deep breath and finally summoned up a semblance of control. She put the car in park and opened the door, stepping out into the crisp cool air. Tall, gently swaying pines bordered the interstate skirting St. Augustine, and they filled the air with a tangy sweetness. The quiet of the setting struck her as strange. The rustle of trees in the middle of a deserted highway was the only disturbance.

Angela walked around to the right side of the Audi and studied the rear fender for a moment, her eyes narrowing in the fading twilight. She bent a little closer, then frowned slightly as she noticed something. There it was. She ran her fingers along the fender's smooth metallic finish, feeling a gouge perhaps eighteen inches long in the paint. On closer inspection Angela discerned that where the metallic coat had been scraped away, a dark blue color marked the area. She straightened and pursed her lips, contemplating what on earth could have happened. Some object lying on the side of the highway had flown up and struck the car, most likely. Well, it didn't matter now. She'd have to see about getting the dent fixed—one more annoying detail to add to her already crammed schedule.

Turning away, she took a few steps, heading toward the driver's side of the car, slowing somewhat as her gaze swept the road behind her one last time. She squinted once more in the dim light and paused as her attention was captured by an object, perhaps fifty yards away on the shoulder. She took a few steps in that direction, unable to make out what it was. A last glimmering ray of the sun slipped through the band of pines at that moment, glinting off the object; its surface was a shiny, silver blue. So there *had* been something on the side of the highway, which had probably hit the car. Whatever it was looked sizable from here. Curiosity got the better of her and she walked on a few more yards. She wasn't about to walk all that way back, but she might as well—

Angela's heart lurched, and she froze where she was. She could see it clearly now, a silver-and-blue bicycle lying on its side, front wheel turned up at a perpendicular angle. "Oh, my God," she muttered, cold fear spreading through her veins. Suddenly, without conscious intent, she took off, running as if propelled, her auburn hair streaming behind her in the evening breeze.

She was racing faster than she ever would have imagined possible in her pumps but was aware of discomfort, of her lungs burning, her side aching from the incredible effort her body was expending. Blinking rapidly and wiping the water from her eyes, she heard her own labored breathing as she began to slow down.

She stopped, her chest heaving. Her frown deepened as she visually measured the distance from the outer lane of the highway to where the bicycle lay on the shoulder. It didn't make sense; it was too far away for her to have simply scraped up against it. But if she had hit it, then it would have slid perhaps a few feet, turned upside down even.... She turned, struggling to make out her surroundings. There was a steadily rising whine of a car approaching, then the glare from its headlights defining the grassy embankment bordering the shoulder. The car's momentum produced a gust of wind that whipped Angela's hair around her neck; then everything was still. But in that brief moment her gaze had caught a dark blurry outline on the grass several yards away.

SHE MOVED TOWARD IT, her heels wobbly on the short, springy grass, making her way carefully, afraid she would trip if she went any faster. Not until she was a few feet away did she stop, recognizing the shape that had caught her attention. She held her breath, her hands clenched at her sides as she struggled for equilibrium. She stared straight ahead, too stunned to move. It wasn't just a shape—oh, God in heaven, it was a person—whoever had been on the bicycle. A tiny moan rose from within her as she began to sway on her feet. Instinctively she sucked in a deep breath as her hand went to her throat. Her pulse pounded crazily against her palm.

A rush of adrenaline shattered her paralysis, and she took the last few steps to the figure on the ground. Her vision had adjusted to the darkness by then, and as she bent she reached out to touch the dark-blue cloth. A parka—no, the material was too thin; it felt more like a Windbreaker. There was no movement beneath it, and all at once she realized it was a child who lay there, a boy, his sandy-colored hair sticking out haphazardly around his head. He lay on his left side, cheek to the grass, right arm and leg hugging the ground; he looked almost as if he were asleep. But a dark trickle painted a line from his nostril, across his lips and down his chin.

"Oh, God." Nausea began to churn within her. "Please, dear God, please. . . ." She was unaware of the childlike tone of her voice, begging for this not to be true. Her hand over her mouth, she turned her head, closing her eyes and swallowing the watering sensation in her mouth. She was trembling; her entire body was trembling.

She turned to look at him again; he couldn't be more than nine or ten years old. Slowly, shakily, she placed her fingers around his wrist. Her heart hammered as she felt a pulse, weak, but steady. He was alive! He was alive. Lowering her face to his, she felt a brush of air against her cheek. He was breathing.

Suddenly she stood up, her eyes sweeping across the highway. Why was there no traffic? There was *no* one on the damn highway! Then she saw the shadowy outline of her own car; she hadn't yet turned on the lights. Her brain was whirling with thoughts of what she must do—what she should do. Backtrack down the highway to the convenience store and call an ambulance—but that would take time, precious time. The child was unconscious—he needed immediate attention. She knew that much. And she couldn't just leave him here alone. *Oh, God,* she prayed in agonized confusion, *please help me!*

One glance back down at the child lying on the grass was all it took to make her move. She was running again, mindless of her shoes, the uneven grass or the pebble-strewn shoulder. Quickly she reached the car, and the engine roared to life as she turned the key in the ignition, wheels churning loudly. She backed the car along the shoulder, brakes squealing as she slammed down hard on them.

She jerked open the car door and bolted out, starting down the embankment toward the boy. Suddenly she stopped. *My coat, I must get my coat.* A northeastern front had finally reached Florida's Atlantic coast yesterday, causing the temperature to drop to the low forties in one afternoon. It was supposed to be even colder tonight, probably already in the upper thirties. She had turned on the heater in the car; her coat was lying on the front seat. Racing back, she opened the car door, banging her head on the frame as she reached inside. She grunted in pain, pulling back and rubbing her forehead.

She grabbed the coat and made her way down the embankment once more to kneel beside the boy, chewing on her lower lip as she determined how to go about picking him up. She got up and flung the plaid-lined trench coat on the grass alongside him. But wait—what was she doing? What if he had a broken bone, a broken neck? Fear mingled with panic and indecision; couldn't she cause him further injury if she moved him?

She closed her eyes and forced herself to think rationally. If she left him here in the cold he might fare worse. She knew enough about shock to realize that a decrease in body temperature could be fatal. And his pulse was already extremely weak. No, she had to do it. She couldn't gamble with indecision now. The child's life was at stake.

Dropping to her knees, she studied the boy. His position didn't indicate any unnatural flexion of his limbs, or his head. It almost looked as if he'd rolled smoothly down the embankment. She reached out and rested her hand on his right shoulder, then gingerly slid her hand along his arm, pressing ever so slightly to check for any break in the bones. She felt none. She probed the rest of the small body, running her hand carefully beneath him to examine his left side. Nothing appeared to be broken. But there was still the possibility of a neck injury.

Again she closed her eyes, racking her brain for a plausible way to handle that possibility. Immobilize. She needed to immobilize his head. What could she use? There was nothing in her car except her briefcase and purse. She hugged herself, vaguely aware that she was shivering. Her fingers plied through the woolen material of her sweater, the only one she'd worn thus far this fall. Her sweater! Abruptly she stood up and pulled it over her head, the polyester blouse she wore beneath providing a flimsy shield against the biting air. But that didn't matter.

She rolled the sweater into an elongated tube, then moved closer to the child's head. With utmost care she slipped the wool under his neck, then pulling the two ends even, tied them securely just beneath his chin. She stood up and looked at the coat lying on the ground beside him. No, that wouldn't do. She grabbed it and spread it over him. Squatting, she slid her arms beneath him, every muscle in her body straining to the maximum as she lifted him, striving to maintain his position as much as possible.

He was a small child, light and not too difficult to carry. When she had him lying on his back in the front seat, his head nearest the steering wheel, she got in the driver's side and turned on the engine. She drove down the shoulder for several yards, checking the rearview mirror for oncoming traffic before entering the highway. There was none, so she made a wide circle and headed the car back the way she'd come.

She steered with her left hand, her right planted on the child's stomach so he wouldn't shift when she turned the car. The small community hospital she was heading for was about eight miles away, and it was all she could do to keep her foot from bearing down on the accelerator. Now was the perfect time to speed, but she didn't want to take any chances.

Her large green eyes were wide with tension, and her normally delicate, angular features tightened as the band of pines, now dark, rushed past the window. Unreality gripped her. This couldn't be happening to her. Only a few minutes ago everything had been normal, a perfectly predictable Saturday evening. Her day at the pharmacy had been hectic. She had thought she'd never get through filling the stack of new prescriptions that kept piling up. Things had slowed down, though, and she'd even managed to let the part-time student go home early.

Never in her wildest imaginings would she have thought. . . but of course things like this gave no warning. She had learned that basic tenet of life well enough.

Images of another sunset, another precious few minutes of wild-eyed panic, decisions, hopeless prayers, invaded her thoughts— *No, mustn't think about that.* Firmly she shoved the threatening memories to another part of her brain, a feat so often practiced these past three years that she had it down pat. Quickly, she reverted to the situation at hand. She turned off the highway and followed the road for another mile or so, seeing the neon sign for St. Augustine General well before she got there. A smaller sign below it, reading Emergency, pointed to the right. Slowing almost to a stop, Angela turned the wheel and followed the drive up the slight incline to the rear of the hospital. An ambulance was parked near the double doors, so she pulled up in front of it, opened her door and got out of the car.

ST. AUGUSTINE GENERAL was an older hospital, with no more than a hundred beds, judging from the size of it. When Angela shoved open the doors and rushed inside, her eyes adjusted with difficulty to the bright lighting. This section of the hospital appeared to be functioning on minimal staffing. Where was everyone? There was no one in sight as she half jogged down the corridor—only two white-sheeted gurneys along one wall. Well, what had she expected? She hadn't called. Still, this was an emergency room, wasn't it? A large rectangular desk stood just off to the left of the corridor, and Angela felt a surge of relief; there was someone behind it. A middle-aged woman dressed in a blue smock and white pants was casually sipping a steaming cup of coffee. Her other hand held a fat paperback book in which she appeared to be engrossed.

"Excuse me," Angela said breathlessly, resting her hands on the high desk counter. She was only vaguely aware of how she must look: her auburn hair wild and windblown, her green eyes wide in fright and fear, her white blouse hanging almost completely out of the waistband of her plaid skirt.

The woman looked up at her, lowered the book for a second, then lifted the cup of coffee and sipped loudly. "Mm-hm?"

Angela drew in a shaky breath and said, "I . . . please, I need some help. There's a child in my car. He's been hit."

Only slightly faster than she'd picked up the cup of coffee, the woman set it down. "Where are you parked?" she asked in an infuriatingly calm tone.

What was wrong with the woman? Why didn't she get off her duff and *do* something?

Forcing control into her tone, Angela answered, "Right outside in the parking lane." The woman nodded once, picked up the telephone and punched a few numbers. Absently she drummed her long red fingernails on the counter.

Angela couldn't hold back any longer. "Please, can't you do something? Isn't someone here to help?"

The woman—Mrs. Georgia Jefferson, her name tag read—calmly adjusted her large-framed glasses and said with condescending patience, "Ma'am, that's what I'm doing. Everyone is on break right now, and— Joe can you get out here? Someone is here with an injured child. Sure. Right." She hung up and looked back at Angela, her round cheeks spreading into a plastic smile. "Someone will be here right away."

Angela gritted her teeth and clenched her fists. Surely this wasn't possible. Emergency rooms were supposed to be manned at all times, weren't they? And by persons a little more concerned than this unrufflable woman. She turned, intending to run back to her car, and almost collided with a white-clad male nurse. Behind him were two female nurses, both of them sipping coffee out of take-out cups.

"Are you—" the male attendant began.

"Oh . . . ! Please," Angela interrupted, "my car is this way. He's hurt badly."

The expression on the young man's face changed instantly, and the other nurses said something to each other as Angela started running down the corridor, the attendant right along beside her.

Angela opened the car door. The attendant slid inside on the floorboards, pulling back the trench coat that still covered the boy. Angela watched as he checked for a pulse, then laid his head against the child's chest, then his face. One of the other nurses appeared, and Angela stepped out of the way, watching as they worked for a couple of minutes, positioning a board beneath the child before strapping him onto it.

"Okay, Patti," the male nurse said. "Let's go. One—two—three." Simultaneously they lifted the child, carried him inside and placed him on a gurney, the boy strapped onto the board. "Room two or three?"

Patti nodded. "Two. Elinor is already in there setting up. I told her to page Dr. Merrill. What's his pulse?" Angela was following behind, listening to the two of them talking in quick, precise medical terms, jargon she herself was familiar with, though at the moment it made no impression on her jumbled state of mind.

She felt herself fading into the background, virtually ignored for the time being, as the ER personnel took over with swift, practiced professionalism. She stood just inside the doorway of treatment room two, watching and listening to the bustle as though taking in a movie. Surely none of this had anything to do with her. But this was exactly how she had felt that other time, in another emergency room.... Again the memory, a shred of it, flitted through her brain. And again she dismissed it, quickly, efficiently.

"Miss?" The male nurse was speaking to her. Angela blinked, focusing on his face. A baby face, she noted, yet somehow strong and capable-looking.

"Y-yes?" Her voice was hoarse, and as she spoke an almost overwhelming weariness washed over her.

"How old is the child?"

Angela moved her head from side to side as though she didn't quite understand. "I...I don't know."

"Are you related to him? Can you tell us his name?"

Angela shook her head again. "No." She swallowed. "I don't know him. He...he was hit by my car."

Just then she was vaguely aware of someone brushing past her arm to enter the room. A man, tall, elegantly dressed in cream wool slacks and a navy blazer. The doctor, of course. He turned toward her as he went around to the head of the examination table, and some detached part of Angela's brain took note of the fact that he was an unusually handsome man. She watched as he spoke with the nurse who was adjusting the IV tubing. He picked up the child's arm, placing his fingers over the inside of the small wrist. Angela listened to the low, authoritative timbre of his voice, watched as his dark head moved very carefully with great assurance, his hands reaching up to remove something from around his neck, a stethoscope. Everyone was still ignoring her, but no one asked her to leave so she remained just inside the doorway, barely able to see the tiny figure who was the center of so much attention.

The matronly looking nurse, the older of the two, had begun removing the boy's clothing, including Angela's sweater wrapped around his neck. She looked at it curiously for a moment before tossing it on the table next to the dark-blue jacket.

The younger nurse finished taking the child's blood pressure, removed her own stethoscope and reported to the doctor, "Eighty over forty." She began unwrapping the cuff from the slender, naked arm.

"All right," the doctor said, straightening up and sliding his stethoscope into an outer pocket. "What do you have there, one-quarter normal saline? Okay. Leave it at fifty cc per hour. Let's get a complete blood count, stat. Call X ray and have them get ready to do a skull series. I want the results immediately."

"Yes, sir," the nurse answered crisply. She handed him a chart, and he scribbled in it for a few minutes. He turned abruptly, then stopped, noticing Angela standing just inside the doorway.

He walked toward her, and Angela's large green eyes widened in unspoken question as she looked up at him. She was scared—her whole body screamed the message. And right now she was scared to death of this tall, imposing man staring down at her, scared of what he was going to say. As a pharmacist she dealt with physicians on a daily basis, holding her own with the most arrogant and condescending of the lot. In this particular situation, however, she was at a distinct disadvantage, and she knew it. He held all the cards at the moment, but she wasn't so sure she wanted to know what they were.

"Would you care to step outside with me, please?" The question was an order. She walked ahead of him back into the bright hallway.

"Is he...can you tell me...." She could barely find her voice, so she clamped her mouth shut and looked away.

"I'm Dr. Patrick Merrill. I'm covering for Dr. Malcolm, the emergency-room physician. Can you explain what happened?"

Angela swallowed. "I...I think the child—the boy—hit my car."

Dark expressive eyebrows drew together as the doctor mulled this over for a moment. "I'm afraid I don't understand."

"I was driving down Highway 1 on my way home, when something struck my rear fender. When I got out to find out what it was I...I saw that he—the child in there—lying on the side of the road. I never saw him until then. He...uh, it's possible he ran into me. I'm not sure...." She sounded every bit as confused as she felt. She gulped once. "How...how is he?"

Dr. Merrill pursed his lips contemplatively. "He's stable at the moment. But I'll need further tests to find out his actual condition." Looking directly at her, he said, "Exactly how fast were you driving?"

Angela flinched at his unexpectedly accusatory tone, and she answered sharply. "I was going the speed limit, if that's what you mean. Fifty, no more than fifty-five miles an hour. I don't see what—"

"Did you see how he fell? Did he hit his head on impact? Was he conscious or unconscious when you found him?"

The questions were rapid-fire. Angela's head was reeling from them. "He was unconscious!" Her voice was rising shrilly. She glanced down at the floor, struggling to control the near hysteria boiling up within. Forcing herself to moderate at least her tone of voice, she continued. "I don't know exactly what happened. All I heard was a grating noise on my right rear fender. As I said, I didn't even see the bicycle until...." She looked up at him fiercely. "I don't see the necessity for all these questions, doctor. I did my best to get him here as fast as I could."

"Which was a stupid thing to do," he answered brusquely.

Angela's jaw clenched. She glared at the presumptuous man. "I resent that. I did what I felt had to be done. I took care to stabilize him as much as possible. I didn't think taking the time to phone an ambulance and wait would be the right thing to do."

The physician seem unmoved by her assertion. "Resent it or not, it was the wrong decision. The child quite probably has a concussion. He very well could have a broken vertebra. Moving a person in such a condition can result in far greater damage."

Pain flashed through Angela's forehead, and she automatically reached up to squeeze the bridge of her nose with her thumb and forefinger. Her hand was shaking, but she managed to answer as calmly as possible. "Doctor, I appreciate what you're saying, but at this moment I really don't need a self-righteous lecture. I did what had to be done at the moment. I was too far away to summon help, and I certainly wasn't going to run off and leave the child lying in the cold on the side of the highway!"

Rubber-soled shoes squeaked against the tile floor as a nurse approached them. "Dr. Merrill, station four is on line two."

"All right. I'm coming."

He turned away, walking down the corridor to the nurses' station. Angela's shoulders slumped, and she leaned against the wall and rubbed her temples, which were throbbing. The door to the treatment room opened. The nurse who had remained inside backed out, guiding the gurney into the corridor. Angela moved toward her, placing her hand on the woman's forearm.

"Please, did you find anything in his clothing? Any identification?"

"Yes. He had a YMCA card in the pocket of his jeans. His name is Rory James Williams. He's the son of one of Dr. Merrill's patients."

"I . . . see."

The nurse went around to the other end of the gurney and began to push it down the hallway. Angela followed alongside for a few steps, staring at the boy's pale face, his golden-tan hair spread against the white sheet, the delicate blue veins of his eyelids. He looked so small, so fragile. . . . She glanced away, pain searing through her at the sight of him.

"This is going to take a while. Why don't you have a seat in the waiting area," the nurse suggested.

"Yes. All right. Are you going to contact his family?"

"Of course." The nurse swung the gurney out to round a corner, and Angela stopped then, turning and retracing her steps down the corridor.

SHE WAS SITTING in a rather uncomfortable blue vinyl chair, her head resting on the wall behind her. Her hair was mussed from her absently running her hands through it. Her smooth ordinarily creamy complexion had a washed-out, almost anemic appearance. Sounds from a television, mounted on the opposite wall, drifted through the cheerless room, canned laughter totally incongruous with the situation at hand.

By now her headache had escalated into a full-blown migraine, and Angela wondered how much longer she could sit there. The thought of the young boy, still in X ray, undergoing all those tests, stopped her from giving in. She kept glancing at the clock, wondering how the hands could be shifting so quickly when time seemed to be dragging on interminably.

Strange, how crazy, how unrelated one's thoughts became at a time like this. Unbidden, Dr. Merrill's image loomed before her mind's eye. She had noticed his imposing height immediately, but little else other than his offensive grilling tactics had impressed her—or so she had thought. Now it was as if he was standing directly in front of her; she could see details of his face, his clothes, things she had given little conscious thought to when she was talking to him. Though his slacks and jacket were obviously of superior quality and design, they were badly rumpled, as though he'd worn them too long. His full head of dark-brown hair was liberally sprinkled with gray at the temples, and his squarish handsome face was deeply lined. Yet he wasn't an older man. Somehow she felt he would be in his late thirties or early forties. Odd, but she couldn't help thinking his face bespoke a life that had seen a good deal more conflict than most. Why was that? Certainly whatever he may have experienced in his professional life wasn't the only reason.

Ridiculous, Angela thought. She'd never met the man until tonight, and here she was speculating as to his character. Her nerves were as taut as strings on a bow. If only someone would just come out here and tell her what was going on! She was about to get up and speak to the woman at the desk when she heard footsteps behind her. She stood up right away, turning to see Dr. Merrill approaching.

"How is he?" she asked immediately, her brow furrowed in lines of worry and exhaustion.

"He's still unconscious," he said, stopping just in front of her. "But most of the tests look favorable. No apparent spinal injuries. There's a possible hairline fracture of the skull, but we'll need other tests. I suspect a fractured collarbone."

Angela slumped back into her chair.

"I'm concerned about what's going on in his brain, however," the doctor went on. "We need to do a CAT scan to determine if there's any internal damage. A CAT scan is an—"

"I know what it is. Do you have one here?"

"No. We'd have to take him into Jacksonville."

Angela bit her lower lip. She said quietly, "I understand you know his family. Have they been reached yet?"

"Yes. They're on the way over."

"I see." Angela looked down at her hands, then back up at him. "Thank you for telling me all this." She sighed heavily. "I'm just so thankful there was no damage done by my moving him."

"You were lucky," he inserted dryly.

Angela's gaze turned into a glare. "I really don't appreciate your condescending attitude, doctor. I'm sure you're quite a capable physician, but you have no business passing judgment, when you have no idea what really happened." She stood up then and said tautly, "Excuse me, but I'd like to—"

She stopped in midsentence at the commotion coming from the corridor. Heavy footsteps mingled with loud voices, a woman's shrill one and a deeper masculine one.

"Where is he? Where is my son?" the man boomed.

"I'm sorry, but are you Mr. Will—" the clerk began, in the same unbearably slow tone she had used with Angela.

"I'm Franklin Williams," he interrupted. "Someone called and said my son Rory is here. Where is he? We want to see him."

Dr. Merrill had already begun walking toward the admissions desk. Angela started to follow him.

"Sir, if you'll just wait a minute the doctor will be—"

"I'm not waiting for a goddamn thing! Where is my son, woman!" The counter almost shook as

Franklin Williams slammed his large meaty hand down on it.

Angela's stomach did a flip-flop, her eyes resting on the overbearing man towering over the now very intimidated Mrs. Jefferson. A woman, his wife presumably, stood nearby, her face ashen as she, too, seemed to shrink, whether from fear for her son or from her husband's threatening presence, Angela wasn't sure.

Angela's instinct was to run, for she had no desire to be a part of the scene that would undoubtedly follow. Reason, however, bid her stay; she had taken responsibility in the situation this far. She would not evade it now.

She took a tentative step forward, then stopped as Dr. Merrill suddenly faced her. He spoke in a very low tone. "Go back into the waiting room. And stay there."

Angela blinked, frowning questioningly, but he'd already turned his back and was walking toward the couple at the desk. Her pride resisted the man's unwarranted order. But something else, an instinctive caution, urged her to do exactly as he said.

CHAPTER TWO

THE RUMBLING, ANGRY VOICE bellowed again. "Where is your supervisor, dammit! I'm not standing here one more minute, do you hear— Dr. Merrill! Oh, thank God, it's you. Have you seen him? Is he all right?" Perspiration dotted the man's fleshy face as he confronted the physician.

"He's still in X ray, Frank. You can see him in a minute. Why don't you step over here so we can talk?"

From Angela's position in the waiting area, she heard their voices grow muffled, then disappear altogether as Dr. Merrill and the couple moved farther down the hall into another room, she presumed.

Shivering, she folded her arms across her chest. Her coat was still in the treatment room, but she wasn't the least inclined to go and get it; her own discomfort at the moment was unimportant.

She started walking, pacing up and down the empty waiting area with its odd assortment of bright-blue vinyl chairs and short, straight-backed blue-and-yellow-striped couches. She longed to turn off the noisy television, but the thing was mounted higher than she could reach, and she wasn't about to ask the desk clerk to do it for her. Anyway, the silence would probably be worse than that indistinguishable racket spewing forth.

She kept up the pacing, glad no one else was around to inhibit her. She was too anxious, too full of nervous energy to sit still right now. What was she doing, anyway? Why should she just follow Dr. Merrill's orders as if they constituted the only possible course of action? She could handle this situation without his running interference for her. She stopped at the end of the room and turned, retracing her steps. Sighing heavily, she grimaced. But she was doing exactly as he'd said. Admittedly, Mr. Williams's tone had been formidable enough. Perhaps it was best for Dr. Merrill to calm him down some before she spoke with the man and his wife.

Still, it irritated her that she'd just run back inside like some fugitive. Obviously the good doctor was trying to protect her. From what? Mr. Williams's irate outburst? Lord knows she'd handled her share of incensed, outraged customers over the years—not a few of those under the crazed influence of drugs. Certainly she could deal with Mr. Williams. This was asinine. She wasn't going to waste another minute pacing around in here when she could be talking to the man and his wife, explaining what had happened. She *had* to tell them, for their sake and her own.

Determinedly she marched out of the room toward Mrs. Jefferson, who was quite alert by this time. The cup of coffee and paperback were stashed out of sight. Angela was about to ask where she could find the Williamses, when a door opened down the hall and the couple emerged with Dr. Merrill. At the same moment, the nurse who had taken Rory to X ray returned, pushing the gurney toward the treatment room.

Mrs. Williams broke loose from her husband's side, rushing up to the gurney just as the nurse rounded the corner with it. "Oh, my baby," she half moaned, half wailed. "Rory, oh, Rory, baby." She sobbed, bent over the small, pale figure, reaching out to smooth her hand across his forehead.

Angela stepped back, biting her lower lip as a knot formed in the back of her throat. The woman's weeping cut through her like a hot, twisting knife. Mr. Williams joined his wife, his round face crumpling briefly when he stared down at his son. He placed an arm around his wife's shoulders for a moment, then let go. As he turned and walked back to the doctor, Angela almost cringed at the barely suppressed anger on his flushed face.

"Frank, why don't you step over here and sign the release papers so we can transfer him," Dr. Merrill said calmly. "The ambulance is already waiting, and all—"

"Is that her?" the man broke in, stopping a few feet from Angela, his livid gaze pinning her to the spot.

Angela swallowed hard, managing to say in a shaky voice, "I'm sorry, Mr. Williams. I should have met you when you first arrived. My name is Angela Carruthers. I found your son on the side of the—"

"Found him!" The huge man's voice thundered. "You almost killed my son, and you're saying you *found* him!"

Angela's eyes widened alarmingly; instinctively she stepped back. Everyone's attention focused on her, but as she opened her mouth to object, the doctor stepped forward to lay a hand on the man's forearm. "Frank, please stop shouting. It's not doing you or anyone else any good."

The man pulled his arm away, but when he spoke his tone was somewhat lower. "Give me the papers. Whatever I have to sign." Mrs. Jefferson handed him the sheaf of papers and he practically snatched them from her, giving them a cursory look then slapping them down on the counter.

"Where do I sign?" The woman showed him, Dr. Merrill standing next to him all the while speaking in an even, reassuring tone. Angela drew in a deep breath, desperately trying to pull herself together. She certainly hadn't expected this dramatic a reaction. God, he really believed she'd run over the child. That wasn't what had happened at all! Her fingers dug into the leather material of her purse, and she took a few steps closer to Mr. Williams as he handed the papers back to the clerk.

"Mr. Williams," she began softly, flinching as the man turned abruptly to face her. "I . . . ." She wiped a film of perspiration from her upper lip. I didn't hit your son. You see, he was—"

The man swung away, demanding of the doctor, "Has she had a sobriety test?"

Angela's sharp intake of breath was audible. "Wha—"

"What are you talking about, Frank?" Dr. Merrill asked, his eyes meeting the taller man's.

"I want a sobriety test, that's what I'm talking about. No drunk driver is going to run over my child and get away with it."

Angela found her voice and blurted out, "I am most certainly not drunk, Mr. Williams. And for you to—"

"Frank," Dr. Merrill interrupted, "a police report will be filed on the accident. That's routine procedure in a case like this. Whether or not you want to press charges is something you'll have to decide." He hesitated, then lowering his voice, asked, "Are you willing to put Miriam through that?" He was looking hard at the florid-faced man, his dark-brown eyes daring Williams to push the issue further.

Damn the man for continuing to interrupt me, Angela seethed. As if she couldn't handle herself in this situation. But he *did* seem to know something about this man who appeared more than eager to condemn her without the slightest shred of evidence. Reluctantly Angela held her tongue.

"Because if you are, Frank, I can tell you you'll be asking for a lot more trouble than it would be worth. This young lady brought the child into the hospital of her own free will, driving her own car. I was here when she arrived and can attest to the fact she was not drunk. I'll do a blood test on her this minute if you want."

Franklin Williams gave Angela a cursory glance, then replied in a grudging tone, "No." He massaged his damp brow with the palm of his hand, smoothing back the sparse strands of hair on his near-bald scalp. "Just get my kid in that ambulance. That's all I want."

"Would you like to talk to Miss Carruthers? You can have some privacy in one of the treatment rooms—"

"What for? What can she do now?" The man stalked away to join his wife, who was standing farther down the hallway, one hand over her eyes, shoulders shaking as she silently wept.

Angela looked down at the floor, trembling inwardly as she considered what else she could do. It would have helped so much to talk with the child's parents, commiserate over their obvious distress, tell her side of the story.

"Miss Carruthers?"

She looked up and was surprised to find Dr. Merrill still standing there. Curious, how much interest he was taking in her. Vaguely she wondered about the reason for it. Despite his concern for the Williamses, he didn't strike her as the overly sympathetic type. "Yes?"

"Are you all right?"

Angela's nod didn't bely the haunted paleness of her complexion. "I just wish I could have talked with them. To explain how it happened."

"How did it happen?"

Angela's gaze met the doctor's; at least he was interested in hearing what she had to say. Her resentment faded somewhat. "Actually, I'm not quite sure. But...I'm positive I didn't hit him. The only thing I can think that happened is that as he was riding along the shoulder he...I don't know, lost control, or wasn't paying attention to where he was, then swerved out onto the highway lane and grazed the fender of my car." She rubbed her forehead wearily. "Dr. Merrill, I know they're upset, but is there any other reason Mr. Williams won't talk with me?"

The physician sighed heavily. "He's been my patient for several years, off and on. He doesn't handle stress very well, which is obvious enough. He's had a serious heart attack because of that unfortunate personality trait, and because of his general physical health. The way he's handling this situation is about par for the course."

"I see." God forbid the man might suffer another attack because of what was happening now. No wonder Dr. Merrill had stepped in the way he had.

Angela adjusted the shoulder strap of her purse, taking a step forward. "Then I guess there's nothing more I can do here...." Her voice trailed off, the lump in the back of her throat expanding to enormous proportions as tears welled up in her eyes. She brushed her cheek roughly with the back of one hand and turned her head away. Feeling a touch on her elbow, she looked down and was surprised to see the doctor's hand cupping it. She glanced up at him curiously.

"C'mon—" he jerked his head sideways "— step in here with me for a moment."

Angela followed him to what appeared to be a small conference room. He indicated that she take a chair, but she shook her head.

"Listen," he said, "are you sure you're up to driving home by yourself?"

"I'm in perfect condition to drive, doctor," Angela said tightly, frowning. "You yourself attested to the fact that I was mentally sound when I got here." She dropped her gaze, hearing the unnecessary bitchiness in her voice. "I'm sorry. Thank you, but I'll be okay."

Dr. Merrill regarded her warily for a moment. "All right. But you do look rather exhausted."

"Well, I am," Angela answered, feeling more than ever the penetrating weariness that had set in hours earlier. Now was certainly not the time or place to give in to it. "Doctor, I...is there, will there be any way I can see Rory? I don't think—" she hesitated, swallowing hard "—I don't think I could stand not to know how he is. And Mr. Williams doesn't seem to want me anywhere near."

"No. I don't think he does." Placing a fist on his hip, he pursed his lips contemplatively, then said, "I'm calling in a specialist, of course, but I'll continue to see the child in Jacksonville." He paused. "If you'll give me a number where I can reach you, I'll give you a call as to his status."

Angela was both surprised and relieved by the unexpected offer. Somehow just knowing she would be finding out something concrete about Rory's condition was enough to ease the pressure.

"Yes. Thank you very much. I would be truly grateful if you would do so. Here." She fumbled inside her purse and withdrew a small green-and-white business card. She started to hand it to him, then reached back inside for a pen to scribble something on the back. "My home number, too."

Dr. Merrill took the card and slid it into a pocket. "I'll get in touch. Sometime in the morning."

"We're all set, doctor." The two of them turned to see an ambulance attendant at the door. "Any other orders before we leave?"

"Yes. Just a moment. I'd like to make a notation on the chart."

"Right." As the attendant left, Angela said, "I'll be waiting for your call, then, Dr. Merrill." She started to take a step forward but strangely, found she couldn't move. His brown eyes seemed to pin her to the spot as they studied her face for a moment. His gaze was disarmingly direct, penetrating; Angela felt herself growing distinctly uncomfortable. An odd sensation crept over her, but she was at a loss to explain it. As it was, he gave her no chance to contemplate her reaction. With a quick nod he turned and left the room.

She followed him into the hallway, stopping at the end of the corridor. A color-coded sign gave directions to the front lobby of the hospital. She would leave that way and walk around the building until she reached the emergency drive, where her car was parked. By that time the ambulance should have left. There was no way she could stand seeing it. Not now.

SHE AWOKE WITH A START, blinking rapidly, smarting from the bright sunshine suffusing the room through the sheer, peach-colored curtains. She bolted upright, swinging her feet to the side of the bed and starting to stand up. Then she stopped, letting out a long sigh and shoving her hair off her forehead.

It was Sunday; she hadn't overslept. But when had she gone to sleep last night? She barely remembered.... Her shoulders slumped, and she looked down at the floor, the memory of everything, the horror of it all flooding back over her. Somehow the events seemed as unreal as they had last night, almost as if she had dreamed them. She hadn't, of course. The child, the accident, the trip to the hospital, the unexpected visit from the police after she'd gotten home; they had wanted her version of the accident. All of it *had* happened. It wasn't a dream, or even a nightmare.

A knot of dread formed in her stomach, and she

glanced at the clock next to the bed. Dr. Merrill had said he would call. Soon, she hoped. The day would be unbearable if she had to wait around for hours without knowing Rory's condition, his prognosis—anything.

Well, one thing was certain. Regardless of her gratitude for the doctor's offer, she wasn't about to depend on his call alone. She didn't care about his advice to avoid the Williamses. The father couldn't be that fearsome. He had been angry enough, there was no doubt of that, but if he'd been serious he would have pressed the issue, wouldn't have backed off so quickly when Dr. Merrill asked if he wanted to file charges against her. At least she didn't have *that* to contend with.

It was almost eight o'clock. If the doctor didn't call by ten o'clock she would phone the hospital in Jacksonville herself, and if she was unsuccessful she'd drive over. Oh, what misery just to wait. Sitting up on the side of the bed, she supported herself with her hands and tilted her head back, stretching her neck to stare up at the ceiling.

Enough, she thought. *I can handle this. This is nothing, really.* In her thirty-one years of life she had already seen a good deal more than people twice her age. She had coped before—she would cope with this. She closed her eyes and squinted hard against the surge of anguish within. *If only it hadn't been a child.* She bit painfully into her lower lip, felt her heart lighten briefly as the picture of another child came to her: soft, golden-brown curls framing a tiny face, heavily fringed green eyes peering so innocently out at those around her, the world. *No!* She knew how to deal with this unwanted memory, too. *Breathe slowly, deeply. Let it out. Again and again. It will pass. As it always does.*

And after a few moments it did. Angela got off the bed and walked over to the long double window, pulling on the drawstrings. The delicate, unlined fabric of the curtains let in almost as much sunlight as when they were open, which pleased her perfectly. Light. How she loved it, any kind of light. Sunlight, twilight, moonlight. Life's light. She didn't mind it waking her in the morning. She *wanted* to get up, relished walking over to this window, her vision soaking up the endless, beckoning panorama of the Atlantic ocean. This was her breakfast, just standing here every morning, feasting on the mesmerizing, blue-green distant waves, white-capped peaks that crested then disappeared as they merged one on top of the other, finally washing onto the shore in curving lines of ivory foam. And the sound—so rhythmic, so reassuring in its constancy. Like a heartbeat.

Sometimes it seemed far longer than three years since Angela had been half owner of the small independent pharmacy on the outskirts of St. Augustine. In the beginning, of course, business had been sluggish, but that had changed due to hard work and dedication on the part of both her and Regi Donaldson.

Oregon. . . her home for many years. . . she'd left it and all the memories behind. Here on Florida's Atlantic coast life was completely different. Lovely, serene St. Augustine, the oldest city in the United States. Soft, sandy soil; towering, gently swaying pines; the ever-surging blue-green water beyond her oceanfront condominium. So soothing, so reassuring. This place was all she needed now. And the pharmacy, too, of course—her own business.

Angela stood at the window for several moments, her reflections providing surcease from the sudden, unexpected troubles that had entered her life. Then, turning away, she walked across the thick plush carpeting to the bathroom. She was beginning to feel hungry. Well, she should. She hadn't eaten a thing since yesterday at noon. And that had only been a snatched sandwich and a cup of coffee.

One thing about living alone, Angela mused as she turned on the taps for a shower, staying slender wasn't a problem in the least. She rarely cooked for herself, although cooking had always been one of her joys when she'd been married. Every once in a while she would give in to the urge, though, and have friends over for a Saturday evening meal. And on Sundays she sometimes enjoyed preparing a really good breakfast. Today, of course, would be something quick and uninvolved, for nourishment alone.

The shower was restorative, and afterward she

toweled off and put on a long terry-cloth robe.
She was padding down the stairway to the lower
level of her two-story condominium when the telephone rang. She hurried the rest of the way to
answer it.

"Angela? Is that you?" The feminine voice
sounded confused.

"Oh, Joyce. Hi." Pushing her damp hair back
from her forehead, Angela sank onto a barstool,
aware that her heart was pounding from anticipation and that she was slightly breathless.

"Did I wake you up? You don't sound like
yourself."

"No. I'm fine. But...well, I'm expecting an
important phone call, so I can't really stay on but
a second."

"Oh. I see." The question in her friend's voice
was obvious, but Angela didn't care to go into any
details at the moment.

"Well, I'm sorry to call so early. I just wanted
to know if you'd like to fill in on a foursome today. A friend of Jonathon's came in to visit Friday night. He loves tennis, and we thought—"

"No. I mean.... Listen, thanks but not today,
all right?"

"Well, yeah, sure." Joyce seemed a little offended, and Angela was instantly contrite.

"I'm sorry, Joyce, I just don't feel so hot today."

"That's too bad. Is there anything I can do? Or
get for you?"

"No, really. I'm just going to stick around the house and get some rest. Yesterday was a killer."

"Well, I've said it before and I'll say it again. You need to take more time off."

Angela, who *had* heard the familiar admonishment, or a version of it, many times before, said, "Well, I'll be resting all day today, all right?"

"Only as long as you really do just that," Joyce insisted. "Well, give me a call later. Bye."

"Goodbye." Angela hung up, then went around the bar that separated the dining area from the kitchen. She filled the glass coffeepot with water and measured fresh grounds into the filter. Opening a bag of English muffins, she split one, buttered it and slid it beneath the broiler. As she prepared her breakfast she thought over the conversation with Joyce.

She wondered about this particular friend of Jonathon's. Angela had made friends with the couple almost three years ago when she'd moved from her apartment into this condominium complex. Her relationship with the Colliers, a married couple in their late thirties, both professors at the university in St. Augustine, had developed into a close friendship over the months. Both of them, but Jonathon especially, were fond of setting Angela up with their seemingly unending supply of unattached male friends and acquaintances.

Out of a sense of obligation, Angela usually went along with their matchmaking efforts, because she often found the experiences pleasant if not overwhelmingly enjoyable. They were usually never more than one-time dates and almost always included Jonathon and Joyce. To say she wasn't in the mood for one of their setups at the moment was a gross understatement, of course, but Angela felt bad about covering up her reasons for declining. She was usually candid with Joyce, a factor that helped make their relationship as strong as it was. Nevertheless, she didn't want to go into last night's accident with her—at least not until she'd gotten more information on Rory Williams's condition.

Again she glanced at the clock; 8:20. The minutes were dragging by. She didn't think she could last until ten o'clock. She felt guilty standing here when the child was perhaps— Panic seized her, and she felt every nerve in her body tensing. She had to *do* something! If only—

The ring of the telephone broke the tense silence, and she leaned across the counter to snatch it up.

"Hello," she answered expectantly.

"Angela Carruthers, please."

"This is she." Her fingers gripped the receiver.

"This is Dr. Merrill. I'm calling about the results of the tests we've done on Rory."

"Yes...?"

"Well, it looks right now as though he's pretty much out of the woods. The CAT scan didn't show any traumatic brain damage. He did sustain quite a severe concussion, however. He also broke his collarbone, as I'd suspected.''

Angela tried to say something but couldn't find the words.

"We had a good sign from him early this morning, however," Dr. Merrill continued. "He regained consciousness.''

Angela thought she might very well slide onto the floor from the sheer relief of those words; good thing she was holding on to the counter. "Thank God," she whispered.

"Yes. It was a good sign. However, we'll be keeping him in intensive care for a few more days for observation.''

"What... what can happen? I mean, what else can go wrong?''

"Well, it's not a good thing to anticipate negative consequences.'' He hesitated, then went on, "I'm not concerned at this point about anything going wrong.''

Angela licked her upper lip. "Did... did he say anything? When he woke up? About what happened or...''

"No. I'm afraid he's experiencing amnesia. But it's not at all unusual with this type of concussion. The loss of memory is almost always short-term. And he didn't stay awake very long. Which is also expected. He'll be sleeping quite a lot for the next few weeks.''

"I see." Angela cleared her throat and struggled to pull herself together. "I.... Thank you very much for telephoning, doctor. Is—do you think I could come and see him? I would still like to talk to his parents. I want to explain how it all happened. And I would like to see Rory. Very much.'' She had to see him. She couldn't just disappear from the picture; for better or worse, her life had been deeply touched, had become irrefutably bound to that child's.

"Well...Mr. Williams is doing a good deal better this morning after I told him the news of his son's improvement. As you saw last night, he tends to overreact to stress rather dramatically. But I'm not so sure he's ready to talk to you yet.''

"I just find that so hard to understand. If it had been my child....'' The phrase struck a painful chord, but she thrust the feeling aside. "I would have wanted to know everything. Can't I see Rory at least?'' Angela's voice dropped to a hoarse whisper; she was close to tears. "It's very important that I do.'' The truth behind the words was almost unbearable. How did one describe the emotions one experienced on having been, if not the cause, then a direct factor in a child's injury, almost death? One couldn't. But she had held that child in her arms, wrapped her own clothes around his small limp body, had prayed with her entire being that he would live, be all right. In a few short, anguishing hours she had imbued him with every ounce of love she was capable of. She didn't care about his father, didn't care about this doctor—she had to see him—she *would* see him. There was no other way.

"Visiting hours are strict in the intensive-care unit," Dr. Merrill was saying. "I don't expect that the Williamses, at least Frank, would be willing to share them with you. However, could you be here at three o'clock? I'll see to it that his parents go somewhere—to eat, home to change, whatever. I'll take you in myself."

Angela was taken aback by the unexpected offer, but her reply was immediate. "Yes, of course! I'll be there."

"Just ask at the admissions desk for directions to neuro-intensive care."

"All right." Angela's voice softened. "Thank you, Dr. Merrill."

"See you later, then. Goodbye."

Angela carefully replaced the receiver, staring at it for a long, contemplative moment. A rush of emotion engulfed her, an odd combination of feelings like none she had ever experienced, let alone could put into words. Relief—immeasurable relief that Rory had improved, was out of danger. And gratitude for Dr. Merrill's unexpected generosity with his time, his understanding, a characteristic that contrasted with her first unfavorable impression of him.

There was something else, too, some other feeling toward this man that went beyond gratitude or respect. She mulled over this surprising realization. Yet that was all it was, a realization of something she didn't really want to define, had she been honest. Well, it wasn't important. Matters of far greater consequence occupied her mind right now.

CHAPTER THREE

POWDER-PUFF CLOUDS dotted a deep-azure sky. Brilliant sunshine gilded everything it touched— branches of distant, lofty fir, the calm, sparkling currents of the bay. Angela crossed the water via the connecting bridge to Jacksonville, and the hour-long drive from St. Augustine seemed much shorter today. Engrossed in thought the entire trip, she had replayed last night's events over and over and over. The loud snap and scrape against her car fender, her recognition of the bicycle, and then little Rory, lying deathly still in the grass on the side of the highway. The nerve-racking emergency-room scene, Mr. Williams's antagonistic behavior. And Dr. Merrill.

What an unusual person he was. At least he was so to Angela. His concern for the welfare of his patient was to be expected, of course. His apparent concern for her involvement in the case was surely directly related to Rory's recovery. He undoubtedly felt her presence would benefit the child; his helping her to see Rory was compelled by that overriding goal. Still, the man intrigued her.

For the second time in twenty-four hours his image came to her with unusual, almost riveting clarity. Features, posture—everything about him was as vivid as though he were standing directly in front of her. His face was handsome despite the deep grooves in his forehead, the three vertical lines permanently etched into the bridge of his nose. He had a hardened look, contradicted by an occasional softness in his dark-brown eyes, an almost melancholy look. The leanness of his body, only natural in so tall a man, lent a contrasting youthfulness to his overall appearance. But why was she dwelling on him? Angela shook her head slightly as if to toss aside the disconcerting, unnecessary thoughts.

By the time she'd crossed the bridge she had dismissed them altogether. She gave her full attention to following the directions she had scribbled down before leaving. Angela visited Jacksonville on occasion, but usually for shopping purposes, and so was familiar only with the area she frequented. Nevertheless the directions were simple, and within a few minutes she was driving into the visitors' lot in front of the multistoried hospital.

Stepping out of the car, she sensed nervous anticipation welling up within her as she locked the door. Perhaps he would be awake again; maybe she could talk to him. She had to know, had to see that he really was all right. Her steps quickened across the asphalt parking lot. She hurried up the stone steps to the front entrance.

Stopping at the information desk, Angela asked for directions to neuro-intensive care. Within moments she was on the elevator, then stepping off on the third floor and pausing for a moment to get her bearings. She glanced at her watch; it was ten minutes to three. She hoped Dr. Merrill was on time. She didn't think she could stand having to wait much longer.

As she rounded the corner and started down the short corridor past the waiting area, her footsteps slowed. Mr. Williams and his wife were seated on either end of a long couch just outside the intensive-care unit. Mrs. Williams was tapping her fingers on the arm of the tweed-covered sofa, while her husband absently leafed through a magazine. Angela stopped, wondering if she should turn and walk away. What had happened? Dr. Merrill had sounded so positive that they wouldn't be here. What a wasted trip for her to come all this way and still not be able to see Rory.

Mr. Williams looked up suddenly. Seeing Angela standing out in the hallway, he put the magazine down on the coffee table. He stood up, and once more Angela was astonished by the man's huge build. Her hands clenching, she opened her mouth to speak.

"Miss Carruthers," Mr. Williams said before she could get a word out, then added over his shoulder, "Here she is, honey."

His wife had already seen her, and was getting up off the couch. Angela frowned, glancing from one to the other, obviously perplexed by the situation.

Mr. Williams spoke up. "We know you weren't expecting us to be here. But Dr. Merrill told us you were coming. Please, can we step over here to talk?" There were others waiting for the three-o'clock visiting period, so Mr. Williams indicated a corner of the room away from the couches and chairs.

Miriam Williams glanced at Angela for a moment, and her lips twitched, spreading into a brief, tiny smile. Angela thought for a second she was going to say something, but the woman lowered her head, deferring to her husband.

Frank Williams cleared his throat rather loudly and said, "We want to apologize for our behavior last night, Miss Carruthers. We were unnecessarily rude. We were wrong not to give you a chance to speak to us."

Angela started to say something, but Mr. Williams held up a hand. "No, it's true enough. Dr. Merrill pointed out to us how anxious you were for our son's welfare. We're thankful—we want you to know this—that it was someone like you who found Rory."

Intense relief spread through Angela. She could only imagine how difficult those words had been to say, coming from such a man. "I'm happy you feel that way, Mr. Williams. Perhaps. . .perhaps I made a mistake in picking up Rory and bringing him to the hospital myself, but at the time I truly felt it was the best thing to do."

"Oh, it was." Mrs. Williams spoke up, her soft brown eyes shining moistly. "I'm sure it would have been far worse any other way. I was wondering if you could tell us please. . . how it happened."

"Of course." Angela related the incident to the Williamses in as much detail as she could recall. They listened quietly, and after she had finished the couple's eyes met, communicating some private message.

"This whole thing was our fault," Frank Williams said finally. His voice was low. Angela was surprised by the degree of contriteness in his tone. "Sometimes we— I should say, sometimes I have a hard time with Rory." He sighed deeply, shaking his head. "I had punished him for something that wasn't really that important. He's our only child and sometimes. . . well, it's hard to let him go his own way."

Angela had to admire the man's openness and honesty; the admission was obviously a painful thing for him.

"Rory was angry with his father," Miriam Williams explained further. "He just jumped on his bicycle and said he'd be back later. We started to go after him, but then decided perhaps it was better to let him go. We thought he would just drive around the neighborhood. We'd told him before he was never to go as far as the highway."

Her voice broke, and Angela reached out and placed a hand on the woman's shoulder. "He'll be all right, Mrs. Williams. I know he will."

The woman lowered her head. Just then the door to the intensive-care unit opened. A nurse stepped out and announced that visitors would be allowed for the next fifteen minutes.

"You go on," Mr. Williams said. "Dr. Merrill told us how much you wanted to see him. We'll wait till the seven-o'clock period."

Angela nodded and smiled briefly. "Thank you. Thank you very much." Preceding the nurse inside, she stopped, taking in the dozen beds along the perimeter of the room. Each patient was provided a degree of privacy, with walls on three sides of each bed and a curtain on the fourth. She had to ask which bed Rory was in, and followed as the nurse led her to a bed in one corner.

"Is he awake?" Angela asked softly.

"He wakes up now and then, but mostly he sleeps. You can talk to him, if you like. He might open his eyes."

The nurse smiled encouragingly, then walked back toward the central nurses' desk. Angela hesitated before moving around to the side of the bed, her eyes on the small boy lying in the middle of it, completely still. Ignoring the lump in the back of her throat, Angela called out to him.

"Rory?" She spoke the child's name in a normal tone, but there was no response. "Rory?" Still he didn't awaken. Very gently she picked up his right hand, which lay on his chest, and held it between her own, stroking his limp fingers. His left hand lay at his side, the IV needle taped to the top of it, near his wrist. A tremor ran along Angela's spine as she looked down at the boy whose life, by some inexplicable quirk of fate, had merged with her own. *One never knows, can never, ever predict such a happening,* she reflected somberly.

"Has he woken up yet?"

Angela turned at the sound of the deep voice behind her, suddenly remembering that Dr. Merrill had said he would be here when she came. And here he was.

"Hello. And no," she answered, shaking her head. "The nurse said he sleeps most of the time. I called his name, but he didn't respond."

Dr. Merrill picked up the chart hanging at the end of the bed, flipping it open. "Did you speak in a loud enough voice?"

"I'm...I'm not really sure. No, not really, I guess."

"Go ahead. Give it another try. Speak loudly."

Angela did so, gratified to see a fluttering of the child's eyelashes, then the gradual opening of his eyes, bright-blue eyes. He looked around in confusion for a moment, finally focusing on the figure of the doctor standing at the end of the bed. How sweet he looked, Angela thought, watching his lips move slowly as he muttered something unintelligible.

"Good afternoon, Rory," Dr. Merrill said in a cheerful tone. "How are you feeling?"

"Okay," the child mumbled, attempting a

smile. He glanced over at Angela, his eyes narrowing in puzzlement.

"This is the lady who was driving the car when you had your accident on your bicycle," Dr. Merrill told him.

Angela smiled brightly. "Hello, Rory."

"Hello." Rory's gaze was still clouded in obvious bemusement.

"Do you remember anything more of what happened to you?" Dr. Merrill asked.

Frowning, the boy cautiously shook his head. "Not too much," he answered in a soft voice.

"Well, that's all right. You'll remember everything in time. Go back to sleep now, if you like."

Already the child's lashes were drooping. His chest began an even rise and fall. "He's already asleep," Angela murmured.

"Hmm." Dr. Merrill wrote something else in the chart, then replaced it on the hook at the end of the bed. He looked up, and once again Angela felt his direct, unwavering stare. She shifted, slightly awkward in the face of his obvious curiosity.

"And how are you feeling?" he inquired, sliding his pen into the pocket of the long white coat he wore over his street clothes.

"Much better now." Angela's gaze slanted to the sleeping child. She glanced back at the physician, her brows drawing together in a questioning expression. "I thought the Williamses weren't going to be here."

He shrugged. "They wouldn't leave. So I talked to them for a while. I had to tell them you were coming."

"Yes. They said they'd spoken to you. They were very nice to me." Angela smiled ruefully. "It seems every time I turn around I'm thanking you for something. Thanks again."

"It's not necessary," he said, his expression warming a fraction as one corner of his mouth tilted into an almost smile. He seemed about to say something else, when one of the nurses at the desk called out to him.

"Dr. Merrill, you're wanted on line four."

"All right." He turned back to Angela. "Excuse me."

She watched as he approached the desk before concentrating again on Rory, reaching out to smooth her hand across his brow. He *would* recover completely; she just knew it. She *had* done the right thing, trusting her instincts in a situation fraught with confusion and unpredictable consequences. And she had been right about another thing, too. Just being here, seeing that Rory was in such surroundings, with competent, caring people, did everything in the world to ease at least some of her sense of responsibility, her worry.

There were only two more minutes of visiting time left. Angela picked up her purse, which she had laid down on the chair next to the bed, and glanced back at the desk. Dr. Merrill was still on the telephone. How odd his expression was. He had almost been smiling when he'd gone over to answer the call. Now his expression was hard, tight with tension, and something else. Anger, perhaps? He certainly didn't appear to be discussing a medical matter. She was wondering why she should even be thinking about him, when his voice rose. She caught very clearly his last words before he replaced the receiver. "*Later,* I said.... Yeah, right."

Angela looked away quickly, embarrassed that he might catch her staring at him. She rather suspected he wouldn't appreciate someone listening in on his conversations, especially this one. She squeezed Rory's hand one last time, then walked out of the small cubicle. Dr. Merrill intercepted her as she was heading for the door.

"Will you be coming back?" he asked her.

"Yes, of course," Angela said, stepping aside so the other visitors could leave. "I'm not sure when, though. I'll be at work most of the time for the next few days. I'll check with the nurses and the Williamses, of course, before I see Rory again."

His jaw worked very slightly, and Angela waited expectantly, thinking he was about to say something more. But he simply nodded once. "Good. Would you tell the Williamses I'll see them in a minute?"

"Sure. Goodbye."

Leaving the hospital minutes later, Angela found herself mulling over those last few words with Dr. Merrill. She was certain he'd had something to add. She couldn't help wondering what it could have been. The man did intrigue her. Ah, well, enough of that particular train of thought. She slid into the driver's seat of her car. It was a purely academic consideration, anyway.

Rory's condition—that was a matter far from academic. She thought of how he'd looked, his small body lying so still in the hospital bed, his wide, round, blue eyes gazing up at her with such obvious bewilderment.

Angela grew still, her hands gripping the steering wheel as tears began to course down her cheeks. The silent, steady weeping brought, at last, a real relenting of the terrible tension and strain of the past twenty-four hours. But with the tears came an even greater relief, the firm, determined closing of the door to memories she hadn't had to deal with in a long, long time. Old, useless, agonizing memories. Once more they were in their rightful place, in some unreachable, unreadable corner of her brain. And there they would remain from now on. Period.

MONDAY MORNING was busy as usual. The telephone started ringing even before the St. Augustine Apothecary opened at nine o'clock. Most of the calls were from customers wanting medications they insisted needed to be refilled immediately, but hardly any of them, Angela knew, would be picked up before five o'clock that evening.

Nevertheless, the calls were answered and taken care of promptly. Angela's insistence on thoroughness and promptness had paid off over the past year. Her business was thriving, supported by a faithful clientele of satisfied customers quite willing to pay her slightly higher prices in recognition of the reliable service she provided.

Regi was taking a day off, part of his long weekend away, so Angela was left to hold down the fort. Dorothy Evers, an affable woman in her mid-fifties, ran the register until one of the part-time high-school students came in around three o'clock. Fortunately, there were no major shipment orders needing to be priced and checked in. Both women had time to catch up on refills in the morning, so that the normal surge of new phone-ins after lunch could be handled without too much trouble. The steady traffic in the store usually left no time for either of them to go out to lunch, but Angela preferred eating in the store, anyway. A sandwich and a cup of coffee were satisfying enough to her, and besides, she liked taking advantage of the extra time to go over some of the pending paperwork that piled up in miniature mountains on a regular basis.

By one o'clock Angela had eaten lunch and reviewed the ledgers, which the accountant needed by the end of the week. She was as caught up as she was going to be for the next few precious minutes, so she decided to take further advantage of the temporary lull. Leaving the dispensary area, she walked slowly down the narrow aisles of the small pharmacy noting the occasional gaps of items out of stock.

As always, she stopped when she reached the front of the store. She paused, looking toward the back of the shop, imagining herself as a customer walking through the front door of the St. Augustine Apothecary. She hoped, she thought they would see it the way she did—a professional, full-stocked pharmacy, small but with a distinct appeal for that very reason. There was no trace, either in layout or in the staff's demeanor, of the assembly-line nature of a chain drugstore.

Competition was stiff from large pharmacies, of course, yet by offering a more personalized service to her customers she had been able to fill a need and had eventually realized the benefits of doing so. The rewards were not only financial; Angela found more opportunity to use her professional knowledge here than anywhere else she had ever worked. It was a rare, satisfying feeling, and she relished it.

"You know," Dorothy said from behind the counter, "I still can't believe what happened to you this weekend. I don't see how you held up."

Angela returned to the back of the store and stepped up to the dispensary. "It was difficult, to say the least." She sat down on a high barstool at the opposite end of the counter and kicked off her low-heeled shoes. She wriggled her toes and flexed her feet. "More than difficult—horrible. But yesterday helped. He's going to be all right. Thank God for that.''

Dorothy sipped the last of her coffee, then picked up the stack of refill cards to begin filing. ''Well, he's certainly in a fine hospital. It's fortunate he was in good enough condition to be transferred when—''

The ring of the telephone interrupted her, and Dorothy's narrow face crinkled as she smiled ruefully. ''Well, there goes the peace and quiet. At least we got fifteen minutes' worth.'' She punched the lighted button, picked up the receiver. ''St. Augustine Apothecary, may I help you? Yes, just one moment.'' She punched the hold button and turned to Angela, who was draining her cup. ''For you, line one. I'll be in the back with these.''

''Okay.'' Angela picked up a pen and pad, ready to take down a prescription order, placing the receiver between her shoulder and cheek. ''Pharmacist, may I help you?''

''Ms Carruthers?''

''This is she.''

''This is Patrick Merrill.''

Angela hesitated, a slight frown etching her brow. ''Yes?''

''Dr. Merrill. Rory's physician.''

Angela sat up straighter, her fingers still poised over the prescription pad. Her senses were suddenly acutely alert—something had happened to Rory. ''Yes? What is it? Is something wrong with him? Did—''

"No. Listen, I'm sorry. I had no intention of alarming you. He's fine. That...wasn't what I called you for."

Angela waited, truly nonplussed.

"I'm here in St. Augustine, and I thought perhaps you could join me for lunch."

She was taken aback. Certainly she hadn't expected him to say anything like that. She would never have guessed he had any interest in her apart from her connection to his patient.

She swallowed and answered in a tone that she hoped covered her inner turmoil. "Actually, I just finished eating. I don't ever take lunch, to tell you the truth. I generally don't have the time."

"I see. I'm due back in my office at three o'clock, but I'll be coming to St. Augustine again tomorrow evening. Perhaps we could make it dinner."

"Uh, well...yes, all right, then. I don't leave until after six. Would that be all right?"

"Of course. I'll phone you tomorrow afternoon, and we can discuss it then."

"All right."

"Goodbye."

"Bye." Angela replaced the receiver in its cradle, tapping the end of the pen on the counter. Dorothy was still in the back filing—a good thing. Angela wouldn't have wanted to answer any questions about the warm flush spreading upward from the base of her neck.

What on earth was wrong with her? She had no

reason to feel strange about accepting his invitation. Since she'd been widowed she'd gone out with a number of men; indeed she took this kind of thing in stride. Yet somehow she felt differently about Patrick Merrill, recognized a response toward him that had been absent with those other men. Perhaps the unusual way she'd met the man accounted for the difference. Yes, of course, that was the obvious reason for her uncharacteristic reaction to his call.

But as the telephone rang again and she reached to pick it up, a tiny voice at the back of her mind suggested, with surprising conviction, that in this case reason had nothing at all to do with it.

CHAPTER FOUR

PATRICK MERRILL SHOOK HIS HEAD in mild annoyance, inscribing blank circles on the chart page with his pen. "Wouldn't you know, just as I'm about finished."

Mrs. Royles, the charge nurse standing next to him, smiled and handed him one of her own pens. "Here you are, use this one."

"Thanks." Patrick finished the medication orders, handing the chart over to the nurse afterward.

She scanned it with a practiced eye, then sat down and began to transcribe the orders into the nursing station's record book. "Will that be all for Mr. Randolph?"

"I think so." Patrick raised an eyebrow. "Assuming our recalcitrant patient informed me of every detail of today's peculiar symptoms."

Mrs. Royles chuckled. "I'm sure he did. He never forgets a thing." She hesitated before asking, "Do you want us to phone in the lab results to your answering service or call your office in the morning?"

"Just leave a note with the office. There's no

urgency. Well, that should wrap it up—" He halted in midsentence as his name was announced over the hospital's PA system. "Now what?" he muttered, reaching for the telephone. "I thought I'd covered just about everything."

The charge nurse shrugged and smiled, continuing to transcribe the chart orders.

"This is Dr. Merrill," Patrick said, hoping there were no further problems.

"Yes, Dr. Merrill," the operator answered. "I have an outside call holding for you. I'll connect you now, if you'd like."

The caller's voice came through immediately. "Pat? Hope I didn't catch you at a bad moment."

Patrick rolled his eyes and clenched his jaw at the sound of his estranged wife's voice. "What is it, Lucille?" He grated out the words, not bothering to conceal his irritation at her untimely call. All her calls, for that matter, were untimely. He would have dearly loved to chew her out on the spot, or better yet, slam the phone down on her, but the nurse was still sitting at the desk. He held his temper.

"I just wanted to tell you," Lucille said in that languid Southern-belle tone that had long since lost its charm for him, "the pool has been getting progressively darker. Kind of a yucky green, you know? I put the chlorine sticks in like you said, but it doesn't seem to be looking any better."

"Have you called Simmons?" He was referring to the pool company they had used since the installation two years ago.

"Should I?"

The nurse got up just then, put the chart back in its slot and walked away from the desk, down the hallway. He was alone on the station for the moment, and suddenly he gave way to his temper. "Come off it, Lucille. You know damn well what to do. Don't play the helpless act with me. If you can't figure it out call Jeremy."

"You don't have to get sarcastic, Pat," Lucille said petulantly.

He could just hang up on her, but she'd manage to find him again; he knew that much. Patrick sighed heavily. "What else do you want, Lucille?"

"Nothing. You told me that if this ever happens to do something quick about it. I assumed it was pretty important. The water looks just like it did last year when we got back from L.A."

"All right. So call Simmons and have them come out as soon as possible. You could have done that on your own. And Lucille, please just leave a message with my answering service next time. There's nothing so earthshaking about the damn pool that you have to page me over the hospital PA."

"Well, I thought you'd want to know."

The perfect measure of hurt was in her tone. Closing his eyes, Patrick answered tiredly, "All right. Thank you. I have to go now."

"Goodbye," Lucille said softly.

Patrick replaced the receiver and started off down the hospital corridor. Goddamn but she was driving him crazy. He'd have to talk to George Cartwright again and see how the divorce proceedings were progressing. "Friendly divorce," was Lucille's term for it. He wouldn't mind if it was the unfriendliest one on the books if that meant he could get her out of his hair. He nodded to a lab technician he knew slightly and rounded a corner, working his way along the maze of corridors to station five, his last stop for the day in the sprawling, one-story St. Augustine hospital. He would call Angela from there.

Such a welcome thought. Just picturing her was enough to settle his mind somewhat after that unpleasant conversation with Lucille. He was planning on taking her to the The Conch Shell, an exclusive seafood restaurant he and Lucille had never visited together. The one place his wife hadn't managed to drag him, he thought sardonically.

But other than the occasional irritation Lucille caused him, such as those infuriating calls for him at the hospital—including the one in intensive care the day after Rory had been admitted—he thought very little about his soon-to-be ex-wife. Indeed, for the past couple of days he'd thought of little else but Angela Carruthers. He recalled her vividly, her gentle character, her unaffected appeal, her intelligence. He'd noticed all those characteristics about her, despite the gravity of their first meeting. Rory was doing much better now, and Patrick was thankful he'd finally been able to talk some sense into the boy's father as far as Angela was concerned. But Patrick was still concerned about her. She'd been very shaken up by the accident, and he'd been almost as moved by that fact as by his immediate medical concern for Rory.

Stopping in on Mrs. Jones, an elderly patient on station five, he looked over her chart, discontinued a couple of medications and added another, then took out the business card with Angela's telephone number on it. An unfamiliar voice answered; he was put on hold for a moment. He tapped his forefinger against the desk; silly how nervous he was.

"Pharmacist, may I help you?"

"Hello, Angela, it's Patrick."

The identification wasn't necessary; Angela recognized his voice instantly. "Hello. Is everything all right with Rory?" Her concern was sincere, but the question also provided a necessary camouflage for the anxiety she'd been battling all day.

Patrick hastened to reassure her. "Oh, yes, he's getting better. He's still not completely out of the woods, so to speak, but his condition is definitely improving."

Angela breathed a sigh of relief. "That sure is sweet music to my ears."

"I thought it would be. You haven't forgotten about this evening, I hope."

"Oh, no, of course not. What did you have in mind?"

"Do you like seafood?"

"Love it."

"Well, I thought perhaps we could drive out to The Conch Shell. Have you ever been there?"

"Yes, it's fantastic. When should I meet you there?"

"Actually, I was planning on picking you up," Patrick said tentatively.

"Thanks, but I think it would work out better if I take my own car and drive over directly from here. I'm not quite finished here—we had a rush of new prescriptions in the past half hour, and I'll have to scramble to get through all the closing procedures. Anyway, it would take me twice as long to drive home first." After a pause she said, "It's no problem, is it, if I just meet you there?"

"Of course not. Shall we meet in, say, an hour?"

"I think I can manage that. All right."

"Okay. See you there."

"Goodbye."

Angela replaced the receiver and hurriedly filled the last three prescriptions. After the final customer had been taken care of, she rushed through the closing procedures and said goodbye to Tim, one of the high-school part timers. Business had been hectic of late, a good indication for the business, of course, but the pace had gradually taken its toll on her physically. Competent as she was in handling things alone, Angela was ready for Regi to return from his vacation. So much had happened recently.

She went into the small bathroom at the back of the store, washed her face and reapplied her make-up. It was chilly out, especially at night, so she'd worn a green tartan skirt, olive silk blouse and pullover sweater, pleased to be able to wear such winter clothes of late. Much as she enjoyed the mild weather in Florida, she often longed for the more definitive change of season she'd known in Oregon.

Walking toward the car a few minutes later, Angela decided she could have chosen an even warmer outfit for the evening. The thermometer must be dipping into the upper forties, and a brisk wind made for an even chillier wind factor. But she didn't mind. The air felt refreshing after her long day, spent standing for the most part in one place, hardly lifting her head and eyes from the counter.

Angela's love and respect for her own profession weren't diminished in the least by the sometimes mundane routine, which occasionally proved tiring. Naturally, the fact that she was working for herself, on her own terms, contributed to her positive attitude. Yet she also found satisfaction in striving for accuracy, such a vital part of her profession. Most of all she valued the opportunity to dispense her hard-earned knowledge. She was fortunate, she realized, to be doing something she really wanted to do, a goal few people realized in their professional lives.

By the time she'd headed the Audi onto the

highway, darkness had fallen completely. She drove cautiously, the incident with Rory three days earlier still weighing heavily on her mind. She knew the way to The Conch Shell, having gone there on one of her "setups" with Joyce and Jonathon only three weeks ago. She had enjoyed herself, but mostly because of her good friends. Her date had been unimpressive, so much so that she couldn't even recall his face or name at the moment. Her state of mind then was definitely a contrast to her present mood. The nervousness she felt was an anticipation bordering on excitement. And she hadn't experienced that kind of excitement in a very long time.

PATRICK'S MOOD IMPROVED CONSIDERABLY after his telephone conversation with Angela. He had even managed to put that latest conversation with Lucille out of his mind.

Yet as he drove down the long, flat stretch of Route 1, his mind conjured up the same old aggravating scenarios that seemed to go on and on and on. Damn but he'd be glad when his marriage was over and done with. He just wanted out—the sooner the better. And so, apparently, did Lucille. The divorce had been her idea, anyway—only she was driving him bonkers with her neurotic hanging on, her insistence that they remain "friends," her refusal to take hold of the "different life" she had claimed was so essential to her happiness.

But then Lucille had always been one to live

with pipe dreams, never really reaching out on her own to establish independence. Patrick knew her well enough to believe she'd never change; she had always been irresponsible and flighty, given to acting on impulse and whim. He hadn't known that, when they first met, hadn't really had time to find it out. He'd been too busy, ensconced in his world at the hospital, entrenched in the never-ending routine of his second year of residency in internal medicine.

He remembered the first time he'd met Lucille, at the annual Christmas party for the hospital residents. He'd been with someone else, a nurse or lab technician, he couldn't recall—one of the few he'd seen back then. Lucille had been a fellow resident's date.

Patrick was attracted to her almost immediately, as were most of the men that night, for she was a ravishingly beautiful young woman, a masculine fantasy of feminine curves, lush flowing blond hair and flashing blue eyes. A tease, an irresistible tease, and he felt no compunction whatsoever in calling her up the day after the party. She accepted a date, and from that point the relationship quickly escalated, growing serious. Lucille was a tonic for him then, a sorely needed commitment to something other than the grim grind of his everyday world. She was also the most restless, easily bored person he'd ever known—it was all he could do to keep up with her incessant demands on his time. But that didn't matter, for she was exactly what he needed then.

He had fallen hard for Lucille, Patrick remembered, unconsciously shaking his head at the
irony. "Fallen" was an apt term, though he was
reluctant now to agree that he'd actually fallen in
love. Had he really ever loved her? He had wanted
her, that was certain, and she had definitely been a
giving woman when it came to the physical side of
their relationship. It had been wonderful to have
someone to come home to, even if coming home
happened every thirty-six hours, for his rotation
would continue for the next year and a half. It
would be better the following year, he had assured
Lucille. He would be a senior resident then, with
all the perks and privileges of that elevated status.
Lucille had been satisfied with that promise, and
they had married the next summer after only six
months of dating.

Again Patrick shook his head, thinking how ri-
diculously naive he had been, thinking he could
know everything he wanted or needed to know
about a woman in such a short time. God, he
hadn't guessed a tenth of what Lucille was all
about.

He speculated as to how long she had actually
been faithful to him. Two, maybe three years.
There was no knowing. She was a consummate
liar. He didn't believe any answer she gave him
about anything. She claimed to have had only one
affair, with Jeremy, which had started just a year
ago. "Only one." That was indication enough of
their different attitudes.

As Lucille had explained it—"excused" might be a better term—she was terribly unhappy with the role of doctor's wife. She didn't care for having to take a "back seat" to his profession. There were other things in life, things she'd always wanted. She was restless and bored and wanted to pursue her ambition to become a professional model. "Fine," Patrick had said. "You could have done that anywhere, anytime." How exactly did that justify her affair with Jeremy?

"You're simply incapable of understanding me," had been Lucille's tearful answer.

That was certainly the truth. He didn't understand a lot of things—like the fact that despite her claims of unhappiness she had enjoyed a certain prestige that went along with being Mrs. Patrick Merrill. After he'd gone into partnership in Jacksonville, Lucille had plunged right into the social scene with never a look back. She had been involved up to her neck in social functions, tennis matches at the club, luncheon after luncheon. From all outward appearances she had been completely satisfied with her life. But time and experience had shown all too well that Lucille was incapable of being satisfied—with anything or anyone. He doubted she ever would be.

Eventually Patrick had come to question his own contentment in their marriage. Admittedly much of the passion of those first few years had dissipated—he didn't really know when. He could have lived with that, he supposed. Wasn't that the case with most marriages? One couldn't expect the fireworks to last forever. Yes, he could have lived with the dwindling passion, his wife's shallow personality, her refusal to take any real initiative, despite her later protests that her marriage to him had stifled her "ambitions." But above and beyond everything, Patrick Merrill valued loyalty, in others and in himself, most of all himself. Lucille had been deficient in that quality.

Self-righteously Patrick had decided she was simply a lazy person, wanting and expecting everything to be handed to her on a silver platter. Time and hindsight had mellowed his perspective, however, so that he recognized an even more significant reason for Lucille's behavior during their marriage. Her lack of responsibility stemmed from basic insecurity about her own capabilities. That insecurity and fear had been manifest in her insistence on not having a child. Though Patrick had wanted to become a father, Lucille had been afraid of the changes a child would bring, afraid she wouldn't be able to fulfill the demands of the mothering role. Patrick had done little to help her face those fears, and now it was too late. There was nothing left between them.

He sighed heavily, for the hundredth time wishing the divorce was over and done with. He was more than ready to kiss his stale, used-up marriage goodbye, to start his life over, *really* over. But George had informed him that even "friendly" divorces took time, another month until this one would be final. One more month for Lucille to hound the hell out of him, he mused wryly.

Shaking himself out of his unpleasant reverie, Patrick slowed the car to turn onto the street leading to the oceanfront restaurant. The parking lot was crowded, but after several minutes he found a space in the back. He walked briskly through the cold, windy night to the front of the restaurant, Lucille completely forgotten. He stood for a moment inside the tiny foyer, adjusted his tie and raked a hand through his tousled hair.

The deep-tufted leather couches in the foyer were filled to capacity with patrons willingly enduring the customary wait for a table. The Conch Shell was like this almost every night of the week. And it was no wonder, Patrick thought. The food and service were worth it. His eyes were slowly searching the crowd when the door opened behind him, letting in a gust of cold air. He turned and saw Angela standing just inside the doorway, her hair a nicely tangled auburn mass around her face. She was a bit out of breath, her expression expectant, pensive, too, and he swallowed deeply as her beauty struck him fully, as if he'd become aware of it for the first time.

"Hello," he said, almost flinching as her large green eyes met his.

"Oh!" Angela smiled gently. "Hello, there. Sorry I'm late, but it took a few extra minutes to close the store."

"You're not late. I just got here myself." Patrick glanced around. "It's really crowded. I called earlier, but they don't take reservations. Why don't I leave my name at the desk and we can scrounge up a couple of seats in the bar."

"All right."

While he spoke to the hostess, Angela looked around, trying desperately to regain her composure. Even though it had only been two days since they'd met, even though a clear impression of him had lingered, seeing him was like meeting a different man, in a sense. Angela was stunned by how handsome he was. She'd noticed that before, of course, but under far different circumstances. His brown suede pants hugged his long, muscular legs, and his sport coat emphasized the impressive width of his shoulders. Angela was most decidedly impressed by his physical appearance, definitely a disconcerting admission.

The bar was as crowded as the waiting area, but Patrick managed to locate an empty table in one corner. Loud voices competed with live music reverberating from the small stage in another corner of the smoke-filled room. Angela and Patrick had to practically yell at each other to be heard.

Finally they were summoned to their table. Patrick managed to convey Rory's improved condition to Angela by that point. As the waiter handed them menus she realized that for the first time since the ordeal with Rory had begun, she felt relaxed.

"You can't imagine how happy I am to hear

about this," she said, shaking her head slowly. "Thank God he's all right now."

Patrick held back the remark he'd been on the verge of adding that Rory wasn't completely out of danger yet. The relief in Angela's expression was too gratifying to mar with any negative references to the child's condition. At the moment he was doing all right, and that was enough for her to know for now.

"How long have you lived in St. Augustine, Angela?" he asked, switching subjects.

"About three years. I'm from Oregon originally."

"Quite a ways away. How did you end up here?"

"Well, it's a long story, as they say," Angela said with a smile. She paused as the waiter reappeared and took their orders.

"Wine?" Patrick asked.

"Yes, that sounds like a good suggestion. But you choose, I trust your judgment."

Patrick decided on a California Chardonnay. They both ordered, then he returned his attention to Angela. "All right. Let's hear the long story."

"Well...." As she talked she was thinking how many times she'd delivered a version of her background to the men she'd dated over the past two years. This time was different. She found she didn't mind at all relating the details—indeed, was almost enjoying herself in the telling.

"As I said, I was born and raised in Oregon.

Just outside Portland. On vacations we often drove down here to Florida. It was my parents' favorite place, mine, too. We'd rent a beach house here in St. Augustine and stay for a week or two. It was wonderful. I suppose the memory of those days was the overriding factor in my decision to move here when I was able to start my own business. I looked around in the area and got lucky. A small, independent pharmacy was on the market and . . . I snapped it up.''

Patrick nodded. "Do you own it outright?"

"No. I'm senior partner with another pharmacist, Reginald Donaldson. I mostly manage the place, though. Regi's been pretty busy with his family this past year. He's married and has a one-year-old son. But he's an excellent worker. Very reliable.''

"And what about you? As far as a family . . . ?"

There was the briefest hesitation before Angela answered smoothly, "I'm a widow."

"I'm sorry. What happened? If you don't take it as prying. . . ."

Angela shook her head. "No, I don't mind. My husband was killed in a car accident." She linked her hands and rested her chin on top of them. "But—that's all in the past. I've started life anew, another one of those sayings.''

"It sounds as if you're not doing half badly, either.''

"I'm not." Angela laughed lightly. "The work is hard at times, but it's worth it.''

Patrick leaned forward, his eyes narrowing slightly. "You really strike me as someone who knows where she's going and what she wants out of life."

"Yes, actually I do have specific goals. I may not know exactly where I'm going, but I do like what I'm doing until I get there."

"There aren't many people lucky enough, or intelligent enough, to have gotten to that point in their lives," Patrick said.

Especially women, Angela silently added. She suspected that's what he was really thinking, yet she wasn't so sure she wanted to tackle *that* subject just now.

"And what about you, Dr. Merrill? Do you know exactly where you're going?" She smiled wryly. "I suppose that's a ridiculous question to ask a medical doctor."

Not really, he thought. *Not at this time in my life. Ask me in a few more weeks and you might get more of an answer.* He said, "Not a ridiculous question at all. Believe me, there are quite a number of frustrated physicians, though personally I'm satisfied. My practice is pretty much what I want it to be. I've worked hard to get it to that point."

"You mentioned before that you were only in St. Augustine because you were covering for another doctor. I take it you don't see patients here on a regular basis."

"No, I don't. My office is in Jacksonville."

"I see. Do you live there, too?"

"Uh-huh."

The waiter returned just then with the wine, and after a few minutes a more relaxed, easy mood was established between them. As they dined the conversation flowed more smoothly, yet something was on Angela's mind, something she couldn't manage to thrust aside, especially since her gaze was repeatedly drawn to Patrick's left hand. The fact that he wore no ring wasn't a reliable indication of his marital status, so she finally decided to broach the subject. She cleared her throat, irritated with herself for doing so, and said, "Patrick, I assumed when you told me you live in Jacksonville that you. . . well, you live alone."

Patrick hesitated briefly, enough time to mull over the answers he could have given her. "Yes, that's right," he said. It was the truth, though he realized he could have been more precise, told her that he was still technically married. He knew that concern was at the heart of her question.

Yet something held him back, something significant, to him, at that point. Even the thought of Lucille was sufficient to put a damper on what had turned into the most enjoyable evening he'd had in a very long time. To speak of her now would be, in some strange way, like inviting her to the table with him and Angela. God knows, Lucille had intruded enough on his happiness, his peace of mind. There would be plenty of time for explanations later, he thought. There was no doubt in his mind that he and Angela would see each other again. That knowledge was enough to set off a thrill of anticipation.

"Actually, I have a companion," he added, and noted the slight frown that creased her brow. He smiled. "Not that you wouldn't like him. Rusty is my very loyal, very devoted Irish setter."

Angela's expression altered immediately with this bit of news. "Really! How interesting—I absolutely love Irish setters! My parents gave me a gorgeous setter puppy on my sixteenth birthday. An odd sort of sweet sixteen present, but the best one of all. His name is Bingo."

" 'Is'? Do you still have him?"

"Oh, no. My parents keep him. He's an old man now. He couldn't come with me when I went off to college, so he became the family dog. Although I still think of him as mine. I really miss him at times."

"Tell you what," Patrick said with a grin, "how would you like to come over sometime and meet Rusty?"

"I'd love to."

"I'd even fix you dinner and demonstrate my superb culinary skills."

"Sounds fantastic."

Patrick asked a few questions about the pharmacy business, and for the next few minutes Angela told him all about her apothecary shop, her underestimation of what had turned into an absorbing, time-consuming job.

"I love it," she said. "I really do." She could have added, *it's all I have,* but that would have sounded slightly—what? *Come on, Angela, get it together.* She kept on talking, as much to cover up her own confusion as to continue the discussion.

Patrick picked up on the implication. As he listened his curiosity was piqued by this woman, truly independent. He'd never known such a woman, though admittedly he hadn't invested much time in attempting to understand the other sex, including his wife, behavior he now considered far from admirable. He was overwhelmed by a desire to know Angela, completely know her, even as he guessed that doing so would take time, perhaps a lot of it. Time he would be more than willing to invest.

CHAPTER FIVE

THE TELEPHONE WAS RINGING when Angela walked in the front door the next afternoon. Hurriedly she shrugged off her coat and piled it and her purse on a dining-room chair, grabbing the receiver on the seventh ring.

"Hello?" she said breathlessly.

"I was just getting ready to hang up," Joyce greeted her. "Sounds like you just walked in the door."

"Yeah, I did. Hang on a sec." Skirting the bar into the kitchen, she slid the telephone across the other counter and placed the receiver between her ear and shoulder.

"Okay. I'm back."

"You sound bushed."

"I am. We had one heck of a morning. Typical Saturday. If I don't get something in my stomach in the next ten seconds I'm going to collapse on this counter."

"Listen, why don't I come over? Jonathon is on the courts with Lonnie, and I've just made a delicious chicken casserole. I'll bring it over. We'll share it."

"You're on."

"Good. I'll be there in ten minutes."

"Okay. Bye."

Angela hung up, walked across the small, efficient kitchen and opened the refrigerator door. She filled a glass full of orange juice and drank it down quickly, refilled it, drained it, then placed the empty glass in the sink. She sighed, smoothing back her hair in a weary gesture.

"What a morning," she muttered, picking up her coat and purse and making her way upstairs to her bedroom. She had left the town house that morning with nothing in her stomach but a cup of coffee, thinking she'd have time to send out for something from a nearby bakery. No such luck. She had handled an unbelievable amount of business today. No sooner had she opened the front doors than a steady stream of customers filed through them. She hadn't been able to stop for a drink of water, let alone to indulge in breakfast. By noon, however, the pace had slowed down enough so that she could finish up all the last-minute refills and new prescriptions, closing the doors promptly at one o'clock. By the time she'd parked the Audi in her carport space she was light-headed from hunger.

The orange juice had perked her up a bit, though, and as she changed into a soft blue velour jogging suit, her favorite at-home attire, Angela thought how grateful she was for Joyce's timely call. How fortunate she was to have such friends.

It was hard to believe she had only known Joyce and Jonathon for just under three years.

Their relationship with her was different from anything she'd ever experienced. Joyce and Jonathon were so much a pair, so equally likable that she couldn't imagine one without the other. Of course Angela discussed some things more openly with Joyce, personal, womanly things, but aside from that both of them knew practically everything there was to know about Angela. Or, stated more precisely, all she wanted them to know.

She still hadn't discussed certain elements of her past with anyone, nor did she care to. The Colliers knew about Gordon, and about Melissa, but they had never pressed her for details of what had happened, of how she had survived that terrible period in her life. Not that they would have succeeded had they tried, for to Angela that part of her life was over and done with. She was very careful to make sure of that, and had been for the most part quite successful in keeping her memories private. Joyce and Jonathon weren't the prying sort, anyway. They simply accepted whatever part of Angela's life she had chosen to share with them. For them it was enough to be terrifically fond of her, to admire her independence, her good-natured cheerfulness that complemented their own.

In regard to Angela's social life—or lack of it, they often complained—the Colliers were persistent in their efforts to rectify it. Much as they loved her, Angela was much too serious, too stubborn about letting go and getting involved with someone. And while they admired her self-sufficiency, they also expressed the opinion that she was wasting precious years of her life. Sharing their lives as they did, with so much togetherness and happiness, Joyce and Jonathon found it difficult to believe others wouldn't want the same.

Any of Angela's arguments were useless. Rarely had she agreed with their assessment of the men they introduced her to, although she never put it quite that way to them. She admitted to herself that another time, another period in her life might have found her much more receptive to at least a few of those men. She might have found someone to develop a relationship with. But here and now, the last thing she wanted was any emotional entanglement.

Joyce and Jonathon were relentless in their "pursuit" of someone for Angela, as they put it. She was touched by their sincerity, even though she would have preferred them to give up. And so she continued to appease them, to accept the dates they arranged on a regular basis. At any rate, she enjoyed the time with the Colliers, which made the effort worthwhile.

The doorbell rang, and Angela called out, "Be right there." She ran a brush through her hair one more time before hurrying down the carpeted stairway, her stockinged feet sliding on the marble-tile entrance as she pulled open the door.

"Hi," Joyce said, moving quickly past her to the kitchen, carrying a casserole dish on a wicker tray.

"Mmm, that smells divine," Angela commented, opening a cupboard and removing plates and glasses.

"It is. New recipe. This is the second time I've made it." Joyce lifted the lid, releasing pent-up steam. "Jonathon absolutely loves it. Today, however, he's more in love with his tennis racket. He snookered Lonnie into being his partner for the tournament at the club this morning, and I guess he must be having a lot of luck or he'd be home already."

"Well, I'm glad, period. His absence is my gain. I'm starved!"

Joyce chuckled as she ladled out a huge portion of the steaming dish. Angela plopped down on the padded dinette chair and dug in. "You must be," Joyce commented. "I've never seen you attack like that."

Angela closed her eyes, held up one forefinger and chewed slowly and dramatically. She swallowed, then sipped the iced tea she had poured for both of them. "First prize. This is outta sight."

"Thanks." Joyce took an exaggerated bow, her straight, wedge-styled blond hair swinging against her cheeks, then sat down and tasted the casserole. "I agree with you completely. I've outdone myself this time."

The two women ate in silence for the next few

minutes, enjoying the gentle, unceasing rush of the surf through a slightly open window.

"Have you heard any more about Rory?" Joyce asked, tearing off a piece of French bread.

"Mm-hm. I had dinner with Patrick last night— Dr. Merrill."

Joyce looked up in surprise. "Oh. Interesting. Dare I inquire how that came about?"

"Yes, you may dare. He called me at work on Thursday to tell me Rory was doing much better, even though the neurologist is keeping him in intensive care. And...he invited me out to lunch. I couldn't go, so he asked if we could get together for dinner last night."

"I see. Where did you go?"

"The Conch Shell."

"Mmm. Nice."

Angela took another bite of food. Joyce sat back in her chair, folded her arms across her chest and said, "Well? You're not going to keep me in suspense, are you? I mean this is something new, almost weird—Angela Carruthers making a date of her very own."

Angela swallowed, grinning as she sipped her tea. Joyce's sarcastic remark was accurate enough; almost every date of hers since moving here had been initiated by Joyce or Jonathon. "I suppose you have a point. What exactly do you want to know?"

"Everything, of course!" Joyce exclaimed, throwing her hands wide. "But wait. Let's hear it over coffee."

"All right." Angela got up and went into the kitchen to start the automatic drip as Joyce cleaned up the few dishes. A few minutes later Joyce was comfortably settled on the living-room sofa, Angela across from her on the love seat. The afternoon sunlight filtered through the pale-blue curtains, casting a cool, refreshing glow about the handsomely decorated room.

Joyce tested her coffee, her soft gray eyes narrowing. "I'm really surprised, you know."

"About what?"

"Well, from what you told me before about this Dr. Merrill, you and he didn't exactly hit it off. Didn't you say you had a few words the night you brought Rory to the hospital?"

"Yes. He really did rub me the wrong way—at the time. I realize now that he was merely trying to get all the facts as quickly as possible. He's not the authoritative snob I had pictured him."

"So he just called you up out of the blue and wanted to take you out?"

Angela shrugged, sipping her coffee. "I guess you could put it that way."

"Then he's definitely interested in you."

Angela laughed. "You and your matchmaker instinct. That's *all* you and Jonathon think about, as far as I'm concerned."

"True," Joyce conceded. "We just hate to stand by and see this wonderful, beautiful intelligent woman wasting away while some poor deserving fellow could be making her happy."

Angela rolled her eyes and sighed. "Just keep on building up my ego, Joyce, keep it up. One of these days I won't be able to get my head out the door."

Joyce waved a dismissing hand at her. "And that's another thing. Are you ever going to learn to sit there and take a well-deserved compliment?" Seeing the pleading look on Angela's face, she said placatingly, "All right. Enough said. So... tell me about this Dr. Merrill. What's he like?"

"Well, as I told you, he's an internist. His practice is in Jacksonville, but he's been covering for a vacationing physician at St. Augustine General. Which is how he came to be there the night I brought Rory in. And as it turns out he's Rory's doctor."

"Mmm. That's a coincidence."

"Well, it was a good thing, in a way. He sure calmed Mr. Williams down. That man is quite excitable, to say the least. He's had a heart attack, Patrick told me."

Joyce smiled curiously. "You're already on pretty familiar ground, it sounds like—true confessions and all that."

Angela finished her coffee, setting the cup and saucer on the coffee table. "Not that familiar. We've only had one date."

"And you're going to see him again."

"I think so. He said he'd call."

Joyce slowly shook her head. "You know, I

never really thought I'd see the day you'd become seriously interested in someone.'' She eyed her friend quizzically, waiting for her to comment.

Angela refused to take the bait and changed the subject. ''So when does the new semester start, Joyce?''

''Oh, not for a while yet, but then we're off for quite a stretch. Can you believe it? We don't go back till the first week of January.'' She hesitated. ''Why do you ask?''

''Just calculating how long it will be till you get your mind on something other than my deficient social life. Not that you ever let up on the subject completely.''

''All right, all right. I'll leave you alone.''

Joyce got up off the sofa, picked up Angela's cup and saucer, went into the kitchen and put them in the sink with her own. ''Something else is on my mind, anyway. And you've heard it before.'' She began rinsing the dishes, stacking them in the dishwasher.

''Tenure,'' Angela said.

''Yeah. We're supposed to get the news in February.''

''That's a long time off, Joyce. It's not like you to waste time worrying about something you can't do anything about.''

Returning from the kitchen, Joyce plopped down in a chair. ''I know,'' she sighed. ''But this is different, Angela. It wouldn't worry me so much if it weren't both of us. I wish it could be

Jonathon this year and me the next—or vice versa.''

Angela frowned. "Surely you don't have to be concerned. You're the best world-history professor they've ever had the good fortune to have on staff. And Jonathon's classes are always packed. Those political-science students love the punishment,'' she teased.

"True, but...."

"And you've both been there seven years. That's a long time. And you're both well published. I don't see how either of you has anything to worry about,'' she insisted.

Joyce answered wryly, "You just don't know the academic field. Anything's possible. And with the current cutbacks in funding, no one knows what to expect.''

"Yes, but I seriously doubt if that will affect either of you. I mean, you're both teaching the nuts and bolts of college education. They could never replace your talent and experience.''

"Thanks, Ange. I'd love to believe you're right, but I can't ignore what's happening. I have to be realistic.''

"Well, I think for now you should just relax and enjoy the holidays. Excuse the cliché, but you'll have to cross that bridge when you come to it.''

"Yeah, that's true...."

The doorbell rang. "You're a popular lady today,'' Joyce commented.

"It looks that way, doesn't it?" Angela crossed the room to the front door. Jonathon was standing there, breathing heavily despite the cool temperature, his sweat-dampened white polo shirt half pulled out of his rumpled tennis shorts, his dark hair plastered to his scalp.

"Good Lord, Jonathon." Angela laughed. "What did you do, join a marathon after your tennis game?"

"Ha, ha." Jonathon plucked at his damp shirt and blew air through his puckered lips. "Is my wife here?"

"I'm here, all right," Joyce said, coming up behind Angela. "What happened? Why aren't you out on the courts? I thought you were on a roll."

"I still am. Our next match doesn't start for another hour, so I thought I'd run by and see if you and Angela would like to watch. If we win this one we're qualified for the next round."

"Jonathon, don't just stand there," Angela said, pulling the door wide open. "Come on inside."

Jonathon shook his head. "I wouldn't dare bring my filthy person into your lovely abode. I was on my way home for a bite to eat, but I had a hunch I might find Joyce here. And I was right. So how 'bout it? Wanna come and watch the match?"

"I'd love to, Jonathon, but I'm just too exhausted," Angela said.

"From slaving away, as usual," Joyce chided

gently. "I'll come with you, Jonathon. I want to see if you can pull this one off. Wait a second, let me get the casserole leftovers. You can finish them."

While Joyce went back to the kitchen Angela said, "Call me later when you get home, Jonathon. I want to know how it turns out."

"You bet. If we're the champs you'll have to come over and celebrate. Champagne—the works."

"You're on. It's not really fair, though, for me to be included in all the celebration, since I won't be there to cheer you on. I tell you what. If you don't win we'll celebrate, anyway. And the treat will be mine."

"What d'ya think, Joyce? Sounds like I can't lose."

"Sure does," Joyce said, stepping out onto the small private patio fronting Angela's town house. "We'll call you later this evening. Enjoyed the lunch, Angela."

"Me, too. Talk to you later. And good luck, Jonathon."

The couple walked off, latching the cedar gate behind them, Angela waving goodbye. She surveyed the multitude of potted plants, geraniums and pansies crowded against the three fenced walls, then went through her biweekly ritual of checking the soil, plucking off dead leaves, watering the plants that needed it. "Two peas in a pod" the saying came to her, and she smiled as she thought of how appropriate a description it was of her dear friends.

Amazing, really, that in a world full of broken and no-commitment relationships, the two of them had made it through sixteen years of marriage, still as devoted to each other, so obviously in love. The fact that her own marriage had been far less a success only made her friends' marriage that much more intriguing. She had often speculated about the key ingredient in their relationship, wondering if there *was* one in particular, or if sharing many interests and needs over the years had kept Joyce and Jonathon together. They had found out long ago, Joyce had confided in her, that Jonathon was sterile, and both had elected not to adopt a child. Neither felt they had missed out, for their lives were rich in experience, satisfying in so many other ways. Angela had no trouble believing her friend. Her own marriage had taught her that children have very little to do with a couple's success and happiness, contrary to old-fashioned belief. Two people had to be right for each other, and even then they had to work, really work at a good, lasting marriage. *That* was definitely not an old wives' tale.

But speculation about Joyce and Jonathon's marriage was academic; all that really mattered was the good friendship the two of them provided her. Straightening from her position over a potted geranium, Angela slapped her hands together briskly, dusting off the soil clinging to them.

Glancing at her watch, she was surprised to see it was almost three o'clock. Joyce and Jonathon had left more than twenty minutes ago. It seemed more like five minutes, but time always passed quickly for Angela when she puttered among her plants— her garden, as she thought of it. It was a relaxing, mentally restorative hobby, and she invariably felt better afterward, no matter what her condition on starting. Even today she felt refreshed, more energetic than when she'd gotten home, though much of that was due to Joyce's opportune visit.

Angela went back inside to find the number for the hospital in Jacksonville. After calling intensive care and talking briefly with the nurse in charge, she decided to drive over. Undoubtedly the Williamses would be there, but they might allow her to go in and see Rory for a few minutes. Even if they didn't, she wanted to talk to the parents again, see how they were doing, assure herself they were handling things all right. She went upstairs to get dressed; if she hurried she could be on her way in the next half hour.

MIRIAM WILLIAMS WAS SEATED in the waiting room outside intensive care and looked up from her crocheting when she saw Angela walking toward her. Angela noticed how much more relaxed the woman seemed this time. "Hello," Mrs. Williams greeted her. "How nice of you to come."

Angela sat down in the chair opposite her. "Hello, Mrs. Williams. How is Rory?"

"He's better—much better. The doctors say he'll be going to a room soon. Dr. Merrill is in with him now."

Angela nodded, surprised and more than a little intrigued by the apprehension she felt at the mere mention of Patrick's name. It was an oddly pleasant sort of apprehension, though.

"Where is your husband? Is he inside with Dr. Merrill?"

"Oh, no. He's at home taking care of a leak in the kitchen pipes." Mrs. Williams plucked at some imaginary lint on her skirt. "Somehow ordinary things have a way of intruding on even the most dramatic circumstances of our lives, don't they?"

Angela was struck by her rather philosophic tone, so at odds with her impression of the woman on first meeting. She remembered vividly Mrs. Williams's expression as she endured the foul temper of her raging, shouting husband. The woman was quiet, rather introverted, but she obviously had more depth than Angela had imagined.

Angela was about to speak, when the door to the intensive care unit opened and Patrick came into the waiting room. Quickly he scanned the visitors, and once he'd seen Angela sitting across from Mrs. Williams his expression brightened immediately. He smiled, walking toward them. Angela felt another curious flutter in the pit of her stomach. Miriam looked up and hastily stowed her needlework, moving to the edge of her seat.

"How is he, Dr. Merrill?" she asked tensely.

"He's fine." Patrick placed a reassuring hand on her arm. He looked at Angela. "Angela. How are you?"

"I'm fine. I thought I'd try to persuade Mrs. Williams to let me steal a few minutes of her visit to see Rory."

"Of course, dear," Mrs. Williams said. "He's asked about you several times. He wanted to know when the pretty lady was coming back to see him."

"Why don't you go in now while I talk with Mrs. Williams?" Patrick suggested.

"Isn't it a little early yet for visitors?"

"I'll speak with the nurse. That way Mrs. Williams can have the entire time."

"Thank you, Dr. Merrill," Mrs. Williams said. "That's very thoughtful."

Patrick returned to the two women a few moments later. He stood in the doorway, holding it halfway open, a nurse at his side. "Angela?" He beckoned her over. "Miss Carlisle will escort you to Rory's bed and make sure you don't get kicked out by any of the other nurses."

"Thanks." Angela smiled, her nervousness reasserting itself; she wondered if he'd still be there when she got back.

His next words answered her. "I'll come and get you as soon as I've finished talking with Mrs. Williams. How does a cup of coffee sound?"

"Sounds terrific."

"Good. See you in a few minutes."

Patrick walked away, and Angela followed the nurse to Rory. The child was lying on his back, his head to one side, eyes closed. He didn't look to be asleep, however.

"Rory?" Angela whispered his name; he turned his head to look at her. The tiny smile on his face was absolute heaven to her.

"Hi," Rory said, his voice somewhat hoarse. "You're the lady who was here before."

Angela smiled. "Mm-hm. How are you feeling?"

"Fine. I just want to get outta here. Do you know when that'll be?" His blue eyes grew round in expectation, as if he thought she would be the one to tell him what he wanted to hear.

"I'm sure it'll be very soon," Angela reassured him, reaching out to smooth back a lock of hair from his forehead. "Rory," she said, then hesitated for a moment. "You do know who I am, don't you?"

"Sure. You're the lady who took me to the hospital. The one who was driving the car I hit."

"That's right. I . . . I want you to know I'm very glad you're all right. You gave me quite a scare the other night. I never even saw you, you know."

Rory looked down at the bedspread. "My dad told me I oughta tell you how sorry I am. It was my fault. I wasn't supposed to be out on the highway."

"Well, it is a very dangerous place to be riding your bike. Especially at night."

"Yeah. I know." His gaze met hers directly. "I'm sorry I caused you a lot of trouble."

Angela laughed softly. "You sure did, you little devil."

Rory smiled back at her; a second later his eyes were closed. Angela gazed down at him, wondering if he was drifting off to sleep. Probably. Patrick had said that would be normal in a case like this. She moved forward a bit and smoothed her hand against the child's hair, pushing back his soft blond hair.

She was surprised when the child suddenly opened his eyes and said, "I want to see my mom."

Angela's hand froze. Her spine stiffened, and she took a half step backward from the bed. She swallowed once and stared blankly, oblivious to the effect her actions had on Rory.

Turning his head slightly, he looked curiously up at his visitor. He frowned, seeing the abrupt, radical change in her. But she really wasn't looking at him at all.

"Hey," he said. "Did you hear me? I want to see my mom. Isn't it time for her to come in now?"

Angela made no move, gave no sign that she recognized what was said or who had spoken.

"Hey, what's wrong?" Rory persisted, trying to push himself up on one elbow. The movement tripped the call mechanism pinned to his pillow, summoning a nurse from the desk.

"Did you need something, Rory?" she asked, glancing from the boy to Angela, who was still standing near the bed, rigid and stony faced. "Ma'am? Is something the matter? Are you all right?'' She touched Angela on the arm, the contact breaking her trancelike state.

"What?" Angela blinked repeatedly. "I...I'm sorry, what did you say?"

Keeping her hand on Angela's arm, the nurse turned to Rory. "I'll be right back, Rory. Your mother will be in in a few minutes to see you."

Angela summoned up a feeble smile. "Goodbye, Rory. I'll see you again—soon."

At the door the nurse asked her, "What happened, Miss...?"

"Carruthers. Angela Carruthers." Angela reached up and pushed at her hair. "Do I look that bad?" She tried to laugh lightly, but the sound stuck in her throat.

"Well, you look all right now. You sure didn't a few seconds ago."

"Why not?" The deep masculine voice came from behind, and both women turned to see Patrick.

"Is everything all right, Angela?"

"Yes, really, everything's fine. Listen, I'll just step outside to the waiting area."

Patrick looked at her with undisguised concern. "Okay. I need to check on a couple of Rory's lab results. I'll be out in a minute."

"Fine." Angela went back to the waiting room, passing Miriam Williams as the older woman went inside to see her son. She sat down on one of the empty couches, then stood up again agitatedly. She had to get hold of herself! Her insides were quivering and her throat ached unbearably with suppressed tears. Roughly she grasped at the sleeves of her sweater, taking in a long, deep breath. *Count, just count. Slowly. It always works. One, two, three. . . .*

It wasn't working; Rory's words kept echoing round and round in her head, bringing back the words she had struggled for so long to put behind her—forever. They ricocheted in her brain like some crazy, incessant chant.

"I want to see my mom." Such a simple, unforgettable sentence, so very like the one spoken by her own daughter, whose sweet, childish voice was barely audible beneath the maze of tubes and bandages. Her hand squeezing, clutching her mother's as Angela bent down, her face next to her daughter's, hope soaring within her while she waited for the next words that had never come. . . .

Angela shook her head several times, determined to rid herself of the onslaught of thoughts and emotions. The scene with Rory was unfortunate, but she wasn't about to cave in over it. In a few moments she would feel better, would have forgotten all about it; her past three years of practice would stand her in good stead. After all, look how she'd managed to get through Rory's accident. This was nothing in comparison.

Life goes on, they had all reminded her three years ago, when she'd only wanted to scream and rant and rave and tell them all to go to hell, that she didn't give a damn if life went on—for her it had stopped. But objecting to the unfairness of it all had been like beating her head against a brick wall, and she had finally relented.

Getting up one morning, after another drugged night of dreamless sleep, Angela decided that dealing with all the emotion and pain was simply too exhausting, too self-defeating. She had thought it all out, very pragmatically, and finally with one superhuman effort, determined exactly how she would carry on with her life. From that moment on there existed in her mind a figurative line of demarcation between the past and the present, the life and plans and dreams of Angela Carruthers Morrison, and the present and future of Angela Carruthers.

She abandoned her married name quite dispassionately, for it would have come to that, anyway. She was different now, and her entire life would be different from then on. She would not, she *could* not live with the memories of what she had once had. The effort to assume this new philosophy was monstrous, but worth it. Within the space of a few days Angela felt renewed again, in control of her life, in control of the emotions that had threatened to cripple her.

There were times, inevitably, when remnants of those emotions would insinuate themselves into her present life, awakening the haunting reality of the past. The events of the past week had brought an onslaught of those feelings; no wonder, really, that she had reacted so radically a few minutes earlier. She would get over it. She was so sure of that. She was only sorry others had witnessed her temporary setback.

The door hinges squeaked, and Angela turned to see Patrick coming out of the unit. His expression was sober, his gaze assessing as it focused on her.

"All finished?" Angela asked brightly.

Patrick nodded. "You look better."

"I'm fine. Ready for my cup of coffee, too."

Patrick pushed back his open white lab coat, his fists on his hips. "Angela, I get the distinct impression you're trying to cover up something. You were definitely not yourself in there."

"Would you stop?" Angela said laughingly. "This is me, isn't it? Same person you saw a few minutes ago."

"Then what was the nurse talking about? She said you looked ill. And you were as white as a sheet."

Angela waved a hand dismissively. "It. . . I just felt a little weird for a couple of minutes when I was talking with Rory. Kind of queasy. I guess tired from the day. And then there was the long drive over."

Patrick came closer. "All right. Let's get you that coffee. And something to eat, too."

As they walked together down the corridor to the elevators, Angela's anxiety eased. It *had* been a long day. Maybe he was right. A little nourishment might make a big difference. They stopped at the elevators, and Patrick pressed the Down button.

"I've got a better idea than the hospital coffee shop, if you're interested," he said.

"What's that?"

"You could come over to my place and meet Rusty. I'll fix you a cup of espresso to go with dinner. How does leftover homemade spaghetti sound?"

"Fantastic. You're making me hungry just mentioning it."

"Good." The doors opened. Patrick followed Angela inside the crowded elevator. "Let's get the hell out of here and do something about it."

As the elevator doors closed and they began the six-story descent, Angela leaned against the wall, ready to forget everything that had just happened. She looked up at Patrick and smiled. He smiled back at her, squeezing her elbow, and she felt better, much better. It *would* be all right, she reassured herself, the scene a few minutes earlier already fading from her mind.

CHAPTER SIX

THE CONTEMPORARY CLUSTER HOME Patrick lived in was located in a bay-front subdivision some fifteen minutes from the hospital. Following his Mercedes, Angela absorbed the night-shrouded details of the new complex. Each building or single unit had been designed to fit into a cohesive ambience of brick, wood and lush, generous landscaping—the whole imparting an enduring quality. After several turns Patrick swung into a private driveway, activating the garage door automatically. He parked inside while she pulled into the driveway.

"Come on back," Patrick called out to her. "I almost never use the front door," he said, opening the gate to the backyard. "In fact, I usually go through the connecting garage door, but I want to make introductions first."

"It's really lovely here, Patrick," Angela said, waiting as he opened the door that revealed a surprisingly large, completely fenced backyard. An Irish setter bounded toward them to sit at Patrick's feet, his tail snapping back and forth as he eyed the unknown visitor with suspicion.

"Okay, Rusty. It's all right. Settle down." The beautiful, russet-haired setter ducked his head submissively, and Angela took Patrick's cue to follow him inside the yard.

"Hi, there, Rusty," she greeted the dog, smoothing her hand over the crown of his head and down the sleek, sinewy neck. "He's absolutely gorgeous, Patrick."

"Thanks. I happen to think so myself."

"How old is he?"

"Almost four. I've had him for about three and a half years now. Got him when he was almost six months old."

Angela appraised the dog. As a teenager, after she'd gotten her own Irish setter, she'd spent hours poring over books on the breed, comparing her own puppy to the champions. "From everything I know of the breed, he appears to have a perfect conformation. Do you ever show him?"

"No. I don't have the time. I just keep his gorgeousness all to myself. Come on, let's go inside. It's getting chilly standing here." He was right, she thought. The cold front that had moved in last week seemed to be here for at least a while longer.

As Patrick hung their coats up in a hall closet Angela walked slowly through the spacious, expertly decorated rooms. His footsteps echoed on the parquet floor of the atrium, muffling as he stepped down into the sunken living room.

"Your place is wonderful, Patrick. I was impressed just driving down the street, but this is something else. Did you decorate it yourself?''

Patrick smiled ruefully. ''Unfortunately I can't take the credit. It was all done by one of my patients, payment for several months' treatment.''

Angela perused the room appreciatively. ''Well, he repaid you with a first-class job, that's for sure.''

''Can I get you something to drink?''

''Are you having anything?''

Patrick rubbed his hands together briskly, walking over to an enclosed bar at one end of the room. ''Yeah, I think I will. I keep a well-stocked bar, so take your pick.''

Angela considered a moment. ''Can you make a kir?''

''Sure can. White wine or vermouth?''

''Wine, please.''

''Coming up.''

Angela sat down on the couch, her hands automatically stroking the navy velour fabric. Patrick stepped from behind the bar to the stereo system a few feet away, and instantly soft, soothing strains of classical guitar filled the rooms. Quiet, peaceful music, she thought. Like the man himself.

''Here you are,'' he said, setting her drink down on the low solid-oak coffee table.

''Thanks. Is there a view of the water?'' she indicated the one large bay window. ''I noticed we were getting closer to the bay as we drove over.''

''Yes, as a matter of fact I'm very close to it.

The one advantage to the place I couldn't pass up. Here, I'll open the curtain.''

It was as if he had unveiled a painting, a breath-taking black-velvet backdrop adorned with twinkling harbor lights and the distant inky shimmer of the water.

Angela's intake of breath was audible. ''Unbelievable.'' She turned to him. ''I do believe you have it all here, Dr. Merrill. Your home is fantastic.''

Patrick swallowed deeply as he looked at the poised, beautiful woman staring up at him, her green eyes so alive, so intelligent and full of curiosity. She was right; at that moment he did have it all. He'd always been aware of the charm and loveliness of his surroundings, yet until tonight he hadn't really thought of this as his home. Despite having lived here almost three months, he often felt like a stranger, as if he'd taken up residence in a very nice, very accommodating but very impersonal hotel. Tonight he was aware of an entirely new feeling; her presence established warmth and familiarity, the missing ingredients. With that realization came, for the first time in months—years, really—a glimmer of the happiness that had eluded him. He smiled, a wide, handsome smile that erased years from his face.

''Yes,'' he said slowly. ''I think you're right. Although I never knew it until now.'' He was looking at her very intently, and suddenly Angela became uncomfortable. She moved toward the coffee table, picked up her drink and took a sip. The momentary discomfort passed, yet she was surprised by what he'd just said, wasn't too sure what to make of it. She should say something, respond in some way, she thought, but how?

In the next second Patrick spoke, relieving the momentary strain of silence. "Tell you what. I'll start getting dinner ready. It should only take about twenty minutes or so."

"Great. Do you need me to help you?"

"Oh, no. I'm a very fussy and very private cook. The kitchen is strictly my domain."

"I see," Angela said, raising one eyebrow and smiling. "Well, then, Dr. Merrill, I shall keep my distance."

"The television control is on the end table next to you, and I've got an entire library in the next room. Why don't you just kick off your shoes and get comfortable?"

"That sounds like a fantastic suggestion," Angela said, immediately removing her shoes. "My legs have been killing me all day."

"I'll get started, then."

She watched him leave the room and thought, for what must have been the twentieth time since she'd met him, how unusual a man he was. Certainly he wasn't the least bit like her late husband. Gordon had never lifted a finger in the kitchen, let alone offered to cook anything for the three of them. It wasn't his duty, he had reminded her, ignoring the fact that she'd been every bit as busy, if not more so, than he. Angela had a sudden, clear picture of him, his handsome face, his easygoing charm. A real liberal, he'd publicly declared himself on numerous occasions. Liberal with himself and his personal needs and desires. Oh, yeah, he'd been liberal, all right.

She leaned farther back on the comfortable couch, staring out the window, concentrating on the chords of the music floating through the room from every direction. She shouldn't be thinking these things. She should be enjoying the moment, not allowing an intrusion of the past. Yet it really wasn't as disturbing an intrusion as she would have expected. This was one of the few times she had ever reflected on hers and Gordon's relationship with such clearheaded dispassion.

She was so different now from what she had been while married to Gordon that it was hard to believe. Had she simply been naive at the time, or afraid? Afraid that if she complained too much about Gordon's lack of attention she would lose him completely. The mere thought of raising a child alone had been enough to make her ignore the dissatisfaction, the unhappiness in their marriage. Now, of course, she realized she could have made it alone, providing as much of a home for Melissa as her daughter had had with both parents.

There was a whistle from the doorway, and Angela spun half-around on the couch. "Oh!" she exclaimed, her self-conscious grin turning to one of amusement at the sight of Patrick in a chef's apron, ladle in one hand, wine bottle in the other. "Sorry, I didn't hear you."

"You sure didn't. I said your name three times. I wanted to know if you prefer red or rosé wine. I have a nice Cabernet Sauvignon."

"That would be fine. Is it all ready?"

"Soon. Are you doing all right?"

"Sure."

"Good. It won't be but another five minutes or so."

Angela returned her gaze to the window, her train of thought interrupted. Which was fine, she mused. She had no desire to ruin a perfectly good evening with such useless reminiscences. Still, it was reassuring to know she had just spent several minutes thinking about Gordon and feeling nothing, no emotion whatsoever. But enough was enough. Reaching for an architectural magazine on the coffee table, Angela thumbed through it, her appetite growing stronger by the minute as a result of the delicious, spicy aromas emanating from the kitchen. She was grateful when Patrick appeared a few minutes later to announce dinner was ready.

The meal was delicious, and Patrick was genuinely flattered by Angela's unending compliments on his culinary talents. She ate everything on her plate, then asked for seconds, which definitely impressed him. Lucille had had the annoying habit of loading her plate only to toy with the food. As if he had sent out some telepathic message, the telephone rang. Patrick had a gut-deep hunch about the identity of the caller.

"Excuse me," he said to Angela as he went to the kitchen extension, hoping against hope that he was wrong. He wasn't. But he had no intention of putting up with any of Lucille's shenanigans tonight, and after one curt, to-the-point sentence, he hung up. He hadn't even listened to what she had to say, and prayed fervently that she wouldn't immediately phone him back.

"Sorry, Angela." Patrick sat back down and picked up his fork. "My answering service."

When Angela nodded her understanding, Patrick felt a pang of guilt over the white lie. He had yet to tell Angela he was still married. He should do so. Yet it seemed highly inappropriate for him to blurt out, "That was my wife calling," without going into a lengthy explanation of why he hadn't said anything about Lucille until then. His reasons might be selfish, but he just couldn't abide the thought of Lucille spoiling another moment of his newfound happiness. Damn, but she had an uncanny knack for picking the wrong time to bother him.

He was determined not to let his irritation get the best of him, though, so he smiled at Angela and said, "More?"

"Are you kidding? I won't be able to walk if I eat another bite."

Angela pushed her plate back, and Patrick got

up and took both their plates to the kitchen. "It was absolutely delicious," she told him, following him with the rest of the dishes.

"Either you really liked it—" Patrick ran water over the plates "—or you're trying to flatter me. Either of which, of course, I don't mind in the least."

"Well, believe me, I'm not just trying to flatter you. Where did you learn to cook that way, anyway?"

From necessity, he thought ironically, but instead he said, "Talent. Pure and simple artistic talent."

Angela laughed heartily. "Leave it to a man to turn ordinary cooking into an 'art'!"

"Aha! Caught you there. Now she calls it ordinary. Before it was superb, delicious, etcetera etcetera."

"A trap," Angela protested, her eyes narrowing. "You set me up for that one."

Patrick started putting the dishes in the dishwasher. "I finally got the truth out of you, that's all that matters." He glanced at Angela, who was taking in every detail of the spacious, well-equipped kitchen. "What are you thinking?"

"Just that you have every possible item a person—or a culinary artist, I should say—could want in here."

Patrick shut the dishwasher door, then washed his hands under the faucet. "You're right. I do. I guess I went overboard. But then with my schedule I need all the help I can get.''

"How long have you lived here?''

"Three months. They only opened this section five months ago.''

Angela nodded and walked back into the dining room, picked up the napkins and returned them to the kitchen. "Where do these go?''

"Just lay them on the counter,'' Patrick answered, thinking that she should have said something else, something like, Oh? And where did you live before? He would have told her then, but she said nothing more, and the moment passed. Back in the living room he offered her an after-dinner drink, which she declined.

"When is your partner coming back from his vacation?'' he asked, sitting on the opposite end of the couch from her.

"Monday, thank goodness. I'm more than ready for *that*.''

"You don't work tomorrow, do you?''

Angela opened her eyes wide and shook her head. "God, no. Are you kidding? I'm not completely crazy.''

"Then how would you like to go for a drive with me? I like to take Rusty for a run on the beach occasionally. It's supposed to warm up a bit tomorrow. We could make a day of it, or a half day, if you like.''

"I'd love it. I'll tell you right now, though, that

my feet won't hit the floor until at least ten o'clock in the morning.''

"That's fine. I've got some things to do around here first. I could pick you up around one. How does that sound?''

"Fine." She paused, looked out the window and said almost wistfully, "It's great, isn't it, having a view of the water?''

"It is. Do you have one?''

"Mm-hm. The ocean. It's what I wake up to every morning." She drew in a deep breath and let it out slowly. "It's what gets me going.''

Patrick's voice was low and unintrusive as he asked, "You almost sound as if you need that. Something to get you going.''

Angela continued to stare out the window, the twinkling lights fascinating, mesmerizing her. "Yes, I suppose I do. But everyone needs something, don't they?''

Patrick didn't answer right away, just rested his eyes on her profile, his interest piqued by this woman he knew so little about, yet whom he felt so close to at that moment. "I guess so," he said quietly, noticing that she didn't appear to have heard him.

Where is she right now, he wondered, wanting to know more, much more about her, yet instinctively understanding that she wasn't the type to open up easily about her feelings. That was all right; he had no intention of prying or asking more of her than she was ready to reveal. That would come in time. And he was willing to wait. It was sufficient, for now, simply that she was with him. He was still concerned, however, about what had happened earlier that day at the hospital.

She sighed, then turned to him, her eyes bright, her expression apologetic. "I'm sorry. I was lost in thought there for a moment. Were you saying something?"

Patrick shook his head. "No. I was thinking, too."

"About what?"

"Oh, just remembering the way you looked today when you were visiting Rory."

Angela laughed lightly. "Was it that bad?"

"I didn't say bad. Disturbed, maybe. Or upset."

"You're too used to hearing patients complain of symptoms all day long, doctor," she teased him. "There was nothing wrong with me. Really, I was just a little tired. When I'm tired I look it. I get sort of pale."

"Ashen would be a more accurate description." He hesitated before saying, "You were frightened of something, weren't you?"

"No, I wasn't frightened!" The harshness of her tone surprised them both, and instantly she smiled self-deprecatingly. "Well, all right, maybe I was. It was nothing important, though."

He shrugged. "Okay, I give up. I'm prying. I apologize."

His backing down was the right tactic, for Angela said, "No, you haven't pried. I realize you were concerned, but...well, it's something I'm not used to talking about, that's all."

Patrick said nothing, just watched as she returned her gaze to the window. After several minutes of silence she added, "I was remembering the night my husband was killed." She paused, surprised that she was saying this. But he didn't seem the type to forget or let matters drop altogether, and she needed to give some sort of explanation. "I spent a lot of time in the hospital, in intensive care. Everything just sort of came back, and...I don't know...."

"I understand." His voice was so full of compassion that she suddenly felt a tightness in her throat. But as sincere as he was, he really didn't understand. There was no way he could, for he could only sympathize with what she chose to tell him. And she had only told part of the truth. The other part was buried too deeply, much too deeply. She would never, ever discuss it with him.

As it had earlier today at the hospital, the memory washed over her, a real-life image, every detail as clear and precise as if the scene were being played out at that very moment. Another intensive-care unit, cold and sterile, a claustrophobic cave of strange odors, fluorescent lights, the constant beeps and whirs of life-sustaining machines. Everywhere machines. And in the midst of it all, her daughter, Melissa, her small body almost hidden by a mass of tubing and catheters and bandages.

Angela was forced to wait outside as a code-blue team worked on her only child, pumping her full of fluids and medications, inflating her lungs with precious oxygen. Then miraculously, Melissa's heartbeat returned to a normal sinus rhythm; she began breathing on her own and regained lucidity. Angela was allowed to go to her. Melissa's lips moved, and her mother bent low, her ear hovering just above the little girl's mouth. "I want my mommy." Her last words, almost the same as Rory's that afternoon.

Angela placed a shaky hand over her mouth, struggling to stem the tears, furious with herself for allowing the memory to get to her again. The distant harbor lights blurred, and she blinked hard, felt a tear coursing down her cheek. She swiped at it with the back of her hand and turned to Patrick with a false grin.

"I'm sorry. I'm acting like an idiot."

"You have no reason to apologize. When did the accident happen, Angela?"

"Almost three years ago. I'm really much better than I seem. I mean, it doesn't bother me too much. Unless something provokes—you know, some unwanted memory. I'm sorry I got all emotional like that."

"As I said, you have no reason to apologize whatsoever. I admire you very much, Angela. Not many people would have had the courage and strength to go on as you did. I'm sure it required a tremendous amount of strength and effort.''

Angela nodded, thinking of those first few hectic, confusing months before she made up her mind to move to St. Augustine. "It did. But I'm here now, and all that's behind me. Thank God.''

Something in her tone struck him as peculiar. He couldn't put his finger on exactly what it was, but the feeling was there nevertheless. He just wondered if it really *was* all behind her now.

Angela glanced at her watch. "Good Lord, I didn't realize how late it is! I'd better get going.''

Much as he would have liked to, Patrick didn't try to persuade her to stay. Besides he would be seeing her tomorrow. That was only a few hours away now. "I'll get your coat.''

He helped her on with it, and when his fingers brushed across her shoulders she was aware of her response, unmistakably sensuous. For an instant she regretted that she had to leave so soon.

"Thanks,'' she said. Patrick opened the back door, and Rusty roused himself from his curled-up sleeping position, trotting over to them. Angela petted the dog's head. "Better get some rest, Rusty. You have a big day in front of you.''

As if he understood completely, Rusty barked, and both Angela and Patrick laughed. Angela's tension dissipated, and she smiled as she opened her car door. "I'll see you tomorrow, then.''

"I'm looking forward to it.'' Patrick shut the

door for her and stood watching as she backed down the driveway to the street. He *was* looking forward to it, much more than she could know. A tinge of a smile touched his lips. A long-forgotten feeling of warmth was beginning to flicker and grow inside him, and that pleased him immensely. At length he turned to walk back to the house.

CHAPTER SEVEN

DESPITE HER CLAIM that nothing could get her out of bed before ten o'clock, Angela found herself wide awake at eight-thirty the next morning. She lay for a few minutes, her eyes closed tightly, willing herself to go back to sleep. Her brain, however, wouldn't cooperate, and after a few minutes of tossing and turning she gave up the effort, deciding she'd do better up and about.

She got out of bed, slipped into her robe and stretched her arms high over her head, twisting a little from side to side. Walking over to the window, she drew back the curtains and looked out toward the ocean. Fluffy pillow clouds dotted the cerulean sky; the sun's rays shimmered across the gently cresting waves. How wonderful to wake up this way, mildly excited, anticipating. Satisfaction spread through her as the memory of last night came back. She recalled every detail of Patrick's face, the deeply etched lines at the corners of his expressive brown eyes, his lightly curling hair dipping across his forehead. She was really attracted to him—there was no question about that—physically, and for a far more compelling reason. They seemed to connect, to share understanding and respect for the differences and similarities in each other's personalities.

Since Angela had known him such a short time, this realization was more than encouraging; it was heartening. Never had a relationship with a man shown such promise so early, except maybe hers and Gordon's. But certainly she and Gordon had shown less and less promise as a couple as time wore on. Her husband had been forever trying to change her, to "improve" her, as he so graciously put it. And Lord knows she had tried, right up until almost the end. Hard to believe now that there was a time when she would have done anything in the world Gordon Morrison wanted her to do.

Angela stared vacantly into the distance, remembering all the times she had given in to him, acquiesced to his every whim and demand. Gordon's decisions had always dominated in their relationship, encompassing just about everything the two of them did. It had been Gordon's decision for them to have a child, though Angela had agreed with that one wholeheartedly. She could excuse a lot of her submissiveness on the basis of her youth—nineteen years old when they'd gotten married, not nearly old enough to know her own mind. Gordon had been older, twenty-five, and at that time in her life twenty-five had seemed to represent so much experience, knowledge. In some ways, she admitted, the first two years of their marriage had been good. She and Gordon had shared many happy times, and she hadn't doubted that she loved him. Later, once Gordon's career had taken off, he had become more demanding, more serious, bringing home the same domineering attitude he was developing in his work.

He grew harder and harder for Angela to live with, yet she had tried, really tried, for the sake of their marriage, their child and the love they had once given so openly.... Thinking about all that now, however, served no purpose. She wondered why she was letting her thoughts drift in that direction. She rarely thought anything at all about her marriage.

Memories and bits and pieces of scenarios from her past kept creeping up on her, more and more in the past few days. Odd how her mind worked. As long as she had remained uninvolved with anyone emotionally, she had managed to block out the past and all the emotions memory evoked.

Reaching up with one hand, she raked her fingers through the hair at her nape. Interesting idea. The obvious implication was that she was no longer uninvolved as far as a man-woman relationship went. She and Patrick were just getting to know each other. It wasn't feasible or realistic for her to assume they were involved. Yet that was how she felt....

Turning away from the window, she reveled in the now-familiar tingling sensation, an anticipation of the day ahead, an eagerness to see Patrick, be with him again.

THE MORNING WENT SLOWLY BY, and Angela was alternately impatient and glad of the fact. On the one hand she wished she had agreed to get together with him earlier, but on the other hand she was grateful for the time to herself. After a huge, satisfying breakfast—her appetite was improving by leaps and bounds lately—she set about straightening the town house, taking care of the laundry and a small amount of ironing, going over her personal finances.

At one o'clock she went back upstairs to change into a pair of jeans, a blue-and-white-striped cotton blouse with a navy sweater tied around her neck and a comfortable pair of runners. She had swept her hair up into a topknot, applied a light amount of makeup and was on her way downstairs when the doorbell rang. Angela took the steps two at a time, and when she opened the door her face was slightly flushed, her expression expectant.

Joyce and Jonathon were standing on the patio, dressed in matching tennis outfits, their "uniforms," as they termed them, each holding a racket and a can of tennis balls.

The words came out before Angela had time to think. "Oh...it's you."

Jonathon turned his mouth down and raised his eyebrows at his wife. "We've made a great impression, haven't we?"

His tone was teasing, but Joyce said, "Have we caught you at a bad time, Angie?"

It wasn't unusual for the couple to appear on her doorstep at odd hours of the day unannounced, something Angela really didn't mind. In fact, she had encouraged the informality, insisting she enjoyed their spontaneous visits as much as the planned ones. She felt embarrassed now by her less-than-enthusiastic greeting, and hastened to open the door wider. "No, come on in. I'm sorry I sounded so—"

"Disappointed," Jonathon finished for her, walking in behind his wife. He flopped down familiarly into a wing-backed chair in the living room, and Joyce was quick to scold him.

"Jonathon, don't be so brash." She turned to Angela. "I'm really sorry we barged in on you. We've got a court reserved for one-fifteen— thought you might like to join us. If you've recovered from yesterday, that is."

Angela loosened the sleeves of her sweater from around her neck. "As a matter of fact, I'm completely recovered, but I'd like to make one thing perfectly clear. And I don't want to have to say it again. You guys are welcome here any time of the day or night. Period. So don't be making any more excuses."

Jonathon winked at his wife. "She's gonna eat them there words some day, mark my word."

"Now, Jonathon, you just hush," Angela scolded, then smiled at both of them. "Can I get you anything to drink before you go play?"

"Does that mean you're not interested?" Joyce

asked, sitting on the arm of the chair Jonathon occupied.

"I can't," Angela replied, walking into the kitchen and opening the refrigerator door, pulling out a large pitcher of tea. She got glasses down from a cupboard shelf, speaking to them through the open bar. "I've got plans. In fact—" she glanced at the clock above the fireplace "—he'll be here in about one minute."

"So we should be on our way," Joyce said, starting to get up.

"No, stay. I'm pouring you both a glass of iced tea. Just the way you like it. Besides, I want you to meet him."

Husband and wife looked at each other, their expressions identical, a mixture of genuine surprise and curiosity. This was definitely a first-time experience with their single friend.

"Who's 'him'?" Jonathon asked.

"The doctor who saw Rory Williams in the hospital last week," Joyce explained.

Angela brought them both their glasses of tea. Jonathon said, "You've been seeing him?"

"I suppose you could say that. We had dinner at The Conch Shell Friday night, and he made dinner for me at his place last night."

"My, my," Joyce exclaimed. "Things are progressing. Come on, Angie, you weren't tired at all yesterday. Why didn't you tell us what you were really up to?"

Angela laughed. "I wasn't lying to you—I was

exhausted. But I went to the hospital later to see Rory. Patrick was there, and he asked me over. It wasn't a planned date.''

The doorbell rang just then; Angela's hand automatically went to her hair, a gesture that escaped neither Jonathon's nor Joyce's attention.

Angela was somewhat taken aback as she opened the door to see Patrick standing on her patio, looking over the array of plants and flowers with interest. Casually dressed in a green-and-blue plaid flannel shirt, snug jeans and worn sneakers, he wasn't at all the serious, careworn doctor Angela was used to seeing. There was a boyishness about his appearance that was immensely appealing, and she felt her stomach flip-flop, a physical response that grew stronger every time she was with him.

''Hi,'' she said, smiling brightly.

Patrick smiled back. ''Am I on time? I didn't wear a watch.''

''You don't need one, in that case. It's exactly one o'clock. Come on in. I'd like to introduce you to a couple of friends.''

Patrick followed her inside, taking in the details of her home. Joyce and Jonathon were standing up when Angela led Patrick into the living room. As introductions were made all around, Joyce winked approvingly to Angela.

''These two highly renowned professors are my very best friends,'' Angela explained to Patrick. ''I don't know what I'd do without them.''

"I'd say vice versa," Jonathon put it. "Except that it would be a vast understatement. This here's one heck of a terrific lady," he added, sliding an arm around Angela's shoulders.

"Jonathon, don't you think you're exaggerating just a little?" Angela asked.

"Not in the least."

"Where are you two off to?" Joyce asked deliberately, to distract Jonathon. She took the empty tea glasses into the kitchen.

"The beach," Patrick said. "We're taking Rusty for a run—that's my four-year-old Irish setter, who at this moment is furiously pacing up and down the back seat of my Bronco."

"Well, you couldn't have picked a better day," Joyce commented. "The weather is absolutely marvelous. Which, by the way, reminds me that we ought to get going, Jonathon." She added to Patrick, "The tennis courts are the main attraction around here. If you're not there on the dot for your reserved time, whammo, somebody else takes over." She tugged on Jonathon's sleeve. "Come on, Johnny, let's hook 'em."

"Okay. Nice meeting you, Patrick. Listen, communal dinners are pretty popular among the three of us. Why don't you and Angela plan on having a meal with us sometime?"

"Thanks. I'd enjoy it."

Joyce rolled her eyes heavenward at her husband's presumptuous invitation and gave him a shove on the back. She looked over at Angela.

"We really would love to get together sometime. Now come on, Collier, let's get outta their way. Move it."

"Bye," both of them said in unison. After they'd left Angela chuckled, shaking her head. "A couple of nuts. Lovable ones, of course." She sobered and said, "Perhaps Jonathon came on a little strong about the dinner.... I mean, you've only just met them."

Patrick smiled. "They're nice people. I wouldn't mind at all taking him up on the invitation. What better excuse to be with you?"

Angela's face colored a little at the unexpectedly forthright statement, and she self-consciously ducked out to the kitchen for her purse and sunglasses. "All set," she said.

"Then let's hit the road." Patrick opened the front door for her with a flourish.

THE SMOOTH, SANDY STRETCH OF BEACH was gloriously deserted, for the time being, at least. But the sky had changed radically in the past thirty minutes. As Angela and Patrick strolled along, heavy, billowing clouds were moving inland and the azure morning was quickly shading into a cold, steely gray. The breeze had picked up, was now almost a brisk wind, and the waves thundered along the shoreline, sending out giant sprays of water.

Angela wasn't bothered in the least by the unexpected change of weather, as she loved the outdoors, respected the ocean in all its various moods.

Rusty was insatiable, flaunting his freedom, reveling in it. He scampered along the shoreline, jumping sideways as a wave crashed a few feet away, then dashing headlong to meet the next. Angela and Patrick followed at a walk, already tired out from an impromptu race from which Rusty had clearly emerged the winner. Angela buried her hands in the pockets of her cardigan and kicked at a rock, sending it skimming across the sand for several yards.

"Nice kick," Patrick commented.

"Thanks. I'm a pretty good rock kicker." She tilted her head to one side. "I don't suppose that sounds particularly impressive."

"Believe me, I'm impressed."

Angela chuckled. "Well, I get enough practice. I should be good at it."

"I take it you come here often."

"Pretty often. But not necessarily here. I know just about all the beaches in St. Augustine. I don't think there's one I'm not familiar with." She looped her hair back behind one ear; it had long since come undone in the persistent wind. "But yes, I do come often. Do you?"

"Mm-hm. Mostly for Rusty's benefit. He's so used to his weekly runs, he'd curl up and die if he didn't get them." Patrick looked upward, squinting slightly. "It's a shame the clouds moved in."

Angela turned her face into the salty spray of

the wind, drawing in a deep breath. "I don't mind. It feels fantastic, anyway." She glanced around, frowning slightly. "Where's Rusty? I don't see him."

Patrick followed her gaze. "I don't, either." He whistled long and loud, and seconds later the setter came dashing out from behind a small dune several yards ahead. He loped toward the couple. Patrick patted the panting dog affectionately on the head. "Having a good time, Rusty?"

Angela knelt down to give Rusty a big hug. "Sure he is. He's having the time of his life, aren't you, boy?"

"Let's take a break," Patrick suggested. "Let Rusty get his breath back."

"All right." Angela studied the various dunes nearby. "Come on, I see something up ahead."

She led them to a large sand dune, its back side adjoining two smaller dunes, providing a crude triangular cove and a very effective windbreak. Angela settled down in one corner, beckoning to Rusty. The two had established a fast and true friendship, so that Rusty eagerly trotted over to Angela and lay down in front of her, his head between his front paws, his big brown eyes shifting from Angela to Patrick.

Patrick sat down opposite them, crossing his legs and leaning on his hands, surveying the natural shelter. "Nice. Did you know about this place, too?"

Angela laughed. "No. It is pretty convenient, though, isn't it?"

"Sure is." Patrick scooped up a handful of sand and sifted it slowly through his fingers. "Tell me something. You don't come here alone, do you?"

"Sure. Why not?"

"Come on. You're an intelligent woman. Why would you put yourself at such a risk?"

"First of all, I think it's pretty safe around here, and secondly, I've taken care of myself for all of three years now. Just little ol' me." She stroked the dozing dog's head. "Anyway, if anything's going to happen it could just as well happen in my town house as here."

"Maybe," Patrick conceded. "Still, I don't think you can be careful enough. You've lived alone ever since you were widowed?"

"Yes. Why do you ask?"

"I don't know. I was just thinking that you *are* a very independent woman."

Angela smiled wryly. "I'll take that as a compliment."

"You should. Have you ever thought of getting a roommate?"

"No. It wouldn't work. I'm much too private a person, and I wouldn't want to start all over again getting used to another person's habits and idiosyncrasies." She paused. "That sounds selfish, doesn't it?"

Patrick had been watching her as she spoke; her

eyes on the blustery, steely-gray sky, her auburn
hair tangled and wispy from the salty mist. He
shook himself out of his preoccupation; he'd almost forgotten what she'd just said. "No, it
doesn't." He hoped she wouldn't take offense at
his next question. "If this is too personal just tell
me, but I was wondering.... How happy were
you with your husband?"

Angela didn't reply, but her face grew taut, and
she seemed lost in thought. Patrick regretted asking. After all, it really wasn't his business.

Angela surprised him by saying, "There's nothing to be sorry about, really. Gordon and I
weren't that happy, especially toward the end. Actually, to be blunt about it, he was unfaithful to
me. I didn't find out until...just before he died.
If we had stayed married, he probably would have
gone on and on doing just as he pleased, if I'd
never found out. Unfortunately, I had very strong
feelings about infidelity. It's one of those things I
found intolerable—and still do. His death was a
terrible thing, so premature, but that's the way
things are in life, you know. Some things we just
can't predict. One adjusts because one has to,
and...in time, one forgets."

She was lying, of course, to herself and to him,
for she had never been able to forget that horrify-
ing night; the memories were still excruciatingly
painful. For the most part her plan had worked,
and she'd been successful in separating that part
of her life from the present. But she was still strug-

gling, even after three years, for the memories had a way of sneaking up on her at odd, unpredictable moments. Lately she seemed to have hit rough waters. The reason, she knew, was the accident with Rory. She was coping, though. And she *would* get over the shock—in time.

Wrapping her arms around her shins, she laid her chin on her knees. "How about you, Patrick? Have you ever been married?"

The question took him off guard, though it shouldn't have. He had spent a good deal of time last night thinking about his marriage, specifically how he was going to tell Angela that he was still married, though in the process of getting a divorce. It was plain wrong to continue withholding such information, he'd decided, and since he knew he wanted to continue seeing her, it would be only wise and fair to get everything up front from the beginning.

"Yes," he answered. "Unhappily also."

"What happened?" Angela asked. Patrick was ready to launch into a description of his failed marriage, when she put up one hand and shook her head. "No. I didn't mean that. It's none of my affair. I really don't know why I asked."

"It's all right—"

"No, it's not. I don't believe in dredging up the past, hanging out one's dirty laundry."

"But you just told me about your past. I don't consider it 'dirty laundry.' It's part of you, and I'm very interested in all the ingredients that make up Angela Carruthers."

He would have expected a smile, a shrug, something to indicate she agreed with him. Instead her expression grew very somber. She stopped petting the dog and sat very still, staring at the toes of her jogging shoes. Patrick realized he'd just stepped over some invisible line, one he hadn't known existed until that moment.

"I'm not sorry I said what I did," she said quietly, "about my former marriage. But you're wrong; it doesn't have anything to do with what I'm all about today. I know that sounds...bitter...."

"Yes. It does."

"It's not meant to. It's just that I believe in being realistic. After my marriage to Gordon ended, so did that part of my life. I have a new life now. I feel very strongly about living in the present."

The solemn force behind her words left him in no doubt of her sincerity. Not that he believed what she had said, but he understood that she believed it. Another piece of the puzzle that made up this beautiful, mystifying woman. He knew very well that what she was today *had* been influenced, shaped by her former experiences in life. That was true of everyone. She was holding back, he decided, and that fact only whetted his curiosity. Yet he was reluctant to push her at the moment, an important reason being his own selfish motives; in spite of his better intentions he was also holding something of himself back. He soothed his conscience with the knowledge that soon—with any luck very soon—that would no longer be the case. Once his divorce was final, the slate would be clean. . . .

The wind shifted, and the sand-dune barrier no longer provided as much protection. Rusty awoke from his siesta, poking his head up high, sniffing the salty breeze. He heaved himself up and walked over to his master, standing at attention in front of him, waiting for the cue that playtime could be resumed. The dog's movement broke the silence, and Angela was grateful for that.

"What's the matter, Rusty?" Angela asked, smiling. "Are you ready for some action?"

The dog barked twice, causing Angela and Patrick to laugh outright. Patrick stood up and dusted off the seat of his pants, then bent down to pick up a short narrow piece of driftwood. "Okay, boy, let's see how fast you can retrieve this one." He drew his long, muscular arm back, throwing the stick out far beyond the dune. In a flash Rusty was off, ready to tackle the form of play he loved most.

Angela laughed as they watched the bounding dog, racing off across the sand, getting sidetracked by the tide, which he couldn't resist jumping and dodging, then turning around in confusion, trying to determine what it was he'd been about to do. Angela moved to Patrick's side to watch Rusty, and was surprised to feel his arm move around her back and draw her in closer to his side.

"You're wonderful when you laugh, do you know that?"

His words took her breath away. Looking up at him, she answered softly, "No. I never think of myself in terms of 'wonderful.' "

"Well, you are." He turned slightly and wrapped his other arm around her, pulling toward him so that their bodies pressed tightly together.

CHAPTER EIGHT

HE SMELLS OF THE OCEAN, Angela thought, knowing she would forever associate him with that aspect of nature she most cherished.

Rusty had come back, dropping the piece of driftwood at his master's side, and now stood patiently waiting for the next throw. But the embracing couple appeared to have forgotten he existed, and when he tried for their attention by nosing between their molded thighs, he was unsuccessful. Finally he turned and ran back to the pounding surf, dodging and leaping the rushing foam tide in pure, unbridled joy.

Lost for the moment in a world of their own, Patrick and Angela knew another kind of joy. The fresh, exciting joy of lips never before united, bodies never before having touched so intimately, breast upon breast, hearts pounding in unison, creating magical passion where there had been only emptiness.

Rusty returned once more, his damp shaggy abdomen heaving, and sat at attention at his master's side, a stick of wet bark on the ground between his paws. He waited, his furry head turning in curiosity, first to one side and then the other, as if trying to figure what was taking so long. Finally the couple pulled apart, and both looked down to see Rusty next to them.

Angela, flushed and disturbed by the unexpected emotion in their kiss, was grateful for the distraction. She drew her sweater tightly against her; the wind was blowing hard now. "Poor Rusty. Nobody's paying you any attention."

Patrick bent and picked up the driftwood. The dog was instantly alert, waiting for the throw. Patrick tossed it in the direction from which they'd come, and as the dog dashed after it Patrick placed an arm around Angela's shoulders. They started back down the beach.

Angela felt the first drop on the tip of her nose, followed by another on the crown of her head. Within seconds the sprinkle had strengthened to a shower. She glanced up at Patrick in surprise. He grabbed her by the hand, and they both started running toward the car, laughing and shrieking like children. Assuming this was the start of a new game, Rusty barked and ran around them in wide circles, heedless of the rain, which was rapidly turning into a downpour.

"Come on, slow poke, run!" Patrick shouted, his words shredded by the wind, drowned out by the pounding surf and increasing downpour.

Angela didn't attempt a response; she was preoccupied in keeping up with Patrick's long stride.

By the time they made it to the Bronco, both were soaked to the skin. Rusty took up his station at the back of the wagon, his long hair dripping huge puddles around him.

"Yuk!" Angela exclaimed as she crawled inside the Bronco. "We're drenched."

Patrick withdrew a few tissues from a box on the seat, the only thing available, and began to mop the moisture from his face and brow. Angela took a few for herself and tried to soak up some of the wet in her hair. The seat and floorboards were rapidly being splotched with puddles from their clothing, and suddenly she started giggling.

"What's so funny?" Patrick asked, a hint of smile on his lips.

"Us. You in particular. Your hair is plastered to your head. You look like Woodrow Wilson."

That image provoked more laughter, and Patrick joined in heartily. Rusty barked his own comment, the sound so loud in the confines of the Bronco that Angela clapped her hands over her ears.

"Rusty, quiet!" Patrick commanded, and instantly the dog lay down, placing his drenched head on his paws.

"Poor Rusty," Angela crooned to the animal, reaching behind her to stroke him. "You don't get a chance to say anything, do you?"

Patrick shook his head ruefully as he gazed out into the solid sheet of rain. "I don't recall hearing any of this on the weather report. It's incredible. We'll have to wait until it stops. The visibility is zero."

"It happens sometimes like this. The clouds just move in and out of nowhere. It's happened to me a couple of times before."

"While you were alone?"

"Yep."

"What in hell did you do?"

"Same thing we're doing now; waited it out."

Patrick grabbed another handful of tissues and patted his hair. A thought came to him just then, reminding him once more of the vast difference between his soon-to-be ex-wife and the woman next to him. Lucille would have been beside herself, griping and fussing over the fact that her precious clothes might be damaged, her hair or makeup ruined, and a million and one other complaints. She had never been able to accept and deal with situations she could do nothing about. If something went wrong, it meant everything and everyone around her was going to suffer as much as she did. What a relief to just sit here and laugh about the whole situation.

"This kind of changes our plans for the rest of the day," he said.

"Oh?"

"Well, I'd intended on taking Rusty home and then taking you out to eat. We're no longer exactly dressed for the occasion."

Angela bit her lower lip, looped a lock of hair

behind one ear and said, "I have an idea. Let's go to my place. I have a nice selection of rib-eyes in the freezer. We can grill them."

"What about Rusty?"

"He can have the patio to himself. And all the trimmings from the rib-eyes."

Patrick stuck out a hand. She accepted it, shaking firmly. "You just got yourself a deal, lady."

"Great," Angela said, smiling. "Do you think we can give it a try now?"

It was still raining hard, but the visibility had improved. "I think so. We shouldn't have any trouble with my trusty four-wheel-drive."

The trip back to Angela's town house was slow and cautious, since the heavy rain continued unabated. A weather bulletin on the radio announced the cause of the unexpected foul weather. A sudden line of thunderstorms were moving slowly inland, and flash flooding was being reported in and around St. Augustine and Jacksonville.

Angela's town house was conveniently designed so that there were entrances in the rear, leading from the carport, as well as the front. Angela's car occupied the one parking space beneath the carport, but Patrick was able to find a curb space directly in front of the town house.

"Wait a minute," he said before they got out. "We can't take Rusty through your front door. He's filthy."

Angela took one look at the dog. "You're right.

We'll just have to race around to the back.'' She placed a hand on the door handle. "Here goes."

They made a mad dash around the side of the complex, splashing toward the back entrance, Rusty alongside Patrick on his leather leash. The temperature had dropped several degrees in the past few hours, and their teeth were chattering as Angela unlocked the door.

Rusty obviously wanted to go inside with them, but Patrick shooed him back onto the covered patio. "Don't worry, Rusty," Angela murmured, stooping to pat the dog. "You just go lie down in the corner and dry off, and we'll get you some water and something to eat."

"First order of business is to get these clothes off," Patrick said, and when Angela looked at him she could see he was shivering. Until then she hadn't noticed that she was, too.

"Right. Listen, all I have for you to put on is an oversized bathrobe. It won't fit, but you can wear it while I wash and dry your clothes."

"I'm not exactly concerned about fashion at the moment," Patrick assured her.

"Me, neither. Just a minute, I'll be right back." She left him standing in the laundry room while she raced upstairs for the bathrobe. While she was there she quickly peeled off her own clothes and changed into a pink velour jogging suit.

She hurried back to Patrick and showed him where the downstairs bathroom was. "There are plenty of towels if you want to take a shower. Just throw your things on top of the washer in the laundry room, and I'll get the heat going.''

She walked into the living room to turn on the central heating, noting the empty fireplace. Perfect, she thought. She'd only used it twice since living there, and even then it had seemed wasteful to do so. The normally balmy Florida temperatures didn't really warrant a fireplace. Indeed, she had assumed when she'd first looked at the place that it was only for decoration. On several occasions she had yearned for a day just like this to put it to use.

Patrick was out of the bathroom in a few minutes, and Angela covered her mouth with one hand to hide a grin as he walked toward her. He'd obviously taken a shower. His hair was plastered to his head again, though he'd combed it neatly to one side. He looked like an overgrown boy. The terry-cloth robe was ample enough but short, so that his legs and arms poked out hilariously.

"Well," he asked cheerfully, "how do I look?" He turned slowly for her inspection, embellishing his movements like a model on a runway, and Angela's smile turned into a giggle, then a hearty laugh.

"What's so funny?" he asked in mock offense.

Her gaze traveled from his head to his feet, taking in the impressive width of shoulder and chest, the powerfully built thighs and calves, the physique of a much younger, athletically trained man.

"You didn't answer my question."

"I was just remembering the time I first saw you," Angela said. "Stern, sophisticated, totally serious Dr. Merrill. I would never have dreamed—" She broke off, laughing all over again.

Patrick walked into the living room, hands shoved into the pockets of her robe, the picture of dejection. He sighed in resignation. "I tell you what. Would it restore my macho image if I did something manly? Like getting a fire started?"

Angela wiped the corners of her eyes and nodded, her mirth finally stemmed. "Yes, I think it would. I was just going to ask you to do that. You get started, and I'll see about the steaks. The matches are there on the mantel."

Patrick bent down to choose a log from the few that were kept in the brass holder next to the grate. Angela turned and started for the kitchen, stopping at the stereo to switch it on to the same classical station they had listened to at his place the previous night.

She hummed along with the familiar Beethoven symphony, not really getting the notes right and not really caring, either. Rain pounded in sheets against the windows, and she thought it a beautiful, perfect accompaniment, to the music, to the day. . . and to the evening about to begin.

CHAPTER NINE

THE RAIN DIDN'T SUBSIDE until nearly ten o'clock. Angela and Patrick had become so used to the steady sound of it that they were surprised when the rain stopped altogether, the only reminder being the erratic patter of drops on the ground outside.

Angela was seated on the love seat, her feet curled beneath her, a crocheted afghan spread across her knees. Patrick, dressed now in his freshly laundered clothes, was sprawled on the floor near the fireplace, his back against the sofa. The fire he'd built earlier was waning. Every few minutes he turned over the large oak log, exposing the glowing underside of the wood to an invigorating breath of oxygen. Two near-empty brandy snifters sat on the coffee table between them, and as Angela picked hers up occasionally to sip at it, her mood was reflective. She couldn't recall a time when she had felt so mellow, so at peace here in her own home.

Her eyes rested on Patrick's back, moved slowly across his strong shoulders, the ample musculature of his upper arms, obvious even through the thick knit of his sweater. His brown hair shone with red from the fire's reflection. His profile was strong and compelling and definitely sexy. There was a swift stinging sensation in the pit of her stomach, and Angela knew the feeling had nothing to do with the liquor. It was Patrick, his mere presence enough to elicit desire within her. But beyond this she sensed security, a contentment she had never truly felt in the past three years. For despite her independence, her ability and success in carrying on her life exactly the way she pleased, there were moments when solitude intensified to an unbearable, aching loneliness.

The evening—the entire day—had been absolutely wonderful in every sense of the word. The meal Angela had prepared had rivaled Patrick's spaghetti last night, and her mind was already buzzing with ideas for other menus. He was easy to please, so easy that she found she wanted to try harder to do so. Conversation flowed between them; even the silences were comfortable. The more they talked the more they discovered they had in common. Medicine, of course, was the most obvious, and there was much in that category to be culled, debated, even argued over. The subject of politics was easy, too, though they disagreed on several points, and in more than one instance, heatedly. That didn't matter to them; in fact, their differences made the conversation that much more enjoyable.

In one regard Angela was secretly very grateful; except for that instance this afternoon, Patrick apparently preferred to leave the subject of their former lives alone as much as she did. She still adhered to the idea that there was no point in dredging up the past—hers or his. She knew enough about him, as he was now, to know they had the basis for a relationship, if that was the way they were headed.

"Hey there, are you with me?"

"Sorry?" Angela started, and the genuine surprise on her face made Patrick chuckle.

"I was saying we'd better let this thing die out now. Otherwise it could keep burning for another couple of hours."

"Oh...yes, you're right. It's stopped raining, too. Did you notice?"

"Mm-hm." Patrick made sure the sliding fire screen was closed securely, then stood up, slapping his hands together briskly. "Well, it's about time for me to head back. I'm sure Rusty is wondering what's taking so long."

Angela felt a pang deep inside; she didn't want him to leave, not at all. The feeling was inappropriate, she reminded herself, considering the length of time she'd known him. But by the time Patrick was zipping up his jacket she was smiling at him, apparently casual. She crossed her arms over her chest when the spasm of a shiver traveled the length of her body.

"Are you cold?"

"A little."

Patrick came to her, placed his hands on her

shoulders and looked deeply into her eyes for a moment, then drew her to him. Angela closed her eyes, inhaling deeply, memorizing the scent of him—his own particular masculine one, mingled with the fragrance of the soap he'd used and the faint smell of burning oak.

As his arms tightened Angela dropped her cheek on his chest, amazed at how compatible their bodies were. *I wish you would stay,* she wanted to say, already missing him. Was this possible, she wondered. Was it possible to feel so close to him, to need him so?

Patrick drew back a little, and she looked up at him questioningly. "How busy are you going to be this week?" he asked.

"Why did you have to remind me of work?" she groaned. "I'd almost forgotten about it."

"I thought you said your partner was coming back from vacation."

"He is. Which means we have a ton of paperwork to go over before things settle down. But by Thursday everything ought to be under control. I hope."

"May I call you before that?"

"Of course. Why would you even ask?"

"Good manners. Actually, I was going to call in any event."

Angela smiled, and suddenly Patrick found the invitation of her lips irresistible. His head lowered slowly, his lips touching gently on hers. They kissed, at first slowly and carefully, then with growing urgency and probing intensity. Angela was the first to pull away; the desire she felt was both tremendously exciting and more than a little frightening. She wanted more from this man— much more, yet it was too soon. But as the two of them walked to the front door that earlier sense of security enveloped her, along with the re- assuring understanding that time was on their side.

"I might see you at the hospital tomorrow if you're there," she said. "I'm going to drop in around one o'clock or so."

"I'm surprised you'll be able to fit that in."

"Since Regi will be back I'll get coverage for a normal lunch."

Patrick touched her shoulder and said, "I haven't really expressed what I feel about what you're doing for Rory. I think the attention you're giving him is highly commendable."

"Thank you, but I don't consider anything I've done especially commendable. It's what I want to do, what I need to do, really. Seeing him regularly gives me the reassurance that he's all right. A self- ish motive, actually." She paused. "I don't mean to bug you about this, but when do you think he'll be moved to a private room?"

"I wish I could give you a definite answer. Dr. Bell will have the final say on that. But I imagine within the next couple of days."

Angela nodded, looking relieved. "Great." Her expression became pensive, though.

Patrick's eyes narrowed. "Now what's on your mind?"

"Oh. Nothing really. I'm just happy he's going to be okay." There was more she was leaving out, but an idea had only just occurred to her, and she preferred to keep it to herself for the moment.

"How about you?" Patrick asked. "Will you be all right tonight?"

"Sure." She frowned slightly, tilting her head to one side. "What a question, Patrick! I've been here on my own for almost three years. I've been handling living alone quite well, thank you."

"Yeah, I suppose. Just don't get overconfident."

The protective note in his voice nurtured a part of her that she hadn't, until that very moment, been aware was needy. She smiled brightly and opened the door, the cool night air whooshing inside the house. Rusty was on his feet in an instant, and they laughed as he made several circles in eager anticipation. Enough was enough, he seemed to be saying. He'd been out here alone for too long already.

"Come on, boy," Patrick said, hooking the leash onto the dog's collar. "Time to head back to the peace and comfort of your own doghouse."

Angela follow them to the Bronco, waiting as Patrick lowered the tailgate and let Rusty inside.

"I do believe he's had enough of my back

porch.'' Angela was standing on the curb, her arms once again wrapped around her for warmth. She was shivering visibly. ''You shouldn't be standing out here,'' Patrick admonished her. ''It's too cold. Go on back indoors.''

Angela waved his comment aside, but took a few steps along the curb. ''See you tomorrow. Bye. 'Night, Rusty.''

She watched Patrick drive away, then turned and ran back to the town house. The brandy had made her slightly drowsy earlier, yet now she felt completely alert. She stood for a moment in the hallway, wondering how on earth she was going to settle down for sleep tonight. However, there was one thing she'd learned from experience: if her body wasn't ready to rest there was no way she could force it to.

She walked into the living room, checked on the fire, which was dying rapidly now, went back into the kitchen to wash the brandy snifters. It was busywork, but she needed it; her mind was still reeling with the events of the evening—the entire day, really—that she and Patrick had shared. An indefinable emotion settled over her and only after several minutes of mulling it over did she label it. Happiness; that was what it was. Genuine, sweet, unadulterated happiness, something she'd long ago given up even wishing for.

She wiped dry each of the snifters, then held them up, enchanted with the way the light glinted off the crystal, dispensing and reflecting it into sparkling, colorful prisms. She smiled, feeling the long-forgotten emotion expanding within, tickling and warming her, almost making her want to laugh. She returned to the living room, stopping in the middle of it, and propped her hands on her hips. She walked around, fluffing up pillows, folding the afghan, checking on the few smoldering embers in the fireplace, finally looking around for something else to do. There wasn't a thing.

I'm in big trouble now. I'll never get to sleep. But for the first time in a very long time, she didn't care. She might feel tired tomorrow, she might not, but she wasn't going to worry about it. For once she was simply going to forget about responsibilities—even those that would rest on her shoulders in a mere nine hours—and savor this wonderful, reborn feeling.

REGI WAS LATE FOR WORK the next morning, which was usual, but Angela didn't mind. She had learned to accept the fact that nothing in the world was going to make Regi Donaldson prompt for anything. Besides which, on the job he was careful to the point of obsession, and more often than not she filled two to every one of his prescriptions. But he was reliable, with an affable, outgoing personality that was responsible to a significant degree for the steady clientele St. Augustine Apothecary enjoyed.

When he walked behind the counter that morning with his usual, "Mornin', hotshot," Angela

shook her head slowly and smiled as she scruti-
nized him.

"Welcome back, Regi. Other than a strong re-
semblance to Rudolph the Red Nosed, I'd say you
look like you had a great time. How was the Epcot?"

"Fantastic," Regi answered, sliding an arm into
his white jacket. "Arlene and I had an absolute
ball. I don't think Tod was particularly impressed,
however."

"I would think most one-year-olds would feel
pretty much the same," Angela commented wryly.
"How was he? Did you get any rest at all?"

"Actually, we did. It wasn't as hard as we'd expected, taking Tod along. But from what I understand, this is just the lull before the storm. The
hard part begins in a year."

"Ah, yes, the terrible twos," Angela said, smiling knowingly. Without warning an image darted
through her mind of a blond, curly headed tod-
dler, an artist at two, unconcernedly creating an
abstract painting on the kitchen wall with spoon-
fuls of peas and carrots. How difficult it had been
to stifle laughter at Melissa's obviously painstak-
ing efforts, to maintain a stern tone and disap-
proving expression. How difficult to deal with her
daughter's temper when the spoon was finally
taken away from her. . . .

"Did he ever call back about it?"

Regi had spoken, and Angela blinked in confusion, the memory gone as suddenly as it had appeared. "Pardon? Sorry, I wasn't listening."

"The Parke-Davis rep. Did he get back to you on that six-week back order?"

"Oh. No, he didn't. I've called him every other day. Half the time he's not in; the other half he has nothing new to tell me."

Regi sighed in disgust. "Business as usual. Where's his card? I'm gonna get a hold of that guy. This is getting ridiculous."

As Angela pushed the card index down the counter to him, their conversation took a more serious turn. There was much to be discussed, and she was glad of it; the unexpected memory of Melissa was disturbing, in more ways than one. Angela wasn't only upset by the memory itself. She was perplexed because lately she had little control over these nostalgic episodes.

Thankfully business as usual soon obscured all other matters. The telephone started ringing at nine sharp. Customers began trickling through the front door, and by ten o'clock St. Augustine Apothecary was buzzing with activity that didn't let up for several hours.

Neither she nor Regi were able to take a lunch break until after one-thirty, and by that time Angela was weak from hunger. Her plans to go shopping would have to wait until later. All she cared to do was sit in the office with a magazine and a sandwich, her stockinged feet propped in unladylike fashion on a cleared-off section of the desk. By the time she took over for Regi she was rested and relaxed, able to plunge back into work for the rest of the afternoon.

On the way home she stopped at a large discount department store, picked up a few items in the grocery section, finally making her way to sporting goods. After almost half an hour of discussion with a salesman, she selected and paid for a flashy ten-speed bicycle, then drove around to the customer pickup in the back to have it loaded into the Audi. She smiled to herself, picturing Rory's face when she wheeled it into his room at the hospital. She had every intention of doing just that, too; no one was going to stop her—even if it took coercing Patrick into writing an order on the chart giving her permission!

The telephone was ringing as she walked in the front door of her house. She picked it up, somehow knowing it must be Joyce. "Hello, Joyce. I just walked in."

"I can tell. What happened? I thought you closed the store doors at six."

"We did. I stopped by Munson's on the way home. You won't believe what I bought—a bicycle."

"Yeah? How come?"

Angela related her plan to Joyce, and her friend approved of the idea with enthusiasm. "I'd love to see his face when you give it to him."

"I'm really looking forward to it, too."

"So? How was the day at the beach?"

"You should ask how was the downpour," Angela said wryly.

"Oh, no, you didn't get caught in it, did you?"

"Yes. We were drenched. And we had to wait almost twenty minutes for it to ease up before we could drive back. Everything turned out all right, though. We had a nice fire going, I made dinner, and...well, to be honest, it was a really lovely evening."

"I can tell. I can hear it in your voice. Unfortunately, Jonathon and I didn't have such a hot one."

"Why, what happened? How was the tournament?"

"We were ousted in the third set. And Jonathon claims it was my fault. Which it was. Anyway, we went out to dinner with Jerry and Cynthia, and they ended up snipping at each other throughout the entire meal. I tell you, we were glad to get home."

"I can imagine. How was school today? You should be letting out pretty soon, right? Can you believe Christmas and New Year's are right around the corner?"

"I can't," Joyce stated flatly. "I just hope we can enjoy them. There's so much on both our minds right now, so much that our future hinges on. It's hard not to think about it day and night."

"Tenure," Angela said.

"Yes. Oh, Ange, I know there's not a thing in the world I can do about it. Yet, still, I worry. The word now is that the cutbacks are going to affect several departments.''

"You've known that all along, haven't you?"

"Yes, but I think it might be worse than we initially thought.''

"Well, you had the right idea before, Joyce. There's not a thing in the world you can do about it. I think you should just forget everything for now. Enjoy the holidays.''

"In other words, cross that bridge when we come to it. You said that before, didn't you?''

"Yep." Angela hesitated. "What does Jonathon have to say about it?''

"Nothing. That's just the thing. He doesn't see the point in talking about it.''

"So—maybe he's right.''

"No, he's not. I think it's something we should discuss and have worked out in our minds as far as alternative plans, in case things don't work out exactly the way we expect them to.''

Angela shook her head, exasperated. "Look, Joyce, I hate to sound unsympathetic, but it sounds to me as if you're begging for trouble.''

Joyce sighed again, lengthily. "I hope you're right. I really do. Oh, listen, I'm sorry to lay all this on you. It's not really what I called about. I wanted to know if you and Patrick would like to come to our place for dinner on Christmas day.''

"Well, sure. That's a great idea. I'd love to. I'll ask Patrick, but I'm sure he'd like to, as well.''

"Boy, you two sure did strike up a friendship right off the bat."

"Not exactly."

"You've only known him a little over a week. That's pretty fast as far as I'm concerned."

Angela laughed. "We're only dating, Joyce. There aren't wedding bells ringing yet."

"You never know," Joyce said in a singsong tone. "Sorry, I'm being silly now. Have you gotten all your Christmas shopping out of the way yet?"

"Pretty much. I've already mailed off the family's gifts. All I have left are you and Jonathon."

"Now don't overdo it."

"That's impossible as far as I'm concerned. I owe both of you far more than I could ever repay."

"That's a bunch of baloney. Period. But before you have a chance to say anything else equally ridiculous, I'm going to let you go. Jonathon just walked in, and it's my turn to make dinner. I'll talk to you tomorrow."

"Okay. Good night."

"Bye."

Angela had taken exactly three steps, heading toward the stairs to change clothes, when the telephone rang again. She went back and picked up the receiver. "Hello?"

"Hi, there. You must have just gotten in."

"Hello," Angela said again, a delicious quiver in the pit of her stomach. "As a matter of fact, I did. And the minute I walked in the door, Joyce called. Where are you?'' The background noise sounded like anything but home.

"I'm at the hospital. I just wanted to let you know, Rory's been sent to a private room.''

Magic words, the very ones she wanted to hear more than anything right now. "That's fantastic! What room is he in?''

"Five-oh-one, station five south. You're not planning on coming tonight, are you?''

"No. Tomorrow afternoon. This is really great news, Patrick. Especially after what I just did.''

"And what was that? You sound particularly pleased with yourself.''

"I went shopping. I bought Rory a new bicycle.''

"Aha! *That*'s what you were thinking about yesterday.''

"Now how did you know that?''

"In case you hadn't noticed, I'm an incredibly astute person. We were talking about Rory, and you got this real faraway look in your eyes. I could see something was going on in your head.''

"Patrick, do you think it would be possible for me to get it up to his room? I know he'd love it. That's what I'd planned on doing, only I wouldn't want to cause a fuss with any of the nurses.''

"I think it will be fine. But just in case, I'll write a note on the chart: one bicycle Q.D., p.r.n.''

Angela laughed. "Oh, would you? That would be perfect.'' Her voice lowered somewhat as she

added, "In fact, if you hadn't offered, I was going
to twist your arm."

"Mm-hm. And you figured I'd give in just like
that, didn't you?"

"Well...I was prepared to do a little per-
suading."

"Now that wouldn't be such a bad idea,
either," Patrick teased.

Just talking to him made Angela wish the week
would fly by. Another new turn in her life, she
thought, remembering all too clearly how, a mere
two weeks ago, she had been in the opposite situation, cooling her heels on the weekends, eager and
ready to get back to the safe and secure routine of
work.

"Before I forget," she said. "Joyce extended an
invitation, and I told her I would talk to you about
it. She wanted to know if we'd like to come over
on Christmas Day for dinner." As she spoke it
dawned on her that he might very well have plans;
she knew relatively little about his family background, so that wouldn't be surprising, really. Her
expectations took a plunge as she realized how
much she was counting on his agreeing to come.

"Sure, that sounds great," Patrick answered.
"It's my turn to cover for the other guys, so I'll be
on call. But things have been fairly quiet, so there
shouldn't be a problem. I was going to ask you as
a matter of fact, what you are doing on Christmas
Eve."

"Well, work, until six o'clock, that is. After

that, I have nothing specific planned." She didn't mention that except for the obligatory long-distance call to her parents' or her brother's home, she had planned on spending the night alone, as she'd done for the past couple of years. Her parents had entreated her this year, as they always did, to fly up to Oregon to spend at least a few days, but she had declined, saying there was too much going on at the store at that time; she couldn't afford to leave. She was fine, she had assured them over and over. She had convinced them with a not-so-white lie about a fictional group of friends who had invited her to a not-to-miss party.

She must have sounded convincing enough, because her parents had backed off...once again. They had finally resigned themselves to the fact that Angela wasn't coming back to Oregon, that she had made herself a new home in St. Augustine, complete with more friends and activities than she cared to part with, even for the sake of her family.

As it turned out, she *had* been invited to parties for both Christmas and New Year's Eve last year and the year before, mostly thanks to Joyce and Jonathon's initiative, and she had dutifully put in an appearance at each. But the parties, crowded with people she didn't know for the most part, and didn't care to know, could never erase the ache that settled on her heart. For all she had managed to put her life back on an even keel, the

Christmas holidays were extremely difficult for her to handle. There was no escaping, it seemed, the memories of that other Christmas....

Patrick's next words, therefore, were more welcome than he would have guessed. "Then how would you like to spend the evening with me?"

"I'd love to," Angela responded readily, thinking how unusual it was to feel actual eagerness for the holidays.

They talked a few minutes longer about their plans, then Patrick said he'd try to schedule his rounds so that he could be with her when she brought the bicycle the next day.

"Do the Williamses know about it?" he asked.

"No. It was just an impulse. But I do plan on calling them and letting them know. You don't think they've done anything as drastic as not allowing Rory to own a bicycle anymore do you?"

"I don't think so. In fact, I doubt it seriously."

"Well, I'll call them just the same. They should know."

"All right. I'll see you tomorrow, okay?"

"Right. Good night, Patrick."

"Good night."

Angela hung up and went into the kitchen, her appetite suddenly demanding immediate attention. She hadn't been as hungry in ages, and there was only one reason for that, she knew. Happiness again. She was absolutely, certifiably happy at that moment. The sound of Patrick's voice lingered in her ear, his face in her memory. She smiled to herself, relishing this mushrooming sensation, filling her with an anticipation that was almost overwhelming.

CHAPTER TEN

HALFWAY THROUGH the morning's schedule of office patients, Patrick received the call from his attorney. At first he instructed his secretary to take a message, but some intuition made him decide to speak to the lawyer right then. He needed a break from the incessant flow of patients, and besides, whatever George had to say was certain to be about one thing—his divorce. And that was a matter of primary importance in his life right now.

"Hello, George," he answered as he sat down in the hunter-green leather chair at his desk. "What's up?"

"I hope you can stand a bit of good news this morning, because that's all I have to offer."

Patrick leaned forward expectantly. "Are you kidding? I can always use it."

"I thought so. Well, you'll be pleased to know you'll be a free man as of the twenty-third of this month."

"Wha—you're joking. What are you saying?"

"I'm saying that your wife's attorney called late last night, and they've agreed to our settlement proposal."

Patrick was astonished. "When you say you've got good news you're not kidding, are you? What the hell brought this on? I was sure Lucille was going to hang in there till the very last."

"Well, apparently she wants to move. Some 'business opportunity' in New York that happened overnight. So she took what we offered with only a few minor objections. We've made some concessions, but believe me they're negligible in the total outcome."

Patrick was silent, absorbing the shock of such welcome, almost unbelievable news. George said, "Patrick? Did you hear what I just said?"

"Yes! Yes, of course. It's fantastic. I was just thinking this is the first time in I don't know how long that I've felt the urge to give Lucille one big kiss."

George laughed. "I wouldn't recommend it."

"Are there any papers to sign right away? Do you want me to come by your office?"

"As a matter of fact, I'll be in your neighborhood some time around seven tonight. If you're going to be there, I'll drop by."

"I'll be at home. And George. . . thanks a lot."

The attorney chuckled again. "Don't thank me too much. It was mostly Lucille's doing. And anyway, you'll get my bill soon."

"Yeah, I'm sure I will," Patrick said wryly. But he would have paid a hell of a lot more than George was charging just to get the whole thing over and done with.

"All right, then," George said. "I'll let you get back to your patients. See you tonight."

"Okay. Goodbye."

Patrick's hand remained on the receiver for a moment after he'd hung up. Sheer relief flooded through him; the wait was finally over. He wondered why Lucille hadn't mentioned the possibility of a move to him, but then that was typical of Lucille. Anything she wanted to do, she would do, regardless of his or anyone else's opinion. In this case her impulsiveness couldn't have pleased him more. In fact, the more he sat there thinking about it, the better he felt. He was going to be free! Free at last of the tentacles of an unwanted, ill-conceived marriage to a woman he had long since ceased loving. The divorce wouldn't be official, of course, until next week, but just knowing the wait wasn't going to take several more weeks, perhaps months, was enough to make him want to jump up and shout with joy.

Instead, inwardly delighted, he stood up, pulling his stethoscope from his pocket and draping it around his neck. As he opened the door to his office, he came face to face with his nurse, her arm raised, her fist poised in midair for a knock on the door.

"Oh! I was just about to come in and get you. Mrs. Lindstrom says she's in a hurry and can't wait more than another five minutes."

Patrick took the chart from the nurse, asking, "Which room is she in?"

"Four."

"Then by all means, let's get in there and take care of the woman."

Gloria Sanford hesitated, raising her eyebrows in surprise at Patrick's tone. He sounded positively ebullient, a turnaround from his mood only minutes earlier. "You never know," she muttered, shaking her head as she followed him down the hall toward room four.

"Did you say something?" Patrick asked, hesitating before going into the room.

"Just talking to myself."

And then he smiled at her, an enormous toothy grin that had Gloria Sanford shaking her head once more, clearly wondering what in the world had happened to the man.

ANGELA LEFT THE PHARMACY that day at four o'clock. Regi had everything under control, and since business was slowing down he told her he saw no reason for both of them to hang around until closing. Especially considering Angela's plans for the rest of the day. She had told Regi all about the accident. He had been shocked by all that had gone on while he was on vacation, but he thought the idea of delivering a spanking-new bicycle to Rory was super and encouraged her to get going before it got dark.

With the bike securely stowed in the trunk of the Audi, Angela headed for Jacksonville as soon as she left the store. She'd spoken with the Williamses the previous night, and both had approved of her plans. Rory would be thrilled to receive another bike, they had said, and presenting it to him in the hospital would cheer him up considerably.

Once there, she went directly to the fifth floor to talk with the nurse in charge. A nurse's aide was summoned, who accompanied Angela downstairs and waited as she got the bike out of the car. She directed the visitor to the service elevators, on the way up expressing her enthusiasm for the surprise idea. They stowed the bike in a supply closet since Angela wanted to go to Rory's room first to make sure he was awake.

As she walked down the corridor her pace slowed somewhat. She noted the number of people, mostly hospital personnel, milling around the doorway to his room. What was going on, she wondered, anxiety stabbing at her. The charge nurse came out of the room, saw Angela standing there and nodded brusquely to her as she closed the door firmly behind her.

"What's the matter?" Angela asked. A number of voices were coming from Rory's room. Among them, she recognized Patrick's.

"We've had a little problem," the nurse said in an officious tone. "Dr. Merrill is in with Rory right now."

The nurse walked swiftly toward the station, and Angela followed, amazed at the change in the woman, who had been so friendly and outgoing only ten minutes earlier.

"Something's wrong," Angela said. "Please tell me what it is."

THEY WERE STANDING NOW behind the glass partition surrounding the nurses' station, and Angela watched as the older woman began drawing medication out of a small vial. She flicked the plastic syringe with her middle finger, replaced the cap, then turned to face Angela, her expression noncommittal. "You'll have to wait and speak with Dr. Merrill. Now, if you don't mind, this area is off limits to visitors." With that she stepped briskly past Angela, her white skirt brushing against Angela as she hurried away.

Angela felt her heart beginning to pound, and when she rubbed her left forearm, noted the goose bumps that had suddenly risen on her skin. Anxiously she searched for someone else to talk to, but the station was momentarily deserted. A film of perspiration dampened her upper lip; her scalp started to tingle. Slowly she made her way into the corridor a few feet from Rory's room, standing with her back against the wall, arms crossed over her chest in a vain effort to still the trembling that had seized her entire body.

No one came out of the room for several minutes, but she was acutely aware of the muted sound of voices from within.

What could possibly have happened in the few minutes it had taken her to go downstairs and come back up? Unwanted memories reared their ugly, terrifying heads, and she squeezed her eyes shut, willing herself to shake them off, to focus on the present situation. Surely Rory was going to be all right, she kept thinking, but as the minutes ticked on and no one came out of the room, the conviction grew weaker.

Finally the door opened, and a nurse walked into the corridor. Angela opened her mouth to speak; before the words were out the nurse was half walking, half jogging back toward the nurses' station. Desperate with anxiety, Angela pushed away from the wall and intercepted the nurse as she was returning to the room.

"Please, can you tell me what's going on?"

The young woman had been there earlier when Angela had spoken to the head nurse about her plans for surprising Rory. The nurse reached out and placed a hand on Angela's forearm. "The doctor will be out in a few minutes. Please...I must go inside."

Angela stepped out of the way, frustration balling up inside like a fist. She wiped a hand across her brow, her fingers pressing gently on her temples, trying to ease the pulsating pressure.

Crossing the corridor, she took up her stance once more at the wall, gluing her eyes to the door opposite. It opened finally, and Patrick walked out into the hallway. Angela started to take a step toward him, but found she couldn't move a muscle.

Patrick saw her standing there, started to say something, but was interrupted by the head nurse. The two of them spoke briefly. When the nurse walked off he turned back to Angela.

"How long have you been here?" He was startled by her ashen complexion, but even more disturbed by the haunted, glazed look in her eyes.

When she answered her voice was quavering. "I—I don't know. What happened to Rory?"

Patrick's frown deepened, and he took her elbow to urge her down the hallway. "He's all right now. It's you I'm worried about at the moment."

Relief mingled with confusion. Angela's gaze was imploring. "Patrick, please tell me what's happened! Is he really all right? Why in the hell do I have to ask so damn many questions? Why doesn't someone just tell me what's going on!"

"I'll tell you everything you want to know. Come in here." He passed the nurses' station, opened a door farther down the corridor. Inside was a staff lounge, a small room with several plastic chairs, an old vinyl couch and a narrow, built-in counter on which stood a coffee machine and various other kitchen supplies. Angela stepped inside, and he shut the door behind them, forestalling what she'd been about to say by directing her to sit down.

"What in heaven's name is the matter with you? You're shaking like a leaf—pale as a sheet."

She *was* shaking, violently, and when she answered, the words came out in a near chatter. "T-tell me about Rory, dammit!"

"He had a reaction to the antibiotic we put him on this morning. An allergic reaction. But he's going to be all right."

Angela swallowed, bit her lower lip, then said in a whisper, "Thank God."

"When did you get here?"

"Half an hour ago. I don't know. Not long. I came up to talk with the nurses about the bicycle I was going to bring up, and the charge nurse sent someone down with me to help. By the time we got back, everything was going crazy." She blinked once and ran her hand across the top of her head. "When did all this start?"

"He had a rash this morning, not a bad one so we weren't too concerned. But after the second dose of medication it flared up drastically. He started having difficulty breathing, and his blood pressure dropped to seventy over forty. The nurses called a code blue. Apparently you were outside when everything happened."

"Anaphylactic shock," Angela stated quietly.

"Yes. I must admit I was rather surprised by the reaction. There was no way of knowing of his sensitivity, however. He'd never been given the drug before. He came out of it pretty fast. He'll be all right."

"Can I still see him?"

"Sure. He's probably sleeping right now, though. The dose of antihistamine was substantial, and he was already getting sleepy when I left."

Angela pressed her palms to her cheeks, and closing her eyes, drew in a deep breath. As she expelled it slowly, Patrick came up to her, placed a hand on her neck and rubbed gently.

"Are you okay now?"

Angela nodded, relaxing gradually as his fingers kneaded her flesh. "Sure. I was just...a little shook up."

More than a little, Patrick thought. *Much more.* He clearly remembered an identical expression on her face that day in intensive care. There had been a world of emotion in her face—pain, grief, shock. As he had then, he understood her concern over what had just occurred, but Angela's reaction had stemmed from anything but simple concern. Much as they'd come to know each other over the past couple of weeks, he was beginning to realize the enormity of the missing piece, or pieces, of the puzzle that made up Angela Carruthers. He suspected he wasn't going to put it together easily, but he was certain that somehow, someday, he would have to.

"I'm all right now," Angela said, lifting her head and summoning a smile. "I know you must think I'm weird, getting so upset...."

"I don't think you're weird in the least. But I do

believe there must be a reason for your becoming so disturbed. Won't you tell me what it is, Angela?''

Instantly she averted her gaze, and a tiny frown etched her brow. In that moment Patrick lost any remaining doubt that there was something troubling her.

"I just have a hard time with...well, you know, handling stressful situations.''

"You certainly didn't give that impression the night you brought Rory to emergency. You held up very well.''

"Yes, well, that was a little different.''

"And a hell of a lot more stressful, to be sure. I don't see how what just happened could make you feel worse.''

Angela got up suddenly and took a few steps toward the door. Her expression was strained, and she gave a false laugh as she said, "Look, I'm really sorry I acted so childish out there. When I saw all the commotion, I guess I just overreacted. I certainly wasn't very professional about it.''

"I wouldn't have expected you to act like a professional,'' Patrick said softly. "The boy means a lot to you.''

Angela nodded, feeling her chin quivering as tears filmed her eyes. "Yes, he does.'' She wiped the corner of one eye. "God, this is so silly! I don't know what I'm—'' But the tears wouldn't be contained. She was crying, great gulping sobs interspersed with gasps for air.

Patrick's arms surrounded her in the next second—she pulled away from him, shaking her head violently. She drew in a deep, shuddering breath and regained control, though she was still visibly trembling. Swallowing, she wiped away the tears from her eyes and finally looked at Patrick, managing a weak smile. "You must think I'm the biggest baby in the world."

His expression was serious, full of concern. "I don't think that at all." He decided right then that telling her about the telephone call from his lawyer could wait. He certainly didn't need to share *that* with her; she was far too upset. "Wha—what should I do? About the bicycle?" she asked, reaching into her purse for a tissue to blow her nose. "You said he was sleeping, didn't you?"

"Yes. It may take him a while to wake up. I'll talk to the nurses and see if they can look it up in the supply closet. You can give it to him tomorrow."

"All right. That would be better." She paused for a moment, adjusted the shoulder strap of her purse before adding quietly, "I really am sorry, Patrick—about the emotional outburst. I'm embarrassed about it, to be honest."

"Angela, you have nothing in the world to feel sorry for. So don't apologize again. Are you going straight home from here?"

Angela nodded. "Yes. Why?"

"I've still got a lot of patients to see, but I'll call you as soon as I get home."

"You don't have to."

"It's not a matter of having to. I think you know that by now. Come on, I'll see you to the elevators."

As they walked down the corridor, he placed one hand at the small of her back. It felt good. He really was an understanding person, she thought, especially considering that she was so unpredictable. She *was* embarrassed that she'd lost control that way, but at the same time she knew there was no sense in dwelling on her reaction. What had happened had happened, and she should be grateful to Patrick for his support. She'd have to work on getting herself back in line from now on; she couldn't let anything like that happen again.

They said goodbye at the elevators, Patrick promising again to call that evening. The drive home, which Angela normally didn't mind—in fact, often enjoyed—seemed tedious and endless that night. As were her thoughts. For despite her intentions to leave it alone, she just couldn't forget what had happened at the hospital. What in the world must Patrick think of her. She had reacted neurotically, had allowed her mind to conjure up the worst possible complications to Rory's condition.

The child was going to be all right, she reminded herself, and even if there were further problems she would just have to be strong. By the time she reached the outskirts of St. Augustine she had managed to pump up her self-confidence to a more tolerable level. Over and over she replayed the mental tape she'd come to rely on over the years, one that eased her into acceptance of those circumstances beyond her control. If something similar happened in the future, she could handle it. The memories might crop up again, but if they did she could deal with them, too. As she always had.

Face it, she thought as she parked the car. *Hospitals just aren't your thing.*

There was far more truth than humor in that thought, so she quickly decided enough time had been spent dwelling on the subject. Letting herself into the town house, she went directly to the living room and switched on the television. She turned up the volume, then took off her coat and set about tidying the downstairs. Fortunately there was an enjoyable sitcom on one of the channels, and within a few minutes Angela found herself smiling, even chuckling in response to the predictable but funny lines. A while later the telephone rang. She was scrubbing the porcelain kitchen sink, simultaneously caught up in the dialogue of another show, so her greeting sounded somewhat preoccupied.

"Angela?"

"Yes.... Oh! Patrick. Just a minute. Let me turn the TV down."

She washed her hands and quickly dried them, then hurried into the living room to turn down the set. "Sorry," she said after she'd picked up the receiver again. "I had the television on so loud, I could barely hear a thing."

The sound of her voice, so different from that afternoon at the hospital, relieved Patrick enormously. Ever since he'd said goodbye to her, he'd hardly had a moment to himself, yet Angela had been at the back of his mind constantly. Worried about her, he'd gone straight to the phone as soon as he got home.

"When did you get in?" he asked, plopping down on a kitchen barstool.

"About an hour ago." She paused, saying in a softer tone, "Hey, I know you're still worried about me, but I'm fine. I promise."

"Okay. I believe you, then."

"Is that all you called about? To see if weird Angela is still freaking out?"

"Of course not. As I said before I understand what happened."

"Good. And I really am fine now. What did the Williamses have to say about Rory's reaction?" She could just imagine Frank Williams, shouting and throwing out accusations about the incompetent staff administering the wrong drug to his son, and so on.

"Actually, he and Miriam took it in stride. After they realized there was no way of predicting Rory's allergic reaction, and that he pulled out of it quickly, they were very understanding."

"Well, that's good. I'll give them a call in a little while."

"Are you still coming to the hospital tomorrow?"

"Sure. Do you think you can make it when I'm there? If things aren't too hectic I'll just do the same thing I did today, leave a little early. I can get there by about five-thirty."

"All right. I'll try to make my rounds then."

"Good. And Patrick? Thanks a lot for... understanding."

He slid one hand down the crease of his slacks, pursing his lips. He understood more than she thought—and far too little for his own satisfaction. "No thanks are necessary. However, what I don't understand is why you're so defensive where your emotions are concerned."

Angela's spine straightened at the subtle change of direction the conversation had taken. "Come on, let's not get so serious about it. Listen—" quickly she changed the subject "—I have yet to call Joyce and Jonathon and tell them we'll be able to make it for Christmas dinner. You still want to come, don't you?"

Patrick laughed. "Believe me, Angela, I wouldn't have said so if I didn't."

She felt embarrassed for having asked something so silly, yet she had been desperate to distract him. "Yes, all right. So I guess I'll see you tomorrow afternoon. Act One, scene two."

"You're on."

"You bet. Say good-night to Rusty for me."

"I will. Sleep tight, Angela."

She hung up the receiver very carefully. The sound of his voice and his words penetrated and reverberated through her brain. As she looked out the bar window, watching the soundless picture on the television, she felt the distinct ache of loneliness. She missed him, terribly so. It struck her that the protective devices she had developed to nurture her independence provided little, if any, help in the face of this new, undeniably intense need.

She could no more deny that need than she could claim the accident with Rory hadn't initiated the rash of painful memories plaguing her lately. She thought of Patrick's face, normally so serious, yet so handsome, so appealingly, undeniably masculine. When he looked at her, he really *looked* at her. He focused every ounce of his attention on nothing but what she was saying or doing at the moment. His presence was such a tangible, lasting thing. Perhaps that was the reason she felt his absence so acutely. It was as though he had filled up her home, yet left some small, very significant part behind.

Angela was engrossed in her thoughts as she stood at the kitchen sink, unseeing, her mind hearing only the expressions of her heart, other yearnings that were as undeniable as they were implausible.

She had the compelling urge to open up to Patrick, to tell him all about the real pain that had stricken her that afternoon, the pain that became more of a struggle to deal with every day. *Why can't you? What harm would it do?*

A lot, a stubborn voice answered. *A hell of a lot.* It would be too much like opening a freshly sutured wound, exposing it anew to all the dangers of infection. She had gone through this alone so far and made it, despite all the odds against her.

Her vision focused once more. Angela turned on the hot-water faucet, scrubbing out the sink, oblivious to the fact that it was already a gleaming white. When she finished she headed for the downstairs bathroom, stopping on the way to turn up the volume of the television set. Forcing herself to listen to every bit of dialogue, even paying attention to the commercials, she finished cleaning the bathroom, then moved on to the living room, dusting and polishing everything in sight.

The ten-o'clock news was over by the time she ran out of things to do, so she went upstairs to take a bath. The housework had exhausted her, and she dropped off to sleep almost immediately.

Her sleep was deep, as though she were drugged, and dream images of the scene outside Rory's room that afternoon predominated.

Angela awoke at three in the morning, her heart pounding, her upper lip moist with perspiration. Terrified, she scooted over to the edge of the bed, flicked on the bedside-table lamp and peered around her room, the pastel amber walls warm and familiar in the glow of the single bulb. She shoved her hair out of her face and drew in a deep shaky breath, then got out of bed and walked through the chill room to the bathroom.

When she came back to bed she picked up the novel she had started more than a week earlier, forcing herself to read. Somehow the ruse worked, for within a few minutes she drifted off to sleep again. When her eyes next opened, the room was suffused with a gentle morning light, and the pale-peach curtains glowed with a soft hue. The memory of the dream flitted briefly into her consciousness, then was very firmly suppressed.

CHAPTER ELEVEN

THE LOOK ON RORY'S FACE the next afternoon when Angela came into his hospital room, wheeling the bicycle alongside her, was all it took to erase the memory of her disturbing dream. She could hardly contain her pleasure as she watched his mouth open wide, his blue eyes growing saucerlike as he stared at the sleek red-and-black ten-speed.

The Williamses were waiting outside in the hallway, having insisted that she deliver the bicycle before they came in. "No," Mr. Williams had said. "The bike is from you. You should be the one to give it to him. We'll wait out here for Dr. Merrill."

She stopped midway into the room, smiled and said, "Good afternoon, Rory."

"Hi." The greeting was muffled. He was clearly puzzled. "What's that?" he asked, sitting up a little in the bed and staring openly at the bicycle.

"What? Oh, the bike." Angela cast a nonchalant glance at it. "It's really nice, don't you think?"

Rory nodded several times, his eyes traveling

slowly across the front fender, the handlebars, seat and back fender.

Angela slid her palm across the narrow leather seat. "I thought so, too. Matter of fact, I just couldn't resist when I saw it in the store the other day, so I snapped it up on the spot."

Rory licked one corner of his mouth with the tip of his tongue, plucking absently at the bed cover.

"Do you like it?" Angela asked, lifting her foot to lower the kickstand.

"Sure."

She crossed her arms and moved toward the bed, then cocked her head in the direction of the bike and grinned at Rory. "That's good, because. . .it's yours."

"Huh?" Rory's blue eyes widened incredulously.

"I said," Angela repeated slowly, "the bicycle is yours."

His mouth hung open for a moment, his eyes moving rapidly from Angela to the bicycle. He swallowed once and nibbled on his lower lip.

"Did you hear what I said, Rory?"

He nodded slowly, but a tiny frown appeared. "Yeah, you said the bike was mine."

Angela smiled brightly. "That's right. What's the matter, don't you want it?"

Rory's eyes met hers. "Of course."

"Then what's the matter? You're not acting very happy about it."

"I don't think I can take it home," he muttered.

"Why not? Oh, you mean because you're still in the hospital. Well, that's no problem. We'll just—"

"No. It's because of my parents."

"What about your parents?"

Rory looked down at the bed covers, and his dejected expression touched Angela. "They're mad at me 'cause of the accident. They don't want me to have another bicycle. Dad said it was a good thing the other one got messed up as bad as it was, and he wasn't gonna fix it again."

Angela sat down on the bed next to the young boy. "Honey, I think your father just said that because he was so upset when you were hurt in the accident. He's not mad at you. Are you sure he said those things?"

Rory looked somewhat confused, then shrugged, his expression still unhappy. Angela smoothed her hand against his forehead and said softly, "Maybe you imagined what your father said, dreamed it or something, because you felt guilty about doing what you weren't supposed to. But even if he did say you couldn't ride anymore, he couldn't have meant it. I know for a fact that he and your mom want you to have the bike."

"Are you sure?"

"Sure I'm sure. Matter of fact, I can prove it right now."

Angela got up from the bed, walked across the room, turning to wink at Rory before opening the door. She signaled to the Williamses, who were now conversing with Patrick.

Miriam Williams went straight to her son's bed and kissed him on the forehead. "Hi, sweetheart. Well, do you like what Miss Carruthers bought you?"

Rory's blue eyes grew wide with hope; he glanced disbelievingly from his mother to his father. "Can I really have it?"

Mr. Williams laughed good-naturedly. "Of course you can, son."

"All right!" Rory enthused, sitting forward as Patrick wheeled the bike over to his bed. "Wow! What a neat racing stripe!"

Everyone chuckled as Rory ran his hand along the front fender, then leaned over to grab the handlebars and began to steer. He looked up at Patrick hopefully. "When can I ride it, doctor?"

"Aha! I do believe our patient is making a great deal of progress."

Rory looked at his parents. "But when can I go home?"

Patrick pressed his lips together, his eyes narrowing in contemplation. "I'd say probably in two or three days."

Rory's expression didn't match his parents'; he was obviously disappointed.

"Isn't that great, Rory?" Miriam asked, smiling. "You'll be home for Christmas." Rory only twisted his mouth in a grimace of dissatisfaction. His expression brightened, however, as he focused once more on the bicycle.

"You're doing much better," Patrick said. "As I was telling your parents before, Rory, you've recovered very quickly. We're going to keep you around, though, to make sure the drugs we're giving you don't cause any further problem. You sure wouldn't want what happened yesterday to happen again, would you?" Rory shook his head, and Patrick went on, "I didn't think so." He smiled along with the others as Rory's hands moved back to the handlebars.

"I tell you what, Frank," Patrick said, turning to Rory's parents, "you and Miriam better take the bike home with you. I don't think I trust Rory not to jump on it as soon as we walk out the door. Next thing you know he'll be speeding down the hallways, knocking down all the patients and nurses."

Rory laughed outright. "Yeah!"

Everyone laughed with him, and Frank said, "Well, all joking aside, I think it's a good idea to take the bike home."

"Oh, dad," Rory complained. "I'm not gonna do anything dumb. I won't ride it, I promise."

"I know you won't, son. I was just planning on getting it ready for when you come home. The chain and axle need a good greasing before you take it out for a spin."

Rory leaned back on his pillow and sighed, giving in grudgingly. "Okay."

"So," Patrick said, "I'll see you tomorrow. Any questions you want to ask me? Anything you need or would like?"

Rory shook his head.

"Well, if you think of something later just ask one of the nurses. She'll take care of it or get in touch with me."

Frank joined his wife at the bedside, and Patrick moved to where Angela sat in one of the visitors' chairs. "Are you going to stay a little longer?" he asked.

"No, I don't think so," Angela said, standing up. "I need to get home."

"Have time for a cup of coffee first?"

She smiled. "Sure. In fact, that sounds like an excellent idea." She picked up her coat and purse. "But first I want to say goodbye to Rory."

"All right. I still have some orders to write. Meet me at the desk."

Angela nodded. When Patrick left she walked over to Rory's bed, taking one of his hands in her own. "I have to leave now, Rory. But I'll be back tomorrow."

"I sure like the bicycle," Rory said shyly. "And I sure didn't expect it."

"Well, I'm glad you like it. I just can't wait for you to get out of the hospital so you can try it out."

"Me, neither," Rory agreed emphatically.

Angela said goodbye to his parents, then left the room. By the time she reached the nurses' station

Patrick was closing the chart he'd been writing in. They headed toward the elevators.

"See? Everything turned out just as you planned," he said as they began the descent.

Angela tilted her head to one side, smiling up at him. "It really did, didn't it?"

Patrick didn't answer directly; he frowned as he gave her a scrutinizing look. "Now that's strange. You look really different than you did in Rory's room. Not too hot, in fact."

Angela clicked her tongue. "Well, I never! You're supposed to say something like, 'How absolutely gorgeous you look, Angela, like a sweet breath of air.'"

"Hmm," Patrick muttered wryly. "Unfortunately you happen to be speaking to a man who is incapable of false flattery. Now 'fess up. Did you have a bad day at work?"

Angela sighed and nodded. "Yes. I did, actually. I had to work my fanny off to get out of there as early as I'd planned." It was a lie, of course, for the way she looked now had nothing to do with work and everything in the world to do with the fact that last night's sleep had been erratic and more than a little disturbed.

The elevator doors opened, and Angela walked out ahead of Patrick. When she turned to look back she caught him giving her backside an open once-over. "Doesn't look like too much damage from here," he commented.

Angela chided him, "I had no idea you were such a chauvinist, Patrick Merrill."

"Chauvinist! Damn, a man can't get away with anything nowadays. Besides, you're the one who brought up the subject of your fanny."

They were separated for a moment by a crowd of people waiting for the elevators. When they met again in the corridor Angela said, "But *I* was only kidding. Leave it to a man to make an issue out of it. Tell me, why is it you never hear women saying the things to men that men say to women?"

Patrick frowned, trying to hide a smile. "Don't they?"

"No. They don't," Angela answered firmly.

They entered the hospital coffee shop, which was crowded with the evening shift. "Why don't you grab that table over there and I'll get our coffee," Patrick suggested. Angela agreed and hurried to claim the small Formica table.

Patrick returned a few minutes later, placed the cups on the table and fished in the pocket of his long white coat, withdrawing packets of sugar and powdered creamer. "So, okay, why don't you enlighten me on the differences between what men and women talk about. Or whatever it was you were trying to get across."

Emptying two packets of sugar into her coffee, Angela said, "I was referring to the fact that when a woman sees an attractive man she just keeps it to herself. She doesn't whistle or make suggestive comments or mutter lewd remarks about a man's appearance, loud enough for him to hear, of course.''

Patrick placed an elbow on the table and scratched the corner of one eye thoughtfully. ''Ah.'' He cleared his throat and said, ''May I ask where all this came from? As I said, you were the one who made the initial reference to your derriere. I merely made another, perhaps more precise one. I had no idea it was going to lead into a discussion of sexism.''

Angela leaned backward and suddenly started laughing. ''You know, neither did I. I don't even know why I got going on the subject.''

Patrick smiled into her eyes. ''Well, I'll admit I understand what you're driving at. And you're right. Some men do act like jackasses in the presence of women. Even the more 'distinguished' of the sex.''

''Why? I never did understand it. Is it the result of some deep psychological need, or instinct—or is it, in fact, the result of male conditioning, the 'power play' we hear about?''

''Peer pressure, mostly. I can remember back as late as my early college years; if a good-looking chick...ah, woman, happened to walk by when a bunch of the guys were together, you were expected to make some sort of comment. Complimentary, derogatory—anything, as long as it indicated you were a real man, capable of noticing a female in the immediate vicinity. I guess what I'm really saying is that noticing the opposite sex is natural, but conditioning has a lot to do with the way guys learn to behave.''

Angela sipped her coffee. ''Oh, most women don't walk around with blinders on, either. Most men would be shocked to hear some of the things discussed among groups of women, I'm sure. But the difference is, as I said, that women generally keep their comments to themselves, or among themselves. I don't think you'll ever run across very many women who feel the urge to give a deafening blast of their car horn simply because a man is jogging or walking along on the side of the road. And believe me, that has happened more times than I care to remember. It's absolutely infuriating.''

The corners of Patrick's mouth quivered into a grin.

''What is it? What's so funny?''

Setting his cup down, Patrick shook his head, the smile on his face reflecting the humorous spark in his eyes. ''You just reminded me of something that happened a long time ago. Something rather self-incriminating, I'm afraid.''

''What? Tell me. You can't bring it up and not say what it is. I hate it when people do that.''

Patrick leaned on the table once more his jaw against his fist, his other hand idly caressing hers. ''When I was about fifteen there was a certain group of guys I used to hang out with—mostly school friends. Back then it was routine procedure to 'make the drag' down Henderson's main street every single Friday night. Didn't matter what the weather was—you did it. Everyone did. Of course, the drive down Main Street didn't take very long 'cause Henderson was really a small town at that time.

"Anyway, one particular Friday night, J.C. Malone—he was the oldest of the group and had a driver's license, which made us legal—he was at the wheel. We had made the drag at least fifteen times already. It was around nine, ten o'clock. The rest of us were getting really thirsty and wanted to pull into Sheps, a drive-in hamburger joint. But J.C. was hell-bent on finding this one chick—excuse me, girl—that he'd spotted earlier walking down the sidewalk. I never did see her, but according to J.C., he was ready to donate his entire body to research the very next day just to get another glimpse of her.

"Well, it was his car, and we didn't want to walk, so we had to go along with it. He finally spotted her, anyway, or thought he did, and was craning his neck to get a better look, when he side-swiped a car parked at the curb. A *police* car. You can imagine the ticket he got."

Angela chuckled, liking the spattering of gray at his temples. Patrick went on, "You should have seen the poor guy. That last look ended up costing him thirty-five dollars and the use of the car for the next three months."

Patrick shook his head, a distant expression of remembrance on his face, reflecting the lightheartedness of his younger years. Angela had a flash picture of him as he might have been at fifteen—happy, carefree, untroubled by the worries and concerns that would affect him later. She wondered how she would have reacted to him as a teenager; no doubt much the same as she did now. But as his expression settled into the one she was more familiar with, she couldn't resist speculating on the cause of the deep, premature creases at the bridge of his nose, the line across his brow, character lines that nevertheless didn't detract from his good looks. What had put them there, what had caused him such stress? The fact that she still had so much to learn about him merely intrigued her all the more.

She drank the remainder of her coffee, set the cup down and said, "Sounds like you led a genuine small-town life."

"Oh, I did. There were only a hundred and two people in my senior graduating class."

"That's incredible. You know, I can't even imagine it. There were almost nine hundred in mine."

"Henderson, Texas, was a small town, all right, with a small-town mentality." He shook his head. "Ever see the movie *American Graffiti*?"

Angela nodded.

"A replica of Henderson. They could have filmed it right there, easily. Nice town to grow up in, but when I left for college I knew I'd never make it back. Not permanently, that is."

"You became a big-city man," Angela said with a smile.

"Not really. I don't like extremes, I guess you could say. Jacksonville is the right size city for me."

"It is nice. St. Augustine is the same. I was never cut out for life in a metropolis, either. I don't think I could stand having to spend two hours every day just getting to and from work. It's enough having to put in the hours as they are."

Patrick studied her curiously. "That sounds rather out of character."

"What do you mean? Oh, about putting in the hours." She laughed lightly. "I didn't mean it to come out sounding that way. I'm very happy with what I do. But, I mean, you have to admit any job can have its aspects of drudgery."

"True. Very true."

"Work itself is enough. If I had to fight just to get to it I'd wear out—like that." She snapped her fingers. "Speaking of which, are you finished for the day?"

"Nope. I still have half a list of patients to see."

Angela reached for her purse and draped her coat over one arm. "Well, I guess I'd better let you get to it."

They walked together toward the front lobby, where they said goodbye, exchanging a rather self-conscious kiss, Patrick promising to call later that night. As she drove home Angela reflected on the entire day. The visit with Rory had turned out beautifully, but the conversation she and Patrick had shared had been even more significant. For it added yet another element to their relationship, a deepening of the intimacy that was growing day by day.

THE NEXT FEW DAYS before Christmas passed in a whirlwind of activity. The store was busy every day right up until closing, and Angela was never able to get away before seven. She had finally bought presents for Joyce and Jonathon, while the store employees were given bonuses in their checks.

Patrick called each night after he got home from the hospital. On Thursday night, when he hadn't called by ten o'clock, Angela found herself sitting in front of the television set, chewing her nails. When she realized what she was doing she jerked her hand away and stared blankly at the set. She hadn't chewed her fingernails since... since, well, anyway, a long time ago.

She got up off the couch and went into the kitchen, poured a glass of milk and stood drinking it, watching the television through the bar window. The distraction was effective, but only to a certain degree; she wasn't chewing her nails anymore, but her mind was still tossing around reasons why Patrick hadn't phoned. He usually did so by nine-thirty. Good Lord, how had she become so dependent on his nightly call? The question worried her every bit as much as what had led up to it.

For three years now she had managed on her own, with no one to depend on to call her every night. It hadn't been easy—in fact, it had been sheer hell at times—but she had adjusted and had developed self-reliance, a life-style that at one time would have terrified her. Tonight here she was, anxiously awaiting a phone call from a man she'd known only a few weeks. True, they had grown close, very close, but certainly not to that extent— she didn't have to hear his voice to get by; a man's voice should never be her only concern.

To hell with all the analyzing, she thought, putting the empty glass in the sink and walking back into the living room. There was one reason for this sudden dependence, and it had to do with timing. Patrick was more than just a good friend—and more than someone she was interested in in a romantic sense. He was a buffer, a very effective human obstacle—between herself and all the emotions she'd had to contend with the past three Christmases. Emotions that were physically and mentally devastating. Without consciously admitting it, she had come to rely on Patrick for more than his company; he offered, at the perfect time, a way out for Angela, out from beneath the heavy cloak of guilt and pain and remorse that descended unfailingly during the very season that was meant for goodwill and cheer and happiness.

She closed her eyes tightly for a moment, then opened them, her gaze resting on the ever-silent telephone. *Oh, to hell with it,* she thought, angry with herself for letting her thoughts veer in that direction. She flicked off the television, checked the locks on the door, turned out the lights and went upstairs.

In her bedroom she turned on her clock radio, then pulled a large paper bag out of her closet and set it on her bed. She removed the box that had been included as part of the purchase, holding up the burgundy sweater by the shoulders. She had no idea what size Patrick wore, but could easily picture the sweater on him, and reaffirmed to herself that she had chosen wisely.

She folded it, carefully placing the gift inside the box before wrapping it in silver foil paper, adding a bow of her own creation made of crimson ribbon. She looked at the finished product approvingly, set it aside, then glanced at the clock; it was almost eleven. Doubting that Patrick would call this late, she changed into her nightgown and pulled back the covers, snuggling beneath the sheets and quilted coverlet, only her hands peeping out beneath her chin as she propped her paperback novel on her chest and began to read.

But after a few minutes the book slid from her hand onto the floor, the sound waking her. Sleepily she turned off the light and rolled onto her side, more than willing to succumb to the soothing, mind-numbing solace of sleep.

SHE WAS STEPPING OUT of the shower the next morning when the telephone rang. Drying off quickly, she slipped into a terry-cloth robe, wondering as she walked into the bedroom if something was wrong at the store. It was Regi's morning to open up; she hoped nothing was amiss already.

"Hello?" She patted her freshly washed hair with the towel.

"Hi, there. You sound like you're up and about already."

"Patrick?" The hand on her head froze just as her heart gave a little leap.

"I know. What am I doing calling so early in the morning? Well, for one thing I just now got my phone working again, and for another I wanted to know if you were angry with me."

Angela laughed with relief. "Of course I'm not angry. Why would I be?"

"Hmm. I'm disappointed. I thought you would be more upset that I didn't call when I said I would."

"I've never assumed your words were carved in cement."

Patrick laughed. "They're not, thank God. Actually, I was busy as hell last night. Didn't even get home till almost ten. And when I did the telephone was dead. Some sort of cable problem in this area.

I had to make two trips to a pay telephone in the middle of the night.''

"That's awful. You must be exhausted. Did you get any sleep at all?"

"Not much. And I've got a waiting room full of patients in approximately forty-five minutes." The thought of the tiring day ahead would have been overwhelming if not for the fact that today his divorce was final. At last!

"You're making me feel guilty," Angela said.

"About my work load? The only thing you should feel guilty about is not noticing that I didn't call."

"But I did." *You have no idea how much,* she added silently.

"Okay, my ego is sufficiently restored. I'm also calling to ask if you have any place special you want to have supper, tomorrow night."

"No, not really. Whatever you choose will be fine with me."

"Good. Listen, I'll try to phone tonight, but in case the telephone goes on the blink again, let's say I'll pick you up around six tomorrow evening."

"That sounds fine."

"Great. Talk to you later, then—and Angela . . . I miss you."

"Me, too . . . bye."

Angela hung up and stood patting her hair dry for a few minutes, feeling absolutely jubilant. *See? See what a total waste of emotion last night was?* She closed her eyes and sighed, and when she opened them again, a small, confident smile pulled at the corners of her lips. Everything was going to be just fine. She was going to make it through this Christmas, and maybe, just maybe, she could really and truly enjoy it.

CHAPTER TWELVE

THE COLD SPELL gripping most of the country intensified during the following twenty-four hours, bringing record-low temperatures to Florida's eastern coast. On Christmas Eve morning Angela awoke to trees and bushes covered with a thick layer of frost. The air in the town house was frigid, and she hurried from the bed to the bathroom, relishing the warmth of the hot water as she stood beneath the shower's spray.

The cold weather invigorated her, however, and she was glad the low temperatures were continuing at least through Christmas day. The past two Christmases, the mercury level had risen to well into the seventies, comfortable weather to be sure, but definitely detracting from the proper Christmas mood, as far as Angela was concerned.

After the pharmacy closed its doors at one o'clock that afternoon, Angela and Dorothy cleared the dispensing counter to arrange a spread of the pastries, sandwiches and cold drinks everyone had contributed for their private Christmas celebration. It was nice having the store to themselves for once. Without the constant intrusion of customers and ringing telephones, the party lasted until almost three o'clock.

Joyce phoned a few minutes after Angela got home, wanting to confirm the plans for Christmas dinner.

"Of course we'll be there," Angela assured her. "I wouldn't miss it for the world, you know that. Is there anything you want me to bring?"

"No, this is my affair. You just bring yourself. And Patrick, of course."

"All right, then. If you insist."

"What are you doing tonight?"

"Patrick is coming by at six. We're going out to dinner."

"That sounds like fun." The comment was made in a blasé manner, which didn't fool Angela for one second. She was well aware of the note of relief in Joyce's tone, and was touched by her friend's genuine if unexpressed concern.

"Where's Jonathon?"

"In the study. Working on his syllabus for next semester already. Can you believe it?"

"Yes. Knowing Jonathon. When are you going to start preparing?"

Joyce laughed. "Are you kidding? I've got my reputation to think about—world's most dedicated procrastinator. I probably won't even look at my class schedule until the night before we go back."

"Well, I think you've got the right idea. You should be enjoying the holidays, not working."

"I agree. And so far I've been doing just that. Well, I guess I'll see you tomorrow. You guys have a great time tonight."

"We will. Merry Christmas."

"Same to you."

THE RESTAURANT Patrick had selected for their Christmas Eve dinner was elegant and expensive, absolutely perfect. "I don't think you could have chosen a better spot, Patrick. And this—" Angela indicated the rich raspberry mousse dessert in front of her "—is fantastic. In fact this is one of the most enjoyable Christmas Eves I've ever experienced."

"You don't miss being with your family?"

Angela hesitated; the unexpected question stung, just a little. "Not really. I know they're doing all right. They're where they want to be, and I know they think I'm doing fine."

"'Think'?"

"You know what I mean. Parents always find something to worry about. I called them this afternoon and told them what my plans were for tonight and the rest of the holidays. They were satisfied— and reassured that I'm surviving."

"And are *you*? Satisfied, that is."

Angela laughed lightly. "Of course!" She looked all around her. "Who wouldn't like being wined and dined in such a setting as this? It sure beats Santa Claus."

Patrick grinned. "Well, okay, I believe you, then."

"You should." Angela took a sip of coffee. "What about your family? Wouldn't you rather be spending the holiday with your relatives?"

"Oh, no. We're scattered all over the place. My older sister and her husband routinely take a couple of weeks off during the holidays for a skiing vacation; my younger brother is in school in London. That leaves my parents in Dallas, and they're very involved with their own social set. None of us misses each other, really. We call and talk if we remember to, but mostly everyone is happy to do his own thing and let everyone else do the same."

"Sounds as though you have a very understanding family."

"Hmm, understanding—if a bit distant." Patrick gently took one of Angela's hands in his and began stroking her palm with his thumb, the gesture eliciting a shiver of anticipation coursing up and down Angela's spine. "Tell you what, beautiful lady. Why don't we skip the after-dinner drink and go to my place. I have the same thing they could offer you here—" Patrick winked "—for a much better price and in a lot more comfortable surroundings."

"So that's it—I've cost you too much already," Angela teased. She let her gaze roam around the antique-filled dining room, oak-paneled walls hung with Impressionist prints, tables covered in white linen, the well-dressed clientele conversing in low tones. "I don't know...this place is *real* comfortable as far as I'm concerned." She looked back at him with a gleam in her eye. "But I agree. We've been here long enough. Let's get outta here. Anyway, we have to make sure Rusty isn't feeling too lonely on Christmas Eve."

Patrick smiled and signaled for the check. "As a matter of fact, that was going to be my very next excuse." Angela sat back and looked all around her one more time, a satisfied expression on her face. How very much she was enjoying herself tonight. Much, much more than she had even hoped for.

TWO LARGE OAK LOGS snapped and popped on the hearth. As Angela watched Patrick prodded them with the poker, sending a shower of sparks up through the damper. The flames grew taller, their heat reaching out to where Angela was seated on the carpeted den floor, propped up in front of a love seat, two plush rectangular pillows behind her back.

Her gaze lingered on the outline of Patrick's body where he knelt in front of the fireplace. She marveled at how lean and fit he was, enjoying the way his thick dark hair, a bit longer now than when she'd first met him, curled slightly upward along the collar of his shirt. *How wonderful that I met him,* she thought. He was an unusual man, kind, dedicated, appealing in a sensual as well as a sexual sense. He took time out for a private life, too, which many successful men didn't.

Strange that in the two and a half years since she'd been dating several eligible men, not one had come close to possessing the characteristics she so admired in this man. Admittedly she hadn't given any of them more than half a chance, either, but still she would have known, wouldn't she, if there had been something there worth pursuing. She had suspected that Patrick had substance from the very beginning—even under the extremely trying circumstances of their first meeting.

He turned away from the fire, catching the pensive expression on her face. Sitting down next to her, he dropped an arm around her shoulders and asked, "What were you thinking just then?"

Angela reached for the snifter of brandy that sat on the low coffee table. "Oh, nothin'."

Something about the way she said that affected Patrick deeply. His arm tightened around her shoulders and he pulled her toward him. " 'Nothin',' my foot. You were lost in thought, I could tell."

"That's right, I was 'lost.' Now I can't remember."

"All right, I get the hint." He gazed into the fire, felt its warmth spreading over both of them. His fingers pressed into her upper arm, kneading lightly. "You know something? I think Rusty was happier to see you than he was me."

Angela's eyebrows raised, and she chuckled.

"You sound jealous!" She hooked a finger thoughtfully over her upper lip. "But you know, he was, wasn't he? He really does like me."

"Sure he does. I'm sure that's mostly the result of the night he spent on your patio—more specifically, the two heavy-duty T-bones you gave him."

"Now what are you tryin' to do, hurt my feelings?" Angela socked him playfully in the arm. "I'd prefer to think he simply liked *me*. Just for myself."

Patrick paused, his gaze locking with hers, the amusement gone from his eyes. "He'd be a fool not to," he said quietly, lowering his head to hers. Angela's head tilted backward, and her eyelids drooped heavily. The warm smell of brandy fanned out across her face, mingling with the spicy scent of his after-shave, the pungent aroma of burning oak and smoldering ashes.

She had remembered his kiss perfectly, missing it greatly over the days when she hadn't seen him. But the memory had nothing to do with the reality of what was happening, making her respond with an ardor that shook her to the core. His teeth gently bit into the flesh of her lips. As she felt his tongue slipping into her mouth, meeting and melding with her own, every synapse of her nervous system awakened and tingled with tension.

Their kiss was long and deep, as full and warm as the flames burning in the hearth. But Patrick had known a need for the woman he held in his

arms since he'd first seen her, a need that would
not be fulfilled by a mere kiss. There could be no
more ignoring it. The time was ripe for what he
wanted to share with Angela, and to his supreme
gratification, she uttered not a word of protest as
he stood and pulled her up by the hand, leading
her out of the room and down the darkened
hallway.

Objection was the farthest thing from Angela's
mind, for she felt the same desire as Patrick, a
need perhaps even greater. She had been with no
other man since Gordon, her normal womanly
passion smothered in the aftershock of grief and
anguish. Now was different. She was at a different
point in her life, and Patrick was certainly a different sort of man than she had ever known. Indeed, there were moments when she wondered if
he really was all he seemed to be, if he were not
too good to be true.

Justification and reasoning were secondary
issues at the moment, however, for the physical
passion she felt and shared with this man was too
great to be denied. As she followed him down the
plushly carpeted hallway, waiting as he switched
on a light, she realized she had probably known
from the beginning that this would happen. Now
that the moment was here, she was filled with an
anticipation erotic in and of itself. She was almost
light-headed, and when Patrick said, "Come in,"
she sucked in her breath involuntarily, aware of a
liquid rush of sensation in the pit of her stomach.

Recessed lighting in the ceiling provided just enough illumination so that each object was discernible. Angela looked at everything in the spacious room, decorated, as was the rest of the house, in an attractive contemporary fashion. An enormous potted ficus plant stood in one corner, the ample branches straining toward the sliding glass doors along one wall.

"This is lovely," she whispered. Patrick let go of her hand, and she heard the plop of his shoes on the carpet.

"You like it, huh?"

"Sure do." She remained just inside the door, watching as he began unbuttoning the top of his shirt, his gaze fastened on hers.

"Is something wrong, Angela?"

"No. Of course not." She laughed lightly. "Why do you say that?"

"Only that you look rather uncomfortable standing there." He crossed the carpet to where she stood and placed his hands on her shoulders, massaging them gently. He sensed the nervous tension beneath her obvious willingness to be here with him.

"That's a wonderful ficus you have," she commented, instantly chagrined by the inane comment. But she was confused by the sudden change in her emotions; she wanted to be here with Patrick, very much—wanted to make love to him. But it had been a long time—perhaps too long.

"Thank you. I've had a lot of luck with it so far."

They were standing now with arms around each other. Patrick didn't seem uncomfortable at all, Angela noticed. Well it *was* his house, his bedroom.

Impulsively she kicked off her own shoes, finding that her chin then rested an inch or two lower on his chest. She closed her eyes, willing away the tension, the doubts that maybe this was all happening too fast.

He kissed the crown of her head, and she relaxed once again, breathing in the familiar aroma of him. He lifted her chin, his brown eyes glowing feverishly. They kissed once more, and she shivered uncontrollably as his thumbs slowly moved up and down her spine, pressing into the hollow just above her buttocks.

They drew away from each other, shedding their clothes quickly, their eyes still fused, expressing a mutual urgency. Patrick sat on the bed, reached out for her, drawing her down beside him.

"You are absolutely beautiful," he said in a soft, vibrant tone, and together they lay back on the huge bed.

Angela moaned gently as his hand rested on her abdomen, the palm flattened across her narrow waist. He kissed her forehead, her eyelids, her cheeks, her nose. His hand slid up her stomach to brush her breast, his thumb circling and teasing the stiffened areola.

Then his mouth moved lower, pressing against

the smooth flesh of her neck. As Angela strained upward in response, he buried his face for a moment between the rounded globes of her breasts, then turned his head, his tongue trailing wetly across one breast, flicking and teasing just as his thumb had done. Hearing her muffled gasp, Patrick suddenly straddled her, his passion heightened to an urgency that demanded release. He saw the desire in her eyes, felt her legs shift beneath him, opening willingly to accept him.

There was resistance as he pushed and entered her only slightly, and he looked down at her in surprise. Angela's face was turned away, her eyes tightly shut; she seemed to be concentrating very hard. He waited, mustering every ounce of patience he possessed, until finally he felt a yielding within her. He pushed again, very carefully, closing his eyes now and swallowing deeply as her feminine warmth surrounded him, bathing him in an exquisitely sensual pulsation.

He shifted his weight, resting his elbows on either side of her head. He undulated his hips slowly, unhurriedly, soaking up the sweet torment of the moment. She moaned, unaware of the sound, and as her teeth sank into the flesh of his shoulder, Patrick began to move rapidly, feeling her respond, their hips merging with each and every thrust. And as her hands fluttered crazily down the length of his back, resting on, then grasping the taut flesh of his buttocks, a deep groan escaped him.

Angela could feel his heart pounding against her flattened breasts, felt tiny rivulets of sweat matting the dark hair on his chest. The initial moment of discomfort had vanished, and she rolled from side to side beneath him, the motion shattering the last vestige of his restraint. Her legs locked around him; his thrusts became quicker and deeper and quicker, until the room was filled with the climactic echoes of their lovemaking.

HE LAY MOTIONLESS UPON HER for a long time. Angela pushed gently against his shoulder, and he dropped his head, nuzzling his face into the auburn hair tumbling across her neck and chin. "Wha..." he mumbled.

"I can hardly breathe," she whispered, pushing against him once more.

His eyes opened, and he looked at her apologetically as he rolled onto his back. "Sorry about that, hon," he said, keeping one arm around her shoulders.

Angela shifted onto her side, facing away from him, nestling into the curve his body made around hers. She hugged her knees to her chest, her teeth chattering.

"What's the matter?"

"C-cold."

Patrick reached down, fumbling for a minute with the tangle of sheets and bedspread, then threw both across them, tucking the edges in securely. "Anything else?"

"Nope, everything else is just fine," Angela answered, feeling very pleased and contented and fulfilled.

"Everything?" Patrick asked, separating the tresses of her hair with his fingertips.

Angela looked back at him, her expression very serious for a moment, then she smiled and nodded. At that moment Patrick felt the most piercing awareness of an emotion he hadn't felt in a very long time—if ever.

"You know something?" he whispered, one hand stroking her forearm, sliding downward to capture and squeeze her hand.

"What?" Angela's eyelids were closing sleepily.

"I think...I think, I just may be falling in love with you."

Angela's eyes popped opened, and she said in a strained voice, "Oh?"

"Oh? Is that all you can say?"

The bed covers crumpled as she shifted slightly toward him, glancing at him out of the corner of her eye. "What?"

Patrick half laughed. "I just said something that I, at least, consider rather significant, and all you can say is 'Oh.' I wonder if you even heard me."

"I heard you."

"What did you say?"

"I said I heard you."

"Oh. She heard me, she says. Nothing else, just she heard me."

"What do you want me to say?"

Patrick propped himself up on one elbow, smiling lopsidedly down at her. "Well, for starters, something original."

Angela rolled completely onto her back and stared up at the ceiling. "Okay, then. I'm a little surprised, I guess. I really don't know what to make of...what you just said." *Hell,* she thought. *You're scared to death. Admit it.*

There was a long silence between them, until finally Patrick said, "There's really not that much to make of it. Look, if I've upset you by—"

"I'm not upset," Angela said. She expelled a long breath and went on. "Look...I guess I'm just not ready to hear such a serious statement yet. We haven't known each other that long, Patrick."

We've known each other long enough to make love, he thought, surprised at the extent of his disappointment. But he kept such feelings to himself and said in a lighter tone, "All right. We'll just leave it for now." He traced his fingertips down the valley between her breasts, then circled them slowly one at a time. "There are certainly things to talk about—and do. Right?"

Angela turned toward him, more than willing to follow his lead. "Right," she murmured, feeling his readiness for her against her thigh, feeling the dampness of her own readiness, too. Her heartbeat quickened in expectation; it was as if, having finally been awakened, her senses were crying out with a hunger that could never be completely sated. Stroking his nape, she slid her other hand down the damp space between their bodies, grasping him and feeling him grow within her palm.

"Sweet heaven," Patrick muttered against her neck, quickly moving above her.

But Angela shook her head. "No. Wait." She pushed against him with her hands until he rolled over onto his back. Then she straddled him, watching his features flush and tighten as she guided him into her. He groaned and gripped her buttocks as she began to move above him, slowly at first, then rapidly, up and down, round and round, a splendid choreography of deliciously tormenting rhythm. When Patrick heard that familiar moan from Angela he grew rigid, every muscle in his body tensing, straining to hold back. When he could stand no more he began to meet her motions, urgently, watching and absorbing the fiery passion in her green eyes. Abruptly she pulled her head back, grasping his upper arms, her nostrils flaring as a deep flush suffused her complexion. The sight of her above him was more than he could handle, the tenuous thread that held his self-control together snapping as Angela cried out— and suddenly the pulsating in his loins released into a warm stream of unbelievable pleasure, sending shock waves of sensation shuddering through him. In his wildest fantasy he had never imagined such sweet, complete sensation.

"My God, sweetheart," he whispered raggedly, continuing to move inside her as he felt her twisting and turning above him. She waited, tensing, then finally caught on to and rode out the next climactic wave washing over her. Patrick's fingers played through her hair as she collapsed on top of him, her quickened breathing gradually subsiding to a more regular rhythm. And then, not caring if it *was* too soon, or whether she heard him or not, he whispered the words into the curtain of auburn hair across his cheek. "I do love you, Angela. I really do."

THEY LAY SIDE BY SIDE on their backs, holding hands, the silence between them almost tangible, yet not uncomfortable. An image came to Angela: a couple standing alone at the top of the mountain they'd just climbed, looking out on the glorious vista surrounding them, dumbstruck by the magnificent beauty they alone had discovered. Exactly the way she felt at this moment, the way she knew Patrick felt. She hadn't known such sweet fulfillment was possible.

They lay in silence for a long while before Angela finally turned to look at Patrick, surprised to see that he was looking at her.

"Thanks," she whispered, squeezing his hand, feeling an emotional warmth spreading through her now, connecting her to him in some deeper way.

"I could say the same thing, you know."

She smiled, rolling toward him, placing a hand on his upper arm. Her eyelids almost closed, and she expelled a long, wistful sigh. "I don't want to get up. I could stay here all night."

"That's what I was planning on."

"You were?"

"Mm-hm. I'm not exactly up to an hour-long drive in the middle of the night."

"I should have brought my car tonight and met you at the restaurant. I didn't even think of it."

"Are you crazy? It's a damn good thing you didn't think of it—I would have been angry as hell if you'd brought it up, that's for sure. I want you to stay."

Angela bit her lower lip. "It is late. And it is Christmas Eve."

"That's right."

"And I sure am sleepy."

"You and me both."

"Okay, then, I'll stay."

"I'm glad you decided that on your own, sweetheart. But I'm afraid you really didn't have a choice."

"I didn't, huh?"

"Uh-uh."

Angela sat up halfway, leaning on an elbow. "You big brute, you were going to keep me here against my will."

"If need be, true."

"Patrick Merrill! One more example of your chauvinistic attitude!"

"When the situation calls for it, sweetheart. . . I can be one of the worst."

She punched him lightly on the shoulder. "Yeah, I betcha can, *sugarplum*."

"Y'know, that's the second time you've done that tonight," he said, glancing at his shoulder.

"So?"

"'So,'" he mimicked her. "So I don't like it."

"Can't stop me."

"No, but I bet I can get back at you."

His next movement was so swift that Angela was stunned when a fat, down-filled pillow was thrust into her face. She shrieked and turned to grab another one, and there ensued an all-out, stand-up, bouncing-up-and-down-on-the-bed pillow fight, the likes of which Angela hadn't enjoyed since her days of all-night slumber parties. She alternately giggled and screamed as Patrick made deep, throaty animal sounds, causing her to jump off the bed and hop back on more than once.

Finally fatigued, she hopped off the bed one last time and ran across the room, crouching behind the ficus plant, her breath coming fast and hard. The room had grown decidedly chillier during the past hour and a half, but she was oblivious to the fact, despite her nakedness.

"Give up?" Patrick asked, standing in the middle of the bed, the down pillow held in front of his stomach.

"Me, give up? Why should I give up? You're the one who started it."

"You're the one hiding in the corner."

"I'm just out of breath."

"Well, I'm waiting."

But Angela knew there wasn't a chance in the world she could continue the game; she was exhausted, totally. Suddenly she burst out laughing, cupping both hands over her mouth and shaking until tears rolled down her cheeks.

"All right, what's the big joke?" Patrick asked.

Angela's breath caught in the middle of a fresh giggle. "You! The dignified, highly respected Dr. Merrill. I just wonder how many patients you'd have if they could see you right now." He was still standing there, king of the bed, his right hand clutching the pillow, which had slid down to a somewhat more revealing position.

"Well, you're going to become one of them," he said, "if you don't get something on that naked fanny of yours. This room is freezing." He said that as though it had just dawned on him, then he turned and jumped to the floor. "Be right back. I'm going to adjust the thermostat."

He left the room, and Angela came out from behind the ficus. It was freezing. She hurried over to snatch up her clothes, bunching them in front of her. Patrick walked back into the room, and by then she was shaking, her teeth chattering, goose bumps raised all over her body.

"I want to take a shower," she said. "A hot one."

"Does that mean you give up?"

"Yeah, yeah. All right, I give up. But I'll get you later—when you least expect it."

"Mmm," Patrick said, unimpressed by the threat.

She took a few steps then turned back. "Um. . . I don't have anything to wear besides this."

"Just a minute." Patrick strode to a chest of drawers on the opposite side of the room, rummaged around for a moment, then tossed something across the room to Angela. It was a pair of men's long johns, obviously much too large for her, but she accepted them gratefully. As she pulled open the bathroom door, she glanced back at him and shook her head.

"I thought you said it was cold in here," she said.

"It is."

"Then how can you just walk around naked as a jaybird, as if it's the middle of summer or something?"

Patrick straightened his spine, drew back his shoulders and said in a very arrogant tone, "Simple. Extraordinary power of mind over matter."

"You're full of it, Merrill." Angela stepped to the bathroom and switched on the light. "I'll be out in a minute." She took longer than a minute, however, opting on impulse for a bath instead of a shower. As she slid down in the oversize brown porcelain tub, she closed her eyes, reflecting on the evening she had spent with Patrick. This had been a special Christmas Eve, and she would remember every single detail of it, always.

She and Patrick slept together in the king-size

bed, lying at first side by side, sometime later in the night slipping away from each other to more comfortable positions. But just knowing Patrick was there with her was a comfort to Angela. She woke once, heard him breathing steadily, then turned onto her side, closing her eyes and drifting off to sleep.

THE SOUNDNESS OF HER SLEEP, however, like the precious hours of passion spent in Patrick's arms, was only a diversion from dark, inescapable re-membrances lingering in the recesses of her agitated subconscious. That night the remem-brances became real once again, demanding a rec-ognition and confrontation she determinedly ignored each and every day. The dreams were so vivid that at one point Angela threw an arm out in front of her, pushing and fighting to be rid of them. Still they were there, pulling her into the past, the night of horror and loss forever branded on her soul. . . .

DARKNESS. EVERYWHERE DARKNESS, stretching out endlessly before them, broken only by the sleek patches of oil and ice dotting the winding, four-lane highway. The frown on Angela's face was rigid by this time, and she could feel the mus-cles in her forehead tightening like a steel band, extending around her head and down her neck. They were going fast, much too fast, but she had long since stopped trying to get through to Gordon about that. *He* was the one driving, he'd growled at her, and she could damn well shut her mouth about it.

Another emotion battled with the anxiety that was escalating into panic: anger. She could feel it in every cell of her body, rage gripping her, blinding in its intensity. Yet she could see very well the blond stranger at the wheel—her husband. She hated him at that moment, hated him with every ounce of her being.

"Thou shall not hate," she had learned as a child, and she never had. She had taught herself to see the good in people, even in those she didn't care for, or who had hurt her. But there was no other definition for her feeling now, and the force of it terrified her. How could it be that she hated this man whom she had vowed to love until "death do us part," to love and honor and cherish forever?

She couldn't stop the words spewing forth, vile words she never would have believed she could utter. The child, fortunately, was still asleep, oblivious of the cruel exchange in the front seat. The whir of tires grew louder and louder as the car accelerated, and Angela screamed at Gordon to slow down. . . .

Suddenly the oncoming headlights of another car flashed brightly, heading straight toward them. Instinctively Angela braced one hand against the dashboard, the other gripping the door armrest, her scream drowned out by the unending squeal of brakes and tires and the frightened cries of a child, the world, her entire world spinning out of control....

"ANGELA! WAKE UP. Come on now, wake up."

She was sobbing uncontrollably, her eyes half open as she struggled against him, one hand pushing hard against his chest, the other clutching his forearm in a deathlike grip. Patrick shook her by the shoulders, and her eyes flew open. Even in the darkness he could see the stark, raw terror there. "Angela, what is it?" he asked softly, smoothing the hair back from her brow.

His voice finally penetrated, and she blinked several times, focusing on his face. Her body remained rigid. She released her breath in a half sigh, half moan, her mouth starting to quiver. She looked as though she wanted to say something, but the words never came out.

Patrick pushed gently on her shoulders until she lay back against the pillows. After several seconds her muscles began to relax, and she was able to absorb the reality of her surroundings. Several seconds passed before she was recovered enough to be somewhat embarrassed. But still the dream hovered starkly in her mind.

Swallowing, she whispered hoarsely, "Sorry."

Patrick, who was still sitting up, looked down at her with concern. "What are you sorry about? You had a bad dream. You certainly don't have to apologize for that."

"I. . . I'm sorry I woke you up."

"I'm sure as hell glad you did. You were terrified." He hesitated. "Want to talk about it?"

Angela shook her head slowly. "It was just some crazy dream. I don't even know what it was about."

Patrick accepted her answer, even as he recognized it for the lie it was. For he could still see the fear written all over her face. The fear, too, that he would try to make her talk about her dream. A dream was a dream, a nightmare a nightmare, but this had been something else, something far more disturbing and significant. And he had seen a similar look in her eyes before. Now he was convinced that there was something about her, her past, something she was concealing from him.

But all he said was, "All right," and settled down next to her. "Think you'll be okay now?"

"Sure. It was crazy. Stupid, really. I have them sometimes, you know. Nightmares. I'm just a big baby."

"Come on, move a little closer."

She did, and he held her tightly within the curve of his body, his lips pressing into the natural part her hair made on the crown of her head.

"Do you think you can go back to sleep?" he asked.

"Yeah, I'm fine, really."

"Okay."

But it was a very long time before he felt her muscles relax and heard her breathing grow steady and even. What was it all about, he wondered, unable to dismiss this dreadful difference in her, this obviously troubled side of her that he knew nothing about. He ached for her, for the pain she was going through, and longed to protect her from whatever demons tormented her. And he would do so, if only she would permit him. If only she would *really* allow him into her life.

CHAPTER THIRTEEN

ANGELA HEARD PATRICK WHISTLING and banging around in the kitchen the next morning as she lay stretched out on the bed, one arm behind her head, her gaze focused on the giant ficus plant. He'd kissed her on the chin a while ago and rolled out of the bed, saying he was going to get dressed, then make breakfast. Angela had smiled at him, hoping she didn't look as bad as she felt. She had slept last night, but only for a few hours, and now she felt totally exhausted, physically and mentally drained.

When she got out of bed she felt a slight pulsing in her temples, an ominous symptom of a possible migraine. Lord, that was all she needed on Christmas Day. Her image in the bathroom mirror only confirmed how miserable she felt, so she went back to the bedroom to get her purse. After vigorously scrubbing her face she took pains in applying her makeup, finally satisfied that she at least looked somewhat better than she felt.

"Breakfast is ready, sleepyhead," Patrick called out from the kitchen, and she yelled back that she'd be there in a minute.

"Hey, you look great in those pj's," Patrick teased as she walked into the kitchen and pulled out a chair at the breakfast nook. He eyed the dragging hemline of the pants, the off-the-shoulder seams and rolled-up cuffs, giving a low wolf whistle.

"The latest in fashion," Angela joked, curtsying dramatically before sitting down at the table.

Patrick put a plate down in front of her, and her eyes widened. "What? You've got to be kidding! I'll never finish all this." The plate was piled with scrambled eggs, hash-brown potatoes and several slices of bacon. He put another plate of English muffins in the middle of the table, along with unsalted butter and a jar of raspberry preserves. "This is ridiculous, Patrick," Angela went on. "We're having dinner with the Colliers, remember? I don't want to get there and be so full I have to waddle in the door."

"Just shut your big bazooka and get busy there, girl."

Despite her headache she laughed, catching some of Patrick's infectious mood. " 'Big bazooka.' Now that's a good one."

"Yeah. The food's good, too. So eat."

She finished a surprising amount of it, along with two cups of coffee. The headache had diminished significantly. Angela began to feel she might just make it through the day, after all.

She and Patrick shared the Sunday paper over

more coffee, mostly in silence, though occasionally one or the other would read aloud some particularly interesting or humorous item. Sunlight streamed through the kitchen windows, bathing the room in a warm mellow glow.

Angela folded a section of the paper she'd just finished and reached for another, taking a sip of her coffee before opening it up. "You know, I really like your kitchen."

"Thanks. It likes you, too."

"It does, eh?"

Patrick nodded, his brown gaze locking into hers. "Mm-hm. It would like to see you here more often."

Angela grinned impishly. "Well, then, we'll just have to do something about that, won't we?" She meant it; Patrick's house had a certain feeling about it, a hominess that attracted one to stay. That quality reminded her of the early years of her marriage to Gordon, when life had been fresh and full of promise. She had been happy as a mother bird, busily creating her own cozy nest. For the moment she ignored the fact that she had been too satisfied, too naive to see what was going on under her nose.

Patrick got up to refill their coffee cups and caught her pensive expression. There it was again. What was she thinking, he wondered. Where was her mind just then? Certainly not in the present, that he knew. He sat back down and broke into her reverie. "This time it's really hot."

"What?"

"The coffee. I heated it a bit extra in the micro-wave." She was still looking at him uncompre-hendingly, so he said, "The last cup—remember? You said it wasn't hot enough."

"Oh!" She clapped a hand to her chest. "I'm sorry, my mind was off on some weird tangent."

"I noticed." He picked up the business section and shook it out, eyeing her from over the edge. "I've begun to recognize that faraway, im-penetrable look in your eyes. I've seen it often, in fact."

"I'm just like that, I guess," Angela said non-chalantly, measuring out a teaspoonful of sugar and emptying it into her coffee. "Out in left field most of the time."

"Hopefully not when you're filling prescrip-tions."

"Me? No way. You're looking at the most con-scientious pharmacist that ever hung up her license."

He realized what she was doing—trying to get him off the track, but he wouldn't be detoured this time. "Angela, what happened last night? What was it you were dreaming about?"

The spoon clinked against the cup as she looked up, startled by his change of subject. "Why are you bringing that up?"

"Why are you answering a question with a question?"

She clicked her tongue exasperatedly. "I told you already. I don't remember any details. It was just a bunch of crazy, jumbled-up, freaky images. The old routine nightmare, wandering down a foggy street, not being able to find my house—something like that."

"It seemed like more than your ordinary nightmare to me," Patrick insisted. "You were living whatever it was in your dream. I saw it in your face—you were going through sheer hell."

Angela slapped the paper down on the table and got up, picking up her cup of coffee and carrying it to the sink. "Look, I'm not really in the mood to be psychoanalyzed, so if you don't mind, let's drop it, all right?"

Patrick said nothing for a moment, just looked at her as she stood with her back to him, rinsing off the cup and saucer in the sink.

"Sorry. I didn't mean to get you upset."

"I'm not upset!" Her hand brushed against the skillet lying on its side in the sink, making it bang against the porcelain. The pulsing in her temples surged again, and Angela squeezed her eyes shut. She turned off the water, wiped her hands on a kitchen towel, then, managing a rather stiff smile, turned to Patrick. "I'm sorry. Really, Patrick. I think I've just had too much coffee. My nerves are all jangled."

She started to pick up the dishes on the table, but he placed a hand over hers, stopping her. "Hey, I'm the one who's sorry. It was stupid of me to bug you like that. You made it clear you didn't care to talk about it. So—subject closed. Period." He stood up and shuffled the newspapers together while Angela finished clearing the table.

"What time are we supposed to be at the Colliers'?" Patrick asked.

"One o'clock is when everyone is supposed to arrive, but Joyce said if we could get there a half hour earlier she'd appreciate it. I think they want to check you out a little more thoroughly before all the others get there."

"Well, we'd better get the ball rolling if you still want to go by your place."

"Oh, definitely. I've got to change, wash my hair... "

"Okay. You finish up here, and I'll feed Rusty. Then we'll get going."

"Will do. Here, don't forget my leftover bacon for your beast."

Patrick gave her a sly look. "You're trying your darndest to win over my dog's loyalty, aren't you?"

"You said it, not me," Angela quipped, opening the dishwasher door, more than a little grateful that things had been so smoothly set to rights.

THE COLLIERS' TOWN HOUSE WAS ALIVE with Christmas spirit. A medley of carols played softly on the stereo, and wonderful smells from the kitchen permeated the air, mingling enticingly with the tangy scent of the eight-foot Scotch pine.

"Your tree is fantastic," Patrick commented. "Really enormous." He was seated next to Angela in one corner of the rose-colored sectional sofa, the focal point of the living room. A hearty fire crackled in the grate, spreading its warmth generously among the five people seated before it.

"It is, isn't it?" Jonathon said, sipping his aperitif and tilting his head to one side, appraising the tree from yet another angle.

"They have one like this every year," Angela said. "At least as long as I've known them."

Jennifer Bronson, one half of the other couple the Colliers were entertaining that Christmas Day, spoke up. "And for as long as we've known them, too. I admire you, Jonathon, for sticking to tradition. It seems a shame not to have a real live tree like this one, especially when this area of the country is brimming with them."

"Well, it's not exactly as if you can go out and chop one down, you know," Jonathon said. "We still have to browse through the lots, argue for thirty, forty minutes about which one is the fullest, and about how ridiculous the prices are. But—we still do it. And we always end up with *the* tallest one, and *the* most expensive."

"Well, it's lovely," Jennifer said. "I wish you could talk some sense into Fred."

Fred Bronson took a slow sip of his bourbon

and slanted his wife a wry glance. "Forget it, Jen," he said in his deep voice. "It won't work. You know I hate the whole mess; making sure the thing doesn't catch fire, pine needles everywhere, which *always* clog up the damn vacuum cleaner."

Angela and Patrick grinned at each other. Despite the fact that Fred had a cynical comment to make about almost everything, he also had a quick, dry wit that was particularly amusing. If one didn't know him as his friends did, one might think he was simply in a terrible mood.

"Come on, Fred," Angela egged him on a little. "What's so wrong with getting in the Christmas spirit just a little. Not everything's as commercial as you say."

"Yeah, yeah. . . . Well, I'm here, aren't I?"

"Everyone just ignore Freddie," Jennifer said. "He's just blowing out a lot of hot air, trying to play Scrooge." She stood up and took her husband's empty glass from him. "I'm going to see if Joyce needs any help."

"I'd go with you," Angela said, "except that I know you'll be right back within thirty seconds. Joyce is a monster when it comes to letting others into her private domain. Especially when she's doing it up big—like today."

"I know, but I'm going to give it a try, anyway."

The men were talking football now. Angela turned back to them but didn't bother to feign interest in their discussion of the upcoming bowl games. She was fairly relaxed by now, having managed to put aside the morning's upsetting talk, and last night's dream. The only reminder was her nagging headache, unaffected by the aspirin she'd taken earlier. She felt Patrick squeeze her hand, and she looked at him. But he was nodding at the other two men, still participating in the conversation. She swallowed, touched by the fact that he had made the gesture unconsciously. The closeness she felt with him at that moment was intense, almost overwhelming. What was it that kept her from staying close, held her back from a relationship she had longed for all her life?

She sipped her drink and turned again to look at the Christmas tree; suddenly it blurred and swam before her vision, and she bit the inside of her cheek sharply. *Stop it!* she chastised herself, blinking rapidly, swallowing hard against the lump in her throat. This was not going to happen to her now; it couldn't. She had had everything under control only yesterday. She could certainly make it through today. She had to.

A solitary tear fell from the corner of an eye, and as she reached up to smooth back her hair, she surreptitiously wiped the droplet away with her thumb. Her head was turned away from Patrick, so she didn't see him looking at her just then, noting the telltale gesture. Jonathon and Fred were engaged in a heated football-statistics debate.

"Angie?" Patrick said in a low voice.

She faced him, eyes bright and moist and lit with false gaiety. "Mm-hm?"

"Something the matter?" He was frowning, the three vertical creases at the bridge of his nose deepening.

She forced a smile. "No. Of course not."

The lie was written all over her faintly flushed face, in her slightly red-rimmed eyes. He was positive he'd seen her wipe away a tear. "Are you sure?"

"Of course." Angela glanced pointedly at the other two men. "What happened, did you lose interest in football?"

"I never was that interested. I'm more concerned about you at the moment, anyway."

"Would you cut it out?" Angela said sotto voce. "They're going to think something's wrong."

Patrick looked at her steadily until she averted her gaze and bent forward to pick up her empty glass. "Actually, I do have a little headache. It's been nagging at me since this morning. I'm sure it's just tension. Would you mind seeing if Joyce has some more sherry?"

"Sure." He took the glass from her, getting up just as Jennifer walked back into the room. "Well, Angela, you were right. She kicked me out."

Angela smiled. The woman couldn't have appeared at a more opportune moment. "I told you so. How's everything going in there?"

"Well, she says it will only be another ten minutes or so. I don't think I can wait much longer. The smell of whatever she's concocting is driving me nuts."

"I'll be right back," Patrick said. Angela nodded.

"Thanks." She turned back to Jennifer and said, "So, are you enjoying the semester break as much as Joyce and Jonathon?"

JOYCE LOOKED UP from the electric range where she was stirring a pot of simmering sauce and smiled as she saw Patrick coming. "Well, hello there. The women I usually expect to invade my territory at least once. The men—never."

"Sorry to bother you. I'm only in search of a refill of sherry for Angela."

"Oh, sure. Look behind you on the counter there. I was just kidding, anyway. The men I'm not so strict about. Especially handsome ones," she added with a grin. "How's it going out there? Is everyone getting sick and tired of waiting?"

"No, I don't think Jonathon and Fred even remember what day it is. They're pretty heavily engaged in a debate over Superbowl contenders."

Joyce rolled her eyes and said wryly, "Ah yes, bowl-game season. I wish—I truly wish—I could become as dedicated a fan as Jonathon, but that seems to be the one area in which we'll never reach a state of mutual enjoyment.''

Patrick replaced the cork in the bottle and picked up the glass of sherry. "I'm what you'd call a fair-weather fan myself. If the Dolphins are doing well—I watch every game. If they're not, I'm busy doing or watching something else.''

"Now that sounds more like my style," Joyce said approvingly. She whacked the wooden spoon against the saucepan a couple of times, then turned off the burner. She swiveled to open the oven door, checking the rack of lamb inside. Turning back, she noticed Patrick still standing there, idly turning the glass of sherry round and round by the stem. He looked up at her with an odd expression, then glanced toward the closed door and cleared his throat.

"Joyce, I was wondering," he said hesitantly. "I was wondering whether you noticed, well, anything in particular about Angela today. The way she looks...." He shrugged and glanced at her questioningly.

"You mean kind of tired? Yes, I noticed that the minute she walked in the door." At the barely concealed concern on his face, she asked, "What is it, Pat? Is something the matter?''

He shook his head a couple of times. "I don't know. I could have sworn she was crying—or on the verge of it—a minute ago. I asked her about it, but she denied it.''

Joyce laid down the potholder and wiped her

hands on her apron. "Oh." She pursed her lips, then sighed. "That's too bad. I thought she was doing so well. . . a lot better this time."

"What do you mean 'this time'?"

"The holiday. Christmas. She had a really rough time of it last year—and the past two years, of course." Joyce shook her head. "Hmm. I don't understand it. I just talked with her yesterday, and she seemed so much more adjusted."

"I'm afraid I'm not following you, Joyce."

"I was referring to the accident three years ago, on Christmas Eve."

Patrick looked steadily at her. "Angela told me her husband was killed. Is that what you mean?"

"But you know her daughter was killed, too."

Patrick's chin jerked up; he averted his gaze from Joyce's.

A dawning realization swept over her. "Lord," she said in a low voice. "You didn't know, did you? About Melissa."

Patrick's silence was answer enough, and Joyce shook her head sadly. "She was a beautiful little girl. Seven years old. I've seen her picture once—though Angela doesn't know it. She absolutely will not talk about her. She mentioned Melissa that one time, and claimed she was over the whole thing. Which is ridiculous, of course. No one can get over something like that in as short a time as she claimed. But she held to it; she has refused ever since to utter one word about Melissa. Jonathon and I know a little more about her husband;

Angela has let slip some items on occasion. But about Melissa—forget it.''

Patrick was staring beyond Joyce's shoulder, out the kitchen window. ''I feel bad, Patrick, that I'm the one telling you all this. It's something she should have told you herself. But...it doesn't really surprise me that she didn't.''

Patrick nodded once, then looked back at her. ''Don't be sorry. I'm grateful to you. It clears up a lot about Angela that I haven't been able to figure out.''

The oven timer buzzed just then, and Joyce turned to switch it off. She slid her hands into a large pair of oven mittens. ''Perhaps you should go back in there. Tell everyone I'll be ready in about five minutes.''

''Yes. All right.'' He headed for the door.

''Don't forget the sherry.''

Silently he turned back around, picked up the glass and walked out. Joyce smoothed her hands down the front of her apron, her gaze blank for a moment. The oven timer went off again, interrupting her troubled contemplation, and she opened the oven door.

ANGELA WAS IN THE MIDDLE of a conversation with Jennifer when Patrick slipped the glass of sherry into her hand. ''Now how is it you didn't get kicked out sooner?'' she teased him.

''Simple. My overwhelming masculine charm.''

"We can't compete with that, can we?" Jennifer said as Angela rolled her eyes.

Patrick dropped down beside Angela on the couch, placed an arm around her shoulders. Taking a sip of her drink, she smiled at him over the rim of the glass. *Everything's fine*, her eyes told him, and for a moment he was tempted to believe her.

Dinner was served a few minutes later, a scrumptious elegant affair, every bit as fantastic as Angela had told him it would be. The conversation flowed smoothly throughout the meal, and Angela gave every appearance of enjoying herself.

But Patrick found it difficult to dispel the pall Joyce's revelation had put on his mood. Everything was explained now, put in an altogether different perspective. Finally he knew the source of Angela's sometimes inexplicable behavior. But if that *had* been a tear she'd been wiping away earlier, she was covering up her feelings expertly now. She was chatting in a lively, witty manner, giving no indication of what was really going on in her mind.

Patrick conjured up a picture of what her life must have been like then, incongruous with the present. She had a husband, a daughter, a family of her own—an average American life-style. Then he thought of her living through the nightmare of the auto accident, losing her family, and he wanted to shake his head to rid himself of the image.

What suffering she must have endured, what unbelievable pain. Three years was three years, and time had surely provided some measure of comfort, but in light of what had happened to her, three years must seem like three hours at times. He remembered how she'd been early that morning, coming out of the nightmare, still terrified, her eyes reflecting the horror and despair of that other Christmas Eve. He knew now that she'd been dreaming of the accident, reliving it, going through a private hell she refused to share with anyone.

Patrick stared at Angela's profile as she listened to something Joyce was saying. She looked the same—the same strong yet delicate beauty, which hinted at the element of her personality that had continued to elude him. Now he saw the other side of this fiercely independent woman, a vulnerability and depth of sorrow that made him ache with compassion for her.

Remembering what Joyce had said about Angela's refusal to speak of the accident, Patrick wondered how he could pretend not to know himself. He couldn't . . . and he shouldn't. For he wanted to share her life; he knew that beyond a shadow of a doubt. Rightly or wrongly, he had confessed something important last night. He was in love with her, and the feeling, almost shocking in its clarity, was only reinforced by what he had just learned.

He and Angela should have started out differently, should have leveled with each other. Just as he was sorry she hadn't told him the truth about her marriage, that she'd had a child, he regretted not having told her at the outset that he was still married. He wasn't anymore, of course, not since two days ago, but still he had held back a huge part of his own life from her, and his guilt was undeniable. It was ironic, he mused, that they had shared so much already, emotionally and physically, yet still they knew little about each other.

Well, no more, he promised himself. It was time to get everything out in the open as soon as—

"Patrick? What do you think?"

Jonathon was speaking to him, and everyone else seemed to be waiting for him to answer.

"I'm sorry, I wasn't listening."

"I was telling Jennifer you might be able to recommend a specialist for her father."

"He's coming for a visit next month," Jennifer said. "His arthritis has been getting progressively worse, and I'm determined to see him do something about it."

Patrick nodded. "Sure. I can give you the name of a friend of mine who's a specialist. He's also done a good bit of research in the field. I'll write his number down for you before we leave."

"Thanks. I'd really appreciate it."

The conversation took yet another turn, drawing Patrick into it this time. Yet in the back of his mind hovered his discovery about Angela, and along with it the determination to set their relationship in an honest direction.

CHAPTER FOURTEEN

DARKNESS WAS FALLING as Angela and Patrick walked the short distance from the Colliers' town house to her own. Reaching the front door, Angela placed a hand over her mouth, ineffectually stifling a yawn.

"Sleepy?" Patrick asked, as she turned the lock and opened the door.

"You bet. Too much wine and good food." Inside the temperature wasn't much warmer than the chill of the outdoors. "Brrr. It's cold in here." Angela went immediately to the thermostat and boosted the heat.

Patrick removed his coat on his way to the living room. He sat down on the sofa, rubbing his hands briskly together to warm them up. "Got any brandy?" he asked as Angela walked in.

"Sure. Look in the little cabinet there. I'm going to run upstairs and change. Be right back."

He found the bottle of brandy and a snifter in the small built-in bar near the window. Sipping a little of his drink, he walked over to the window. The ocean beyond was barely visible, the moonlight occasionally filtering through the offshore fog and glinting off the inky surface.

He couldn't do it—not tonight. He didn't want to exchange true confessions. She seemed so peaceful, obviously recovered from the unpleasantness of the night before and the little scene this morning. Another thing was certain; he wouldn't leave her, not tonight.

"I see you found it."

He turned to see her standing at the bottom of the staircase, buttoning the cuffs of the shirt she wore beneath a lavender Shetland pullover. Her jeans were worn and comfortable-looking, a washed-out blue. He whistled dramatically, and Angela cocked her head to one side with a curious look.

"Now what's that all about?"

"You," he said, putting the snifter down on the table and walking over to her. He hugged her deliciously, linking his fingers just above the small of her back. "Did I ever tell you how foxy you look in a pair of jeans?"

She raised one eyebrow. " 'Foxy'? Did you actually say foxy?"

"Sure. Something wrong with the word?" He actually looked offended.

She laughed. "No. It just doesn't sound like you. And anyway, I don't think I've ever heard the term applied to me."

"Well, there's a first time for everything." He kissed the tip of the nose, asking, "Want me to start a fire?"

"Sure. At least it's cold enough. This will be the second time this year I've used the fireplace, which I can hardly believe. There are a few more logs in the storage closet on the patio if you need them."

"Okay."

While Patrick started the fire Angela went into the kitchen. She found a wedge of brie and arranged it on a small platter along with a selection of crackers. The meal at Joyce's had been substantial, so it was odd that she was feeling slightly hungry again. She poured herself a glass of chilled white wine, put everything on a tray and carried it into the living room, setting it on the coffee table.

The fire was well-established, Angela was pleased to see. She threw a few pillows on the floor, against the couch, and slid downward contentedly. After washing his hands Patrick joined her.

Angela handed him the brandy snifter and picked up her glass of wine. They clinked glasses, and she added, "To a wonderful Christmas."

"Here here," Patrick said. They both took a sip of their drinks.

Laying her head against his shoulder, Angela closed her eyes. "It really was nice today, wasn't it? Isn't Joyce a fabulous cook?"

"Yep. She sure is."

"Did you like Fred and Jennifer?"

Patrick laughed lightly. "Yes."

"What's so funny?"

"You sound so worried. Believe me, I had a great time. Only one thing could have made it better."

"What's that?"

"If I'd have had you to myself the entire day."

"Mmm. . . ."

"Hey. What's the matter, aren't you listening to me?"

Angela nodded and muttered some other unintelligible response. The wine and the warmth and the lack of sleep the night before were finally taking their toll; she was finding it an effort to keep her eyes open. Her hunger was secondary all of a sudden. Patrick adjusted his position so that she sat between his legs, her head resting on his shoulder.

"There," he said, reaching out behind him to grab the afghan lying on one arm of the couch. He spread it over them both. "More comfortable?"

Angela nodded and turned slightly, resting her cheek on one hand, her forehead pressed to the woolen fabric of his sweater. Patrick stared into the fire for a time, took another sip of brandy and looked down at her. Her hair, gleaming with red-gold highlights, fell away from her face. He watched her until he could see she was asleep, then leaned his head back against the couch. Drawing in a deep breath, he settled himself a little more comfortably, letting his own drowsiness drift over him, reminding himself not to forget to check on the fire before he went to sleep.

DECEMBER TWENTY-SIX dawned clear and cloudless. The record-low temperatures that had affected the Atlantic Seaboard and much of the rest of the States appeared to be relenting at last.

Patrick lay on his side, wide awake and staring at the partially opened curtains in Angela's bedroom. Sunlight streamed through the gauzy fabric, yet still she slept, half on her side, half on her back, one arm thrown over her head, the other tucked in at her side. They had awakened together earlier that morning, before sunrise, and made love. Patrick had just awakened for the second time a few minutes earlier, the grumbling in his stomach getting louder by the minute. He was hungry, as he always was in the morning.

Angela turned over and opened her mouth, scratched a corner of it, then sighed, her lips making a soft smacking sound.

"Hey," Patrick said, gently nudging her shoulder. "Wake up, sleepyhead."

Angela mumbled something onto her pillow. "Wake up, sleeping beauty. I'm getting hungry, Angie."

Her eyelids opened to a bare squint. "You what?"

"I'm getting hungry."

"Are you kidding?" she asked hoarsely. "The day after Christmas, no work, nothing to do except sleep, and he's trying to yank me out of bed." She yawned and stretched, pulling the covers tighter around her neck. "You already woke me once this morning, fella. Can't you give a girl a rest?"

He burrowed under the covers and drew her to him, hugging her tightly. "You didn't seem to object too much, you know. And you sure didn't act sleepy then."

"Well... I am now."

He kissed the crown of her head. "Sure you don't want to come downstairs with me and show me where everything is? I was going to cook breakfast. You don't have to do a thing."

"What time is it?"

He twisted to glance at the digital clock radio on the nightstand. "Eight forty-five."

"Really? Great! I really slept late, didn't I?"

"You got enough hours' sleep, that's for sure. Do you know what time it was when I got you up here last night? Eight-thirty. And that was after almost two hours' sleep in front of the fire."

"Yeah, well, I must have needed it."

"Either that or you're coming down with something."

"Well, you're the doctor." She looked up at him, pulling down one lower eyelid. "How do I look?"

"Fine. Healthy as an ox."

"Gee, how romantic. He compares me to an ox."

"That's a compliment, my dear. Now come on, let's hop outta here and rustle up some grub," he drawled, getting out of bed.

Angela rolled over and stretched long and hard, moaning and groaning loudly. "You're right. We ought to get up. Besides, I've got a lot to do today."

Patrick was already stepping into his pants and zipping them up. "Like what?"

"Mostly preinventory stuff for the store. What about you, do you have to see any patients?"

"Yeah. I have to make rounds at the hospital."

"You know, I *am* starting to get hungry. Bring the paper on your way back up, will you?"

"Ha! No such doin's. You get your lazy fanny out of bed and hightail it downstairs."

"Rats. I was hoping you were really going to treat me right."

Patrick's expression was sly. "I thought that was already taken care of."

"Well. . . yeah, but it wouldn't hurt to get in a little more practice—in a different manner, of course."

Patrick shoved his arms into his new sweater and shook his head, tossing the hair off his forehead. "There's a saying, you know—don't push your luck when you're ahead."

"All right—" Angela dragged out the words "— I'll be down after I take a shower. You'll just have to find everything for yourself." She smiled. "You look good in burgundy."

"Thanks. You look better in gold."

Angela fingered the 18 karat gold chain necklace he'd given her for Christmas, knowing she'd never take it off. "I tend to agree with you on that."

"I'm glad." He bent down and planted a loud kiss on her forehead. "Now up and at 'em."

He bounded down the stairs two at a time, and a

few minutes later she could hear doors opening and closing as he rummaged around in her kitchen. Instead of getting up immediately she propped both pillows behind her back and simply lay there, gazing out through the curtains, mulling over all that had happened in the past forty-eight hours.

Last night's sleep had done wonders to restore her emotional equilibrium, which had been so precarious ever since the night before at Patrick's. Once they'd arrived at Joyce's yesterday she had thought she was under control, despite the aching, nagging awareness of the dream that had taken both her and Patrick by surprise. It could have been the Christmas tree, the sudden, haunting remembrance of an excited child dancing around another Scotch pine, that had brought the tears to Angela's eyes. She had almost believed enough time had gone by now, enough to erase the memories. But she'd been wrong, very wrong. Fortunately the other guests at the Colliers' had helped her to get her mind back in the present. Patrick especially.

Her eyes remained unfocused as the light in the room became even brighter, the morning rays warming the chilly air. She swallowed, aware of some other deeper emotion when she thought of him—deeper than gratitude—when she thought of the way he looked, the sound of his voice, the sensual, magical way they made love. She loved everything about him, every nuance, every gesture, every precious minute they spent together. She loved him.

There it was. Those three short words that she

had believed would never be a part of her life again. They were true, though, despite her brain's cautious warning that she hadn't enough time. Time was irrelevant; she and Patrick had been right for each other from the start. And then she remembered, with a tinge of excitement and a stab of fear, Patrick's own expression of love. *Let it be true, dear God,* she silently prayed. *Let it really be true.*

AS THEY HAD DONE the day before, Patrick and Angela enjoyed a leisurely breakfast, taking turns with sections of the morning newspaper and sipping numerous cups of hot coffee. Angela thought she could very easily grow used to such an arrangement, so that by the time Patrick left shortly before noon, she was feeling pangs of regret. The Christmas weekend hadn't lasted nearly long enough. She began to miss him even as they stood together on her patio saying goodbye.

"Thank you, Patrick. I had a marvelous Christmas."

Though he wondered about the truth of her statement, he could see that at that moment she really believed it. That was fine; eventually she would open up enough to share her past with him, as he would with her. He realized the subject wasn't something they could jump right into, and he was as reluctant now to mar her good spirits as he had been last night. Developing a truly honest relationship would take time, but they had all the time they needed. Gradually they would come to trust each other, completely.

"I did, too," he said, kissing her lightly on the lips. "I'll call you tonight."

"Okay. Don't work too hard."

"Same to you."

After opening the patio gate, she watched until he got in his car and started the engine. She waved once, then shut the gate and went back inside the house. There was so much to do, all the book work for the store and a mountain of laundry she'd been ignoring for the past week.

Good, Angela thought, heading up the stairs to get started. The more there was to do, the easier it would be to forget that Patrick was gone, that she was left alone once again to think too much.

THE FOLLOWING TWO WEEKS WENT BY in a blur, it seemed. On New Year's Eve Angela and Patrick went to a party at the Colliers', then spent the night at Angela's. The next day, the first of the brand-new year, they drove to Patrick's house, put Rusty in the Bronco and drove to the beach. The temperature was a good deal warmer than two weeks previously, but the ocean wind was strong and buffeting, and Angela was glad they had taken care to dress warmly. Walking and sometimes running along the shoreline, they laughed at Rusty's antics as he jumped and chased the waves, wearing himself out by the end of the afternoon.

Almost before she could adjust to it, the New Year was well into its first week. The distance between St. Augustine and Jacksonville precluded

Angela's and Patrick's seeing each other on a daily basis, especially as business for both of them had picked up considerably. They spoke every night on the telephone, however, sharing daily events.

The second week of January was even busier. Angela was astounded by the number of prescriptions, new and old, that were being called in. It seemed everyone had made it through the holidays, only to decide to give in and get sick.

One Thursday afternoon the telephone lines were ringing incessantly, and a steady flow of customers kept the stack of new prescriptions at least three inches high. Dorothy, who never left the front register, couldn't assist Angela and Regi, who worked feverishly side by side.

"Did you get a hold of Tim yet, Angela?" Regi was returning from the back wall behind the vertical rows of medicine shelves as he spoke, his arms loaded down with an assortment of bottles and jars, boxes of creams and ointments.

Angela mumbled to herself as she finished counting out one hundred tablets, then emptied them into a brown plastic vial and punched a button before picking up the ringing telephone. "Yes," she said to Regi before speaking into the receiver. "He'll be here as soon as he can make it. About a half hour or so— St. Augustine Apothecary, may I help you?" She reached for a pen and began scribbling down yet another set of prescriptions. Hanging up, she said in exasperation,

"Can you believe this? I don't think we've ever been this busy."

Regi tilted his head back, rolling it from side to side to ease the tension. "Tell me about it. The holidays seem like a light-year away."

Angela punched another line, greeted the caller, then said, "Oh, hi, Linda. Geez, I'm glad it's only you. Yes, he's right here. No kidding, we're going nuts. Here, I'll put him on."

Regi picked up the receiver and spoke to his wife for a few minutes as Angela kept typing, trying desperately to finish at least half of the stack of new prescriptions. If things didn't slow down for at least a few minutes, it was going to take forever to catch up before closing time.

"My feet are killing me," Dorothy said, walking over and sliding several new prescriptions beneath the stack next to the typewriter. "And I'm starving to death."

"You and me both. I appealed to Tim's merciful nature. He's bringing us all something to eat."

"God bless Tim," Dorothy said. "He's such a sweetheart. But I hope he hurries. My stomach is growling so loud the customers keep giving me the strangest looks."

Angela's stomach was rumbling, too, but at that point anything would have satisfied her, a cup of coffee, even a glass of water. It seemed as if she hadn't looked up from her work for hours, and the backs of her calves were screaming for a change of position. Yet despite the discomfort and stress of the heavy work load, Angela was undeniably satisfied, proud that everything was going so well, and she knew Regi shared her feelings. After almost three years of hard work and dedication on both their parts, St. Augustine Apothecary was firmly and successfully established in the community.

Tim brought in a bag of hamburgers, French fries and cold drinks. Then he took over the register for Dorothy. For a few precious minutes there were no customers in the store, and he was able to handle the incoming calls, too, allowing Regi and Angela to take a break. They quickly finished off the hamburgers and fries, taking time to sip leisurely at their drinks while seated on the two barstools at the end of the counter.

"By the way, Linda told me to tell you she was really sorry we couldn't make it New Year's Eve," Regi said. Angela had extended the Colliers' invitation; Joyce and Jonathon had met the Donaldsons through her and had entertained the couple on several occasions.

"That's all right," Angela said. "I'm just sorry Tod was sick."

Regi shook his head, draining the remainder of his drink. "Leave it to Tod to pick New Year's Eve to come down with the measles. I think he did it on purpose, just because he didn't want to be stuck with a sitter."

Angela chuckled. "He's got your number, Regi. Better watch out. He's going to be spoiled rotten before you know it."

"I know. Can you imagine what's going to happen when and if he gets a little brother or sister?"

Angela smiled. "Yes, I can. You're going to go crazy."

Tim called out to Angela, "I hate to interrupt, but Dr. Merrill's on line two."

"Oh. All right, I'll get it." After tossing her hamburger wrappings in the trash can, Angela washed her hands and dried them off quickly. It always sounded funny when someone referred to Patrick as Dr. Merrill. The others hardly knew to refer to him any other way, however, since they weren't aware that she saw him socially, let alone that she was involved with him. Angela had always been private about her personal life; neither Regi nor Dorothy attempted to pry.

Their phone conversation was short. Patrick was calling to tell her he had a hospital staff meeting that evening, which he'd forgotten about; he and Angela would have to cancel their plans for supper. Angela was disappointed, for their weeknights together were few. But judging by how the day had gone so far, she knew she'd be exhausted by the time she got home that evening, anyway. He would call her at work tomorrow, he promised, and they would make plans for tomorrow evening.

As she hung up, Regi said offhandedly, "You know, Linda said something out of the blue yesterday about him."

"Who?" Angela frowned as she struggled to

decipher the illegible scrawl of the next prescription.

"Dr. Merrill." Regi opened up a bottle of tablets, poured them into the small blue counter and screwed the cap back on. "She said she got a Christmas card from Lucille Merrill. She was surprised—she hadn't heard from the woman since her divorce in December. And the next thing Linda hears, she's left Jacksonville for New York to become a 'big-time model.' " Regi snorted lightly. "Sounds typical of Lucille. I've only met her a couple of times when she's come by the house to pick up Linda—they used to belong to some sort of social club or other—anyway, she's a looker, all right, but Lord, what a flaky one."

Angela's fingers paused over the typewriter keys. She felt a peculiar numbness spreading across the backs of her knees. She managed a preoccupied, "Mmm," and finished the label she'd been working on, then started to line up the prescriptions on the counter top. Regi's comment had taken her completely off guard, and something sharp and quivering seared through her middle. Surely he couldn't have meant....

Regi went on talking, oblivious to the effect he was having on Angela. "She was something else, according to Linda. Really flaunted the doctor's-wife bit—then whammo, she was divorcing him."

Angela continued typing, amazed that her fingers were keeping such an even rhythm, when her heart was racing crazily. She was rattled. She could think of no comment to what Regi had just said, but apparently he hadn't expected one.

The telephone rang again; Regi took the call. A few moments later there were four customers standing at the register with new prescriptions to fill. Conversation, what little of it there was, was focused on the work at hand for the next hour and a half, and Angela couldn't recall ever having been so grateful for the mind-numbing effect of the count-and-pour routine, her movements precise and automatic.

Her partner's words kept going around and around in her brain. She felt almost sick to her stomach. She simply couldn't fathom it—Patrick had been married and hadn't said one word to her about it. Regi had mentioned a December divorce, but when in December? The possibility—the likelihood—that she had been dating a married man, was unbelievable. That not only went against one of the strongest principles she'd adhered to over the years, but devastated the foundation of her relationship with Patrick.

Thinking of him, she froze in the middle of typing the last label for the stack of new prescriptions. Impossible to absorb it all. Who was Patrick Merrill, really? She didn't know. She absolutely didn't know. It was several minutes before she got hold of herself and finished the work in front of her.

As the last customer was leaving the store, Regi plopped down in a chair and ran a hand through his hair. "Man alive, this has been one hell of a day."

"No kidding," Tim agreed. "You guys should have called me first thing this morning."

"I wish we had." Regi pulled his hands back over his head, combining a stretch with a yawn.

Scooping up an armful of bottles, Angela began replacing them on the shelf. "Hey," Regi said. "You don't have to do that. Tim and I will take care of them. You look like you're about to fall on your face."

"I'm all right. You guys have been working just as hard."

"But I know you spent a lot of time on the books yesterday," Regi insisted. "And you look like hell."

"Thanks," Angela said absently.

"You're welcome. So don't worry about it. I'll close up. You go on home."

Exhausted as she was, home was the last place she wanted to be right now, for there would be no distracting her from the confusion and turmoil and anger churning inside. Regi persisted, though, and finally she agreed.

Lucille. The name resounded over and over in Angela's mind as she drove home, until she thought she would scream. His wife. How could Patrick not have told her—how could he have been so dishonest? All right, he'd said he *had* been married, but she had assumed he'd been referring to several years ago. A suspicious woman might have checked into the matter, but she wasn't that type.

Okay, then, so what if he'd been married when they were first going out. He was divorced now, what difference did it make? Plenty, she answered herself. His status meant all sorts of things, but most importantly it implied that he hadn't respected her enough to tell her he was still entangled when they started seeing each other regularly. And this was the one man she'd chosen to become involved with after so long—the man she loved.

Absently Angela shook her head, wanting to scream and curse at having been deceived. She refused to dwell on the possibility that she was being unfair, declaring him guilty without giving him the opportunity for a defense. Dammit to hell, there was no defense for it. He should have told her, period. Earlier she had been almost relieved because they wouldn't be seeing each other tonight; now she was angry, furious that she couldn't have it out with him.

THE EVENING PASSED with excruciating tedium. Angela was worn out from the physically exhausting day, yet she couldn't go to bed. She sat with her eyes glued to the television set, unable to focus on it, or to comprehend the voices bombarding her. Even Joyce's phone call at around seven-thirty had little effect on her tormented mental state.

"Where's Jonathon?" Angela asked after a few minutes of chatting.

"He's got an evening class." Joyce sighed heavily. "Angela, do you have a minute?"

"Sure." Lord help her, but the question sounded serious, and she really didn't feel like listening right now.

"Oh, Ange, I know you're tired of hearing me go over and over this, but I'm just so nervous I don't know which end is up."

"You mean as far as tenure is concerned."

"Yes." Joyce's voice was shaky as she added, "There was a memo from the department chairman in my box today."

"Is that good or bad?"

"Could be either. But I have a strong suspicion this is it."

"I thought you said you wouldn't find out anything until February."

"That's the way it was supposed to be, true. Everything's different now. Everything. The rumors have been flying around about the budget cuts we'll all be facing this year. I tell you, they're scalping us." Joyce continued in a plaintive tone, explaining the consequences and implications of the administrative changes at the college.

Angela drummed her fingers on the kitchen counter, struggling to keep her mind on what her friend was saying. This was very important to Joyce, and she deserved to be listened to, yet Angela found it a struggle not to interrupt with some excuse to hang up. Her impatience and lack of understanding made her feel ashamed, so she forced herself to concentrate on the conversation.

"Well, what does Jonathon say?"

"Nothing. That's why I'm bending your ear about all this."

"I don't understand. Jonathon is certainly more involved than I am."

"Exactly. The changes will probably affect him the most, since the political-science department will be getting the worst of all the cutbacks. He's more worried than I am. He's all clammed up, won't talk about anything."

Angela was silent for a moment. "I hate to be critical, Joyce, but this doesn't sound like you two guys at all. I mean, of all the couples I've ever known, you two have always had excellent communication."

"Yeah, well, we're not exactly communicating now." Joyce sighed heavily. "Gee, Ange, I'm truly sorry to be crying on your shoulder this way. I had to talk to somebody, though."

"Joyce, don't apologize to me. I'm your friend, remember?"

"And you're the greatest. But listen, I'll let you go. I know you've got things to do."

"All right. Give me a call as soon as you find out what the dean has to say."

"I will. Wish me luck. Wish *us* luck."

"You know I do. Even though I don't think you'll need it."

"Well, talk to you later."

"Bye."

Angela hung up but stood right where she was, her back against the kitchen counter, her gaze focused on the blank television screen in the living room. She closed her eyes and rubbed her temples. "Damn!" she muttered. She was nothing but a hypocrite, and a big one at that. She had hardly been able to stay on the phone with Joyce, let alone work up any real sympathy for her friend's problem. In the face of her own, Joyce's seemed minor. Perhaps she and Jonathon really did have a problem on their hands, but when was the last time they hadn't been able to work out their troubles? Hell, they'd never had troubles. The fact was they had each other, for better and for worse, and that alone was more than most people could claim. Especially her.

Her discovery about Patrick's marital status was par for the course, anyway, Angela thought cynically. Nothing was ever exactly as it seemed. Everyone had something they were hiding—she included—and happiness was an elusive state at best. A rather jaded philosophy, some would say, but it was the truth.

Flipping off the light in the kitchen, she walked back into the living room, opened the rolltop desk and sat down to open the mail she'd received today, hoping that would get her thoughts going in another direction. Pausing, she tapped the stack of letters against the heel of her hand and calculated the length of time she had known Patrick Merrill. A month and a half. Only six weeks. No time at all, really. She was naive to have begun to trust the closeness and intimacy that had developed between them, should have expected something like this to pop up. She stared down at the maple desk top for several minutes, then looked at the envelope on the top of the stack. A bill. There were several more beneath it.

Angela picked up a stainless-steel letter opener and started slitting the flaps one by one, thinking this was certainly the first time she'd ever felt grateful for having a stack of bills to pay. But then tonight she would have been thankful for any diversion, anything to get her mind off Patrick Merrill.

CHAPTER FIFTEEN

THE WORK FLOWED MORE MANAGEABLY at St. Augustine Apothecary the next day, giving Angela and her co-workers a much-needed respite from the postholiday crunch. There were several mixture preparations to be filled, Regi's least favorite, so Angela volunteered to take care of most of them.

Shortly after lunch, she was working diligently on an ointment preparation when Regi said, "For you, Angela. Line three." She finished weighing out powdered hydrocortisone, set the glassine paper to the side, then washed and dried her hands. She punched the button for line three. "St. Augustine Apothecary, may I help you?"

"It's me. You sound busy."

Patrick's voice produced a resurgence of resentment, and Angela answered crisply, "I am. What's up?"

"What's up is that I'm calling to ask what time you think you can be ready this evening. I made reservations at The Conch Shell."

Angela hesitated for several seconds before answering. "I hope you don't mind canceling them."

"No. No problem. Would you rather go some-where else?"

"Not really."

Patrick had been scribbling down a notation on a patient chart he was reviewing. Suddenly he stopped, fully alerted by the tone in Angela's voice, a tone he'd never heard before. "All right," he responded carefully. "If you're too tired to go out I certainly understand. We'll just cook some-thing up at your place. I can stop by the grocer's on the way over."

Again Angela hesitated. Angry as she was with Patrick, she knew the only way to come to terms with that anger was to confront him. And the tele-phone was certainly not the way to do it. "I have some steaks in the freezer," she said finally. "But I don't think there will be enough time to thaw them out. I won't get home until around six-thirty."

"No problem. I'll just bring something. Any-thing you'd like in particular, or will you settle for potluck?"

"That's fine."

"Okay, then. See you around seven-thirty or so."

"Right. Goodbye."

Patrick hung up and stared thoughtfully at the quartz clock on his desk. Another nine hours until he saw her, until he found out what was wrong. He couldn't imagine what had happened since the last time they'd spoken to warrant the coolness in her attitude. Maybe her job was getting to her; maybe he'd just caught her at the wrong time. But a niggling, deeply felt suspicion told him there was something else, something else altogether.

ANGELA STOOD WITH HER BACK to the shower nozzle, her eyes closed and her arms wrapped tightly around her chest as she absorbed the massaging needles of hot water. She felt better, much better than she had that morning. In fact, she had begun to feel better shortly after the phone conversation with Patrick. At least she knew when she was going to see him, therefore when she could confront him with the monstrous lie he had thought she would never discover.

After her shower she dressed in slacks and sweater, pulling her hair back in a ponytail. She didn't bother with makeup, just applied a moisturizer and a touch of blusher. What would be the point, anyway? They weren't going out, and she certainly wasn't going out of her way to get dressed up for him.

You're being childish, a part of her mind accused, as she caught a glimpse of her expression in the mirror. She looked exactly as she felt, angry and hurt, but worst of all, betrayed. Maybe she was overreacting, but dammit, that was the way she felt.

She turned away from the mirror and left the

bedroom. When she was halfway down the stairs she heard the doorbell ring. She didn't bother with her usual, "Just a minute," but purposely took her time descending the rest of the way, stood for a moment near the front door, checked the peephole, then finally opened it.

"Hi, there, beautiful," Patrick greeted her, planting a kiss on her cheek before walking quickly past her into the kitchen, where he deposited the two grocery bags he was carrying on the counter. "I hope you like pork chops, 'cause I had some cut special."

Angela said nothing, just walked into the living room and began straightening the throw pillows on the couch.

"Angela?"

"Yes. That's fine." She continued what she was doing, listening as Patrick opened and closed the refrigerator door, then the cupboards, moving around her kitchen as though he lived there. An unexpected, bittersweet nostalgia swept over her, and she thrust it aside quickly.

"What are you doing in there?" Patrick called out in a cheerful tone. "C'mere. Take a look at these things. You won't believe the size of 'em."

She stopped what she was doing. She turned and walked to the kitchen, pausing just inside the doorway. Patrick opened a huge, freezer-wrapped package and flipped it over so she could see the three butterfly pork chops. She stared at them blankly.

"Well? Don't they make your mouth water? I've got one hell of a recipe I thought you might like. It'll take at least an hour, but in the meantime—" he reached inside one of the grocery bags, withdrawing a bottle of wine, two packages of cheese and a box of crackers "—*voilà*! I got all this in the deli department. I hope you're hungry, 'cause I—"

"Stop." Angela was looking directly at him, her tone as expressionless as her face.

"What?"

"I said stop."

"What do you mean?"

"Stop what you're doing. The playacting, the entertaining. I'm not interested."

Patrick placed everything on the counter, folded the paper back over the meat and turned to her, one fist on his hip, his head cocked a bit to the side. His eyes narrowed cautiously. "I wasn't aware that what I was doing was playacting. Entertaining, maybe, but that's even stretching it." He hesitated. "What is it, Angela? What's wrong?"

She shifted her weight, pushed her thumbs through the belt loops of her jeans and looked down at the floor, then back up at him. "I found out...about Lucille, your wife. About your *marriage*."

Patrick said nothing at all, simply chewed an inside corner of his lower lip as he gazed at her, a strange mixture of surprise and resignation washing over him.

Angela waited for a moment, shifted again and said, "Well? Are you going to deny it, admit it—or what?"

Patrick shook his head slowly several times, keeping his eyes on her. "No. I'm not going to deny it. It's true. I was married. But I told you about it already. Remember?"

"Yes, I remember. You also gave the impression that it had been quite some time ago." Her jaw clenched and unclenched, and she said in a bitter tone, "When exactly *did* you get your divorce?"

"In December. December 23rd, to be exact."

Angela's laugh was short and mirthless. "A month ago. Well, then, that certainly confirms the fact that you *were* married while we were dating."

"I was separated."

"What difference does that make? Married is married. Until you're divorced."

"Baloney." Patrick's expression was taut, impatient. "You know damn well there is a difference. A big one. Lucille and I weren't living together at the time I met you. Don't you think you're coming on a little strong? After all, you have absolutely no idea of the circumstances leading up to the breakup of my marriage."

"No. I don't." Angela swiveled abruptly, heading for the living room. "And I really don't care to."

Patrick looked at the white package of meat, picked it up and put it in the refrigerator. He should have known something like this would happen. Damn! Walking into the living room, he saw her standing at the window, arms over her chest in a very obvious don't-touch-me attitude. He sat down in a chair, crossed the ankle of one leg over the knee of the other and rubbed the bridge of his nose with his thumb and forefinger, waiting for her to say something. She didn't.

"Angela, look, just sit down and let's talk this over. It's not as dramatic as you're making it out to be."

She whirled to face him. "Don't be condescending with me, Patrick. I don't happen to consider the subject dramatic in the least."

"All right, I worded that wrong." Patrick sighed heavily. "All I meant was that if you'll listen to what I have to say, you might not be so condemning."

Angela's fingers squeezed and plucked at her sweater as she held his gaze. The air between them was rife with the tension of her anger, and Patrick said finally, "Please, sit down. You'll be more comfortable."

"I'd rather stand, thank you. All right, go ahead. What is it you have to say?"

He placed his hands on either arm of the chair, his fingers tapping there distractedly. Then he plunged in. "I was married to Lucille for nine and

a half years. We met when I was still a resident.
The first two years were happy ones, the rest not
so happy. Miserable at times, to be honest. I
couldn't take it anymore, and Lucille had. . . other
things on her mind, so I asked her for a divorce
last August. When I met you I had already been
living alone for several months. The divorce was
final in December, and I haven't heard from her
since." He shrugged. "That's it—that's the whole
story."

"Why didn't you tell me?"

"Angela, you can't imagine how many times
I've asked myself that same question." He ran a
hand through his hair. "Look, it was wrong of me
not to tell you, I admit it. But I was so thoroughly
sick of Lucille by the time I met you that the last
thing in the world I wanted was to let even the
mention of her name intrude into what I had just
found." He paused again and rubbed the crease
on his forehead with a middle finger.

"This isn't exactly easy for me, Angela. I'm not
the self-analytical type. I don't have every little
quirk and idiosyncrasy of my personality figured
out. But I suppose a big reason for my holding
back had to do with fear. Meeting you was the
first time in ages that I'd had a glimpse of something other than what I'd lived with for years. You
and Lucille were like night and day. You were exactly what I needed and wanted—and still are. I
guess I was afraid I would blow it by telling you
everything right off the bat."

His gaze locked with hers. "But there was more to it than that. The circumstances of our first meeting weren't the norm, and you were obviously upset for quite a while after that. Nevertheless, the opportunity arose a few times shortly after, times when I could have told you but—I didn't. It was pure selfishness on my part, I admit. Since I hadn't told you at the beginning, it became more and more difficult to do so. But, Angela," he said imploringly, "you have to remember you didn't exactly encourage my telling you about my marriage, anyway."

"What does that mean?"

"The time at the beach—when I really did want to tell you. I tried to, in fact. You were the one who stopped me, remember? You said you didn't believe in people sharing every last detail of their lives, in dragging out their pasts for inspection— or something like that."

Angela lowered her eyes, that day at the beach suddenly coming back to her. He was right; there had been that moment when he'd been about to say something more to her. She had never suspected what that something was.

Glancing back up at him, she said, "All right. That's true. But you could have told me some other time. There were plenty of other opportunities."

"You're right. There were. Only every time one came up, something got in the way of my telling you. The day Rory had the antibiotic reaction, for example. I was going to discuss Lucille with you then. How could I? You were beside yourself. I wasn't about to tell you something that might upset you further.''

Angela's hands dropped to her sides, and she took a few steps to the couch. She picked up a pillow and patted it a few times, fluffing it out, then tossed it back and sat down. ''I wasn't that upset.''

''You weren't?'' Patrick was incredulous. ''As I recall you were white as a sheet. And you cried for—''

''Okay, so I was a little upset. I told you I'd had a bad day at work. I was really tired. That's not the point, anyway.''

''Isn't it?'' Patrick said, leaning forward slightly. ''Isn't it the point, Angela? Isn't that another one of the issues here?''

Angela frowned. ''What are you talking about?''

Patrick closed his eyes briefly, then turned his head to stare absently into the fireplace. Angela watched his profile, his somber expression causing a nervous tingle to race up and down her spine. She grabbed the same pillow she had just fluffed and put it on her lap, punching it down with a fist. She lifted her heels, bouncing them up and down on the carpet as her gaze shifted to the window.

Patrick looked at her again, and when he spoke

she knew he meant business. "There's more than the issue of my not telling you about *my* past, Angela. You haven't told me about yours, either."

Angela's posture grew rigid. "I have too told you about my past. But to be honest, I didn't think you cared that much."

"You're damn right I care. I care very much." His eyes narrowed. "To the extent that I believe I love you, I care. You can count on that."

Angela said nothing, just continued to squeeze the edges of the pillow.

"And because I care, I have to say that what you've withheld from me, Angela, is as important, if not more so, than the fact that I neglected to tell you I was still legally married when we first met."

Her chin came up sharply, and she glared at him. "Look, why don't you quit beating around the bush. I don't know what in hell you're talking about."

"Angela, you said it before to me, and I'm saying it to you now. Let's cut the games. They're not necessary—not anymore. I know about your daughter." He hesitated for only a second before adding, "Why didn't you tell me about her? You told me about your husband, why not about her?"

Angela stared at him dumbly, feeling as if someone had thrown cold water in her face. She was unaware of her blanched complexion and the vacant, haunted look in her eyes. When she answered, her voice was strained and distant. "Who told you about. . .her?"

"Joyce did. On Christmas Day. But that doesn't matter, Angela. I've suspected all along that you were holding something back. It—"

"I don't believe it," Angela interrupted, coming alive with a flash of resentment. "I don't believe Joyce would walk right up to you and tell you something so personal, so private about me."

Patrick held up one hand. "Now wait a minute, it wasn't like that at all. When I went into the kitchen to refill your drink *I* brought it up."

"Brought what up?"

"I asked her if she happened to know if anything was bothering you." He paused and said in a lower tone, "I saw that you were crying."

"I wasn't crying!" Angela jerked her head away, her chin quivering. "God, I don't believe this." Patrick waited, and she added reluctantly, "All right, there were a couple of tears, sentimental ones. Big deal."

"The point is, Angela, I was concerned. I did ask you what was wrong at the time, and you wouldn't tell me anything. And I certainly hadn't forgotten the night before. So I mentioned my concern to Joyce. That's when she said she thought this Christmas would have been better for you. She kept on talking, assuming I already knew. Angela, she didn't purposely reveal something personal about you. So don't hold it against her."

Angela said nothing, just continued to stare at him, acutely aware of her body's abnormal vital signs. Her heartbeat was racing like wildfire, her respiration was quick and shallow, and there was a liquid sensation of dread in the pit of her stomach.

"You told her," Patrick said softly. "Now why don't you tell me?"

"Tell you what?"

"About your daughter." He spread one palm outward. "Were you *never* going to tell me?"

She nodded curtly. "That's right. I wasn't. I don't see that my past has anything to do with you."

Patrick caught his breath and shook his head disbelievingly. "But it does. Very much so. It was one of the reasons I was unable to tell you about mine."

"Don't use me as an excuse, Patrick."

"I'm not. I don't need to, anyway. I take full responsibility for my actions. But it's true, Angela—don't try to deny it any longer." He studied her thoughtfully for a moment, his elbows resting on his knees. "That was what you were crying about, wasn't it? You were remembering the accident. You can tell me, Angela, I want—"

Angela shot up off the couch and yelled at him, "I don't care what you want! *I* don't want to discuss it with you!"

Patrick was taken aback by her vehemence, but he spoke in a calm, steady tone. "I don't want to know every single detail of your past, Angela, and believe me, I wouldn't even be pressing you like this if I didn't think it necessary. But God, look at where we are now. Why can't we start over, wipe the slate clean and tell each other who we really are? I'm glad you found out about my marriage. I'm glad we're having this discussion. We need it.''

Angela stood behind the couch, her arms once more crossed over her chest, her hands agitatedly tugging at the sleeves of her sweater. Patrick wanted more than anything to go to her, to take her in his arms, to soothe away the fright that had taken hold of her. He didn't dare. She was like a terrified kitten, its spine arched, ready to hiss and claw at the enemy, the danger—him.

''I don't agree with you. I don't feel a 'discussion' is necessary at all.''

''What good does it do to act as though our pasts never existed?'' Patrick argued fervently. ''We *know* what happened—why can't we talk about it?''

''That's just it. As you say, we know already. What's to talk about?''

''Your daughter, dammit!'' Patrick slammed the heel of his hand down on the arm of the chair and stood up. Angela took an automatic step backward, astonished by the abrupt anger in him. ''She existed, didn't she? And I know she was killed in the accident with your husband. And I know it was a terrible, tragic thing you went through. I can't pretend I don't know any longer. It would be faking it, and I hate faking.''

"There's nothing to fake," Angela said. "Okay, you know. Great. So now it's all out. My big dark secret, you know all about it. I know all about your divorce, as well—there's no more faking. That should satisfy you.''

"It doesn't.''

"Well, too bad. Look, Patrick, you're pushing this too far. This is...." She was chewing on her lower lip, which was quivering threateningly. She strove to control the quaver in her voice. "It's not fair of you to push me into talking about something I've managed to put behind me. It happened to *me*, it's all a part of my past, and...and maybe I was wrong not to have told you, just as you were wrong not to have told me about the divorce. But...I just *don't* want to talk about it. I don't think I should have to explain anything more than that.'' Her voice shook with the last few words, and she swallowed hard, blinking back a film of tears.

Patrick walked over to the window, pulling back the curtain to stand staring out the window. He didn't turn as he spoke. "It's obvious, Angela, that the subject is extremely painful for you. I don't blame you, believe me. I...." He shook his head. "I can't even imagine what it must have felt like. But your refusal to talk about it is going to

come between us. It already has. And not because,
as I said, I need to know every single thing about
your past.'' He faced her.

"It's just that I can see it written all over you,
this hurt. It's an enormous part of you, harming
us.'' His voice dropped, and he asked, ''That's
what happened Christmas Eve, isn't it? When you
had the nightmare. You were dreaming about the
accident, and your daughter.''

Angela glared at him, then spat, "Yes! Yes, yes,
yes! What is it you want—to wring every last detail out of me? All right, then. I *was* dreaming
about it then, and it's what was bothering me
those other times when you saw me crying. I'm
sorry, but it happens sometimes. The holidays are
the worst, because that's when the accident happened.'' The lump grew hard and rigid in her
throat, and her eyes swam with tears. Her next
words came out sounding garbled. ''You want to
know the whole truth, all right, I'll tell you. I was
responsible for my daughter's death. That's right,
me. And some...sometimes the truth comes back
to haunt me. I—'' She cleared her throat and
brushed the heel of her hand against her cheek.
She couldn't go on.

Sniffing, she looked away from him, staring at
the door. There, so she'd told him. Now everyone
could know about it—what difference did it make.
She breathed in ragged, shallow spurts, her chest
expanding and contracting visibly. She chewed the
inside of her cheek until it hurt, determined not to

break down in front of him. Damn him for making her say all this.

Patrick said nothing for a long time. He sat down on the couch where Angela had been and picked up the pillow she'd been holding. He stared into the empty fireplace, remembering the time that they'd shared in front of its warmth, the tenderness, the intimacy of their togetherness. He couldn't lose her over this. He just couldn't. Yet what she had said had shaken him to the core, making him realize the extent of the damage, the emotional scars that still afflicted her. He wasn't sure what angle to take now, how to approach the subject, how to get her to tell him everything. That's exactly what she needed; he knew it as a physician, as a friend and as a lover. She had to get it out, somehow, with someone.

He looked at her, wanting with his entire being to reach out and draw her into the circle of his arms, to soothe and caress her, to make her see that he loved her. And that she could and would get over this. But the scars were deep, much deeper than he had suspected, than even she realized.

"Angela?"

She didn't move, so he repeated her name. Her head inclined slightly. "Angela, were you driving the car the night the accident happened?"

For a moment he thought she either hadn't heard him or wasn't going to answer. Finally she shook her head in denial.

"Then it was him, your husband driving, right?"

Angela slanted her gaze toward him. "Yes. Why?"

"I don't understand how you can say you were responsible for her death, when you weren't even driving."

"I was, believe me. . . I was. I didn't have to be driving."

Patrick was encouraged; if he could only get her going, get her talking about it, he didn't care what kind of scene ensued—in fact, he was hoping for one. He wanted her to get it out in the open; then they would at least have something to deal with. He wanted her to know he was there for her, that she could tell him anything.

"I still don't get it," he persisted. "If you weren't driving, how could it have been your fault?"

"You don't know the circumstances. You don't know what was happening in that car." Her eyes were glazed with remembrance. "I wasn't myself," she said, her voice not much more than a whisper. "I was angry, terribly angry. I was practically screaming at Gordon—I don't know how Melissa didn't wake up." She swallowed, the glazed look becoming feverish. "I kept asking him to slow down, not to drive so fast. It was raining, the roads were slick and there was a lot of fog. I wanted to stay at my parents' house that night, but no, Gordon had to leave. It was too much to ask of him to go along with my wishes. If only we'd stayed...." Angela's lips began working, tears running down her face in an unbroken stream. "Then I might not have found—" her voice broke for an instant before she went on "— then I wouldn't have found the letter."

"What letter?"

Her voice was nasal and watery now. "The one from Sarah. I...I should have known what was going on, of course, but I...." She shrugged, and her voice rose somewhat. "I thought they were only friends." She attempted a laugh that came out a moan. "Friends. What a joke. They'd been having an affair for ten months, just when I'd started to believe things were really going well between me and Gordon. At that moment I knew the real reason for Gordon's happiness."

"The letter, you mean."

"Yes." She coughed slightly and began rubbing her hands along her upper arms again. "I found it in his overcoat pocket when we were leaving my parents' place. It wasn't even in an envelope. I didn't need to read very much of it—" Her voice broke again, and she sniffed loudly. She looked directly at Patrick, yet he could see she was really looking through him. "So I asked him about the letter once we were in the car. We got into this horrible fight. Melissa was exhausted. She slept soundly through the whole thing. Gordon kept telling me to shut up, but I wouldn't listen. He was driving like a maniac—I kept at him to slow down, I wouldn't let the subject of Sarah drop, either. I was furious, crazy with disbelief that he'd been cheating on me. Then...then...that's when the accident happened." She shuddered slightly. There was nothing more to say.

A cavern of silence enveloped them for a long time. Patrick sat quietly on the couch, hoping she would go on. But Angela stood completely still, her head down, eyes closed, hugging her chest as if she were freezing.

Finally Patrick spoke. "Angela, I still don't understand why you blame yourself. I don't see the rationale behind it."

"Oh, believe me, there's plenty of rationale," she choked out scornfully.

"You weren't driving," Patrick countered with conviction. "Your husband was. You just said he was driving too fast, in bad weather conditions. The fact that you were arguing with him wasn't the cause of the accident."

"You think not? Well, you're wrong. Dead wrong. If I'd kept my mouth shut, he probably would have been more careful. He wouldn't have acted as he did, driving like a fool and losing control of the car."

"But, Angela, you can't take responsibility for the way he was behaving. My God, you'd just found out—" Patrick was interrupted by the beeping of his pager, which he wore on his belt.

He pulled back his jacket to turn it off, then went on. "Angela, nobody in his right mind would accuse you of being at fault. It's ridiculous. Look, I'm not trying to—" The pager went off again; once more Patrick silenced it. "Damn," he muttered.

Angela knew the double page was the signal for an urgent situation, so she said, "Go ahead. Answer it."

Patrick ran a hand agitatedly through his hair as he went to the kitchen bar. Whatever the message, it had certainly come at the wrong time. He dialed his answering service and was immediately connected to the hospital emergency room in Jacksonville.

Angela moved toward the window, listening as he spoke, his conversation mostly monosyllabic responses. When he hung up she knew what he was going to say.

"Angela, I've got to go. One of my patients has just come into emergency with gastric hemorrhage." He pulled the set of car keys from his pocket and jangled them for a second. Angela turned to face him.

"All right," she said.

"Angela, I'm sorry. Dammit, I don't want to go. I can't leave you here like this."

"Like what?" Her expression was calm now, her face wiped clean of the tears.

"Upset the way you are."

"I'm fine. You'd better get going."

Patrick jangled the key chain again, then walked toward the door. "Yes. I have to. I'll try to make it back."

"No. Don't do that. It's too far to drive. And anyway...I'm really tired. I'm going to bed."

"I'll call you when I get home." There was a world of frustration and regret in the words.

"No. Don't worry about it. I'll be asleep, anyway."

His hand lingered on the doorknob, his gaze on her now-stoic features. "Then I'll call in the morning."

She said nothing, merely shrugged lightly.

"Are you sure you'll be okay?"

"Yes. Of course." Her voice was placid, her demeanor perfectly controlled.

But as Patrick opened the door and stepped outside, he was filled with an irrepressible doubt and a sense of dread. The feeling never left him that night, nor the suspicion that he'd opened up a Pandora's box that was far too big for either of them, alone or together, to deal with.

CHAPTER SIXTEEN

SUNLIGHT STREAMED through the parted curtains, sunbeams glinting off copper highlights in Angela's hair as she stood before the dresser, mesmerized by dust motes dancing around the mirror. A memory flitted through her mind, seizing her with an intensity that mimicked reality; she was back in Oregon, a twenty-five-year-old married woman with a very rambunctious, talkative three-year-old who kept demanding every moment of her attention. . . .

Angela averted her gaze and forced herself to focus on the task at hand, the first of her Saturday-morning chores. She finished dusting the mirrored perfume tray and the top of the dresser, then moved on to strip the sheets off the bed.

She had crawled into bed half an hour after Patrick left last night, completely exhausted. All she'd wanted was to sleep, sleep, sleep. No more memories, no more true confessions. She had wanted to simply float away, forget everything that had happened and that had been said.

Now, with the clearer perspective the new day

brought, she was able to recall the scene with Patrick in a detached, unemotional light. He was right, of course. They had both started off on the wrong foot, each omitting or concealing from the other very significant matters about their pasts. Now that that was all out in the open, she wasn't sure how she really felt. Knowing Patrick had tried to tell her about his marriage was reassuring, and to be totally honest with herself, she had to admit she had played a large part in keeping him from doing so. So okay, everything was clean on that score.

Her own deep, dark secrets were another story. It was better that he know about everything, she supposed, and in a way she was relieved Joyce had told him about her daughter. Angela seriously doubted that she herself ever would have. Still, knowing he understood about Melissa and how the child's death had affected her didn't make the situation any easier or better for her. In fact, awareness only served to put a serious dent in her carefully wrought self-control. Of course the accident with Rory had tapped the memories anew, but the effects would have faded in time. Patrick's knowing everything only brought him and Angela that much closer, creating a situation she wasn't at all sure how to handle.

Angela *was* certain Patrick's idea was to force the issue for that purpose, to bring them closer together. She respected his conviction, even thought him right and admirable for his insistence. There were plenty of men who wouldn't care enough to hear such a painful truth, much less think it of paramount importance. But if he imagined she was going to open up completely, sharing every last emotional detail of her relationship with her daughter, or of the accident in which she'd died, he was wrong. Last night had been enough, more than enough. She couldn't go through these exploratory sessions again and again—not with him or anyone.

Well, she reassured herself, she was coping for now. Everything was under control, and that's the way it would stay. She balled up the sheets and pillowcases and the few wash items in the bathroom. There was plenty to do, and Angela was glad of it. A busy schedule would give her mind a sorely needed release.

PATRICK CALLED at ten o'clock that morning. He sounded tired and preoccupied. When he explained what was going on Angela could understand the reason. The patient he'd been called in to see last night had required surgery, and he'd spent several long grueling hours in the hospital both before and after the operation. The patient, a man in his mid-forties, was now in intensive care and doing poorly. The next forty-eight hours were crucial to his survival, so Patrick couldn't leave Jacksonville. He wanted Angela to drive out and spend the weekend with him, admitting that it might not be much fun, since either his beeper or the telephone repeatedly commanded his attention. Not to mention the time he must spend with his regular patients.

Angela declined, saying she had a ton of chores to catch up on and that she probably would get in the way. Patrick sounded disappointed. She imagined he would feel better were she with him, despite his hectic schedule, but she was firm. What she didn't tell him was that the night before was too much on her mind, and she needed to be alone for a while to get herself back together before they saw each other again. She put on a good front, she thought, in convincing him that she felt fine, that she wasn't still disturbed about what had happened, and Patrick sounded as if he believed her. He promised to call later on, either that night or the next day, depending on how the critical patient was faring.

Angela kept busy that day, doing all her washing and ironing and grocery shopping. She dropped by the Colliers' for a cup of coffee with her good friends, though Jonathon wasn't there. Joyce was nervous about her upcoming meeting with the department chairman and could talk about little else. Angela was on the verge of mentioning the scene with Patrick, but the moment never arose. She found it hard to tactfully interrupt Joyce's preoccupation with her own problems.

After she got home, she dressed in long underwear and a hooded warm-up suit, setting out for a run on the beach. The brisk wind gusted mightily at times, but Angela paid it no heed, simply pulled the hood over her head, tucked her chin inside the front of her jacket and took off, occasionally passing another stalwart soul. The run was good, just what she needed, and when she got back to the town house she felt renewed, free of the cobwebs of confusion in her mind. She settled down that evening in front of the television with a bowl of popcorn and a glass of tea, ready to enjoy a cable movie she hadn't seen yet.

After thirty minutes of watching and listening and understanding nothing of the plot or the characters, she got up off the couch, turned down the volume and went to her desk. Sitting down, she found a box of stationery crammed into a back corner of one drawer and drew out several sheets. She picked up a pen, poised it over the cream-colored paper and stared at the wall. *To hell with it,* she thought, dropping the pencil and crossing the room to turn off the television.

She pulled the telephone through the bar window and dialed her parents' house in Oregon. Her mother answered after the third ring. "Hello-o" in that warm, singsong tone Angela used to mimic as a child.

"Hi, mom. It's Angela."

"Angela! Of course it's you. Do you think you have to identify yourself to your own mother? Just a second, honey. Law-rence! Lawrence! Grab the extension, it's Angela!"

The excitement in her mother's voice warmed Angela with a sense of familiarity and belonging. "He's outside working on the car, but he'll be right in," Molly Carruthers said. "Honey, I'm so glad you called today. I've really been thinking about you a lot lately."

"I've been thinking about you guys, too, mom."

There was a click on the line, and Angela's father cut in. "Hi, baby. What'sa matter, such a boring Saturday night that you can think of nothing else to do but give the old folks a call?"

"Oh, dad, come on." Angela smiled at her father's typical teasing.

"Your brother called today, too," Molly said. "He's getting along pretty well on his mountain in Washington."

"Wait till he gets tired of going to the bathroom in the woods," Lawrence said dryly. "He'll be back."

"He's still into the naturalist thing, is he?" Angela asked. Steve had always been attracted to the outdoors and was determined to live his life as a modern-day pioneer.

"Yes, he sure is," Molly said with a resigned sigh. "He said to say hello to you if and when we talked to you."

"Which is hardly ever," Lawrence complained.

"Now that's not true. I talked to you just before Christmas."

"And I loved the perfume, honey. You know

it's my favorite. Lawrence's slippers fit perfectly. Did you get my note?''

''Yes. About a week ago. Thanks for my gifts, too. The nightgown and robe were just what I needed.''

''How's the store doing?'' her father asked.

''Great. Business is very steady. The week before Christmas was slower than usual, but after New Year's it was unbelievable. Regi and I were swamped. We're back to normal now.''

The three chatted for a few minutes longer about Angela's work, her parents' upcoming golf tournament and the possibility that they might come down to St. Augustine for a visit in late spring.

''That would be really nice,'' Angela said, more excited at the prospect of seeing them than she would have expected. ''Let me know when you get things worked out.''

''You can count on it,'' Molly said.

''Well, I just wanted to check in with you and see—''

''Honey,'' her mother cut in, ''um...are you doing all right—you know, not just in your work, but....''

Angela had been expecting her mother's routine question, but her reaction to it this time was different. She had always been ready with the reassurance her mother and father needed to hear—that she was handling her widowhood and the loss of her child as she had all along, calmly and intelligently and with a minimal amount of lingering grief. But this time was different, for she felt an immediate thickening in her throat and a smarting at the back of her eyes.

"I'm fine, really, mom." Somehow the words came out sounding as convincing as always.

"She's doing fine, Molly, you can hear it in her voice," Lawrence said. "But, baby, if there's anything you need, anything at all, you don't hesitate to give us a call. Okay?"

"Sure, dad." She was glad the conversation was coming to a close, for the ache in her throat was intensifying. "Write and let me know how the tournaments go."

"Oh, we will," Molly said.

"Great. And I'm looking forward to your coming down."

"We are, too. Bye, honey."

"Goodbye, sweetheart."

"Goodbye, mom and dad."

The connection was broken; Angela replaced the receiver. Tears filled her eyes, and she brushed them away, a wave of homesickness she hadn't felt in a very long time washing over her. She wondered why she had gotten the urge to call them. A combination of reasons, she supposed: a sense of obligation, the simple need to hear their voices, and something else, some other, deeper reason that was the most important of all.

After years of refusing to talk about the accident, even with her parents, she had felt an overwhelming need to hear them mention Melissa, to just say her name, to give credence to the child's existence. It was Angela's fault that her mother referred to the past in the vaguest way. Molly and Lawrence had long since given up trying to broach the subject—Angela had simply refused to let them. Any grief they had experienced over the death of their granddaughter and son-in-law, they had to deal with between themselves, with no commiseration from Angela.

Now, after all this time of keeping things that way, Angela felt almost resentful that neither of them had said a word about her daughter—their grandchild. "Dammit," Angela muttered aloud, asking herself how long it was going to take her this time to get her emotions—her life—back in order. None too soon, that much was certain.

SOMEHOW SHE MADE IT through the weekend. She hadn't looked forward to a Monday morning in a long time, not since before she'd met Patrick. And busy as the store was, it wasn't busy enough as far as she was concerned. Her concentration level was at its highest ever; she desperately wanted to block out any thoughts that didn't pertain to the present.

As the days went by with reassuring regularity, however, the nights became increasingly difficult for Angela to cope with. They continued to be filled with dreams and memories and recountings of that horrible turning point in her life three years earlier. She would wake in the middle of the night—her heart pounding, her face covered in sweat, terror ripping through her heart, a scream ready to break through her lips. Gradually the fear would abate, and she would relax, obtaining a few precious hours of sleep before dawn arrived.

Patrick called every day. His patient had made it through the crucial forty-eight hours and was doing better. But crises seemed to develop all at once, he'd lamented. Not only had he had an unbelievable number of emergency cases crop up over the weekend, but his office had scheduled patients one on top of the other for the rest of the week, leaving only the evening hours to make his hospital rounds. He sounded genuinely exhausted, and Angela sympathized with him. Still, she withheld some part of herself when they talked, the part of her, she later realized, that was still angry with him, angry that he'd provoked her into revealing painful details about her feelings and her past. Unburdening herself, so-called, hadn't had a beneficial effect, for now she was constantly on edge, irritable from lack of sleep. It was hard to dismiss the fact that Patrick's insistence had caused her to feel so completely out of sorts now.

On Wednesday he didn't call until eleven o'clock that night.

"Hi, sweetheart. Did I wake you?" He sounded tired himself.

"No. I was watching television and reading a book," Angela answered. Somehow, despite the resentment she harbored, she couldn't deny her relief at hearing his voice.

"I don't see how you do both things at the same time."

"It's easy, really. I alternate boring parts of the book with boring parts of the television show."

"That's crazy. Why don't you get a really good book, or watch a really good show? The book would probably be the easier to find."

"I don't know, I haven't come across a really riveting book in a long time."

"You just haven't been looking hard enough. Tell you what, why don't you come over here Friday night, and you can go through my bookshelves? I guarantee you'll find something you'll like."

Her lack of an immediate response was telling, and Patrick said, "Come on, Angela, it's been almost a week now since we've seen each other. That's too long."

"I know. But you've been busy, and so have I. Won't you have to see patients Friday night, too?"

"Yes. I've discharged quite a number already, though, so I should be home no later than seven o'clock. I'll cook dinner, something really mouth watering. Bet you haven't had anything mouth watering all week long."

"Well. . . that's true."

"Then come on over. I'd come to your place,

but it's better that I stick around here, close to the hospital.''

The temptation was too strong; besides, she was getting sick and tired of nothing but her own company. Within the confusion of her feelings there was one very strong, very compelling one that determined her final answer—the simple, inescapable desire to see him, to be with him again.

''All right, I'll come. But I'm not sure I'll be there by seven.''

''That's all right. Make it eight, eight-thirty, even. That'll give me plenty of time to cook.''

''Okay. Well, I guess I'll see you then.''

''Good. Angela . . . ? Is something the matter?''

She laughed lightly. ''No. Not at all. Why do you ask?''

''I don't know. You just don't sound like yourself.''

''There's nobody here but li'l ole me,'' she quipped.

Patrick wasn't fooled by her tone of voice, but decided to let the matter drop. ''I'll try to call you tomorrow. If I don't I'll see you Friday.''

''Okay. Good night.''

''Good night. And sleep tight. I'll be thinking about you.''

Patrick hung up, then walked to the living-room bar and poured himself a brandy. He swirled it, staring into the golden liquid, mulling over his conversation with Angela. There was no doubt in his mind that she was still upset over the discussion they'd had Friday night. "Discussion," he thought ironically. What an inappropriate term. "Scene" would be more accurate. He hadn't forgotten it for one second during the past five days. He'd hated seeing her that way, hated making her reveal something so painful. It was like opening up a wound, a badly scarred one, and watching it bleed freshly. As a physician he was dedicated to healing, but he was also well aware that at times a great deal of pain must be inflicted before the healing process could begin.

He sipped the brandy, then abruptly set it down on the bar. He didn't want it. Good God, he wasn't a psychiatrist, and he was too close to this situation to deal with it. Yet he knew something must be done, because he hadn't been exaggerating when he'd told Angela her problem was going to be their problem. It already was.

JOYCE CALLED ANGELA AT WORK on Thursday, which was unusual; her friend hardly ever spoke to her from the college. Could Angela come over for a cup of coffee as soon as she got home that evening, Joyce wanted to know. Angela assured her that she could and asked if anything was wrong, but Joyce was brief and only said they could talk that afternoon.

Angela hung up, puzzled by the strange tone in Joyce's voice, then remembered that it probably had something to do with her meeting with the department chairman. She hoped the news wasn't bad, but she wasn't able to give the subject more thought until she got home. As she drove into her parking space and switched off the engine, she decided to walk over to Joyce's right away. A cup of coffee was exactly what she needed right then, and her curiosity about what Joyce had to say had taken hold.

Joyce opened the door almost as soon as the bell chimed. There was no smile on her face. She just pulled open the door and said, "Come on in. I've got the coffee ready in the kitchen."

Angela noted with some alarm the strained expression on her friend's face; even the way she walked, very erectly and stiffly, indicated something was amiss.

"Smells fantastic," Angela said as she followed Joyce into the kitchen, taking a seat on one of the high barstools next to the island in the middle of the room. Joyce handed her a mug of steaming black coffee, which Angela sweetened and creamed generously. "Listen, I hate to sound tacky, but you wouldn't happen to have any cookies, or cake, or anything to go with this, would you? I'm absolutely starved."

"Sure." Joyce turned and went into the oversize pantry that Angela had wished, on more than one occasion, had been an option in her own town house.

When Joyce came back with a covered plate holding a tall, lemon sponge cake, Angela's eyes grew wide. "Mmm. Looks scrumptious. Did you make it?"

"Are you kidding? It's been strictly takeout around here for the past three days. I don't think the burners have been lit in at least five."

Angela blew slightly on her coffee, then took a sip. The seriousness in Joyce's tone was enough to make her forget the cake for the moment, no matter how hungry she was. "Joyce, what's wrong? I've never seen you like this, or heard you sound so...so, I don't know...."

"Try bitter." Joyce was standing across the island, her thumb absently circling the rim of her mug. Angela was surprised to see a certain brightness in her friend's eyes, the glimmer of unshed tears.

"Tell me," Angela said quietly.

Joyce drew in a deep breath and held it for a moment before expelling it in a loud, shaky whoosh. "Oh, hell, I don't even know where to begin. So much has happened since I last talked to you."

"Joyce, that was only four days ago. What could have happened in four days? You sound like the sky's falling in on you."

Joyce's gaze met Angela's, her gray eyes glinting with an emotion Angela had never seen in them—fear. "It is," she said in a barely audible tone. She picked up the mug of coffee and brought it to her lips, took a sip and set it down, staring down into it abstractedly. Angela waited, her curiosity overcome by downright concern.

Finally Joyce spoke. "I had my meeting with the chairman of my department. I was granted tenure."

Angela looked perplexed. "But that's great, Joyce!"

"Not so great. Not so great at all."

"I don't get it."

Joyce raised an eyebrow, and her lips twisted into a sardonic grimace. "Just so happens that Jonathon heard on Monday from his department chairman. His tenure was rejected."

"Oh." Angela could have kicked herself for the inane comment. Yet she was stunned; she had no idea what else to say. Joyce was silent, and at last Angela said, "Did. . .did they give a reason why? I mean, even I know how well respected Jonathon is in his field. You're both extraordinary. Why would. . . ."

"Why would I obtain tenure—something we've both worked our tails off for, for the past seven years—and Jonathon be rejected? The budget cuts. Exactly as I feared. As I told you, the college has been operating with an outrageous deficit for the past couple of years—something everybody knew about—and it finally had to take action. Big action. Unfortunately, the political-science department got hit the hardest." Joyce shook her head. "Oh, Angela, I knew something like this was going to happen. I had this—I don't know, premonition, I guess you'd call it—for a long time. It's as if I've finally woken up to find out the nightmare isn't a dream, it's reality."

The pain in her friend's expression was so real, Angela's heart went out to her. "Does it mean Jonathon doesn't have a position—at all?"

"He could stay on. With a reduced schedule—and pay, of course."

"Then it's not a nightmare, is it? I mean, if he still has a position—"

"He doesn't," Joyce answered flatly. "He turned in his resignation already."

"What! But why? What will he do?"

"That's the sixty-four-thousand-dollar question." Joyce's eyes shimmered as she looked at Angela. "Oh, Angie, he won't talk. He's all closed up like a clam. I've tried and tried, and I just can't get through to him."

Angela's eyes narrowed, and she shook her head. "I can't even picture Jonathon not saying anything. He's never kept his mouth shut—about anything. And I certainly can't imagine you two guys not talking. In fact, I've never seen a time when you actually shut up for any length of time."

Leaning an elbow on the table, Joyce rubbed her cheekbone with the heel of her hand. "I know. God, how I know. But it's true. It's even worse, really."

Angela waited, watching while Joyce picked up her mug of coffee with a shaking hand. "He's already started checking out other possibilities."

"What other possibilities?"

"Other college and university positions. He has friends all over the place, you know. One of them, an old graduate-school chum, told him he knew of a strong possibility of an opening at his university. In Dartmouth."

"Dartmouth? That's in New Hampshire."

Joyce laughed sardonically. "Yes, I know."

Angela's concern increased as she began to realize the extent of Joyce's predicament. "So what if he got it, the position? Where would that leave you?"

"Right here." She raised one eyebrow, and her voice was laden with sarcasm. "Care for a roommate?"

"Come on, Joyce, that's not funny! This is beginning to sound more serious by the second."

"Now you see why I called you."

"Yeah. I sure do." Angela drummed her fingers on the counter. "There *has* to be some sort of solution. For God's sake, you two have been married—how long?"

"Twelve years."

"Twelve years! So, Joyce, this is nothing. You can make it through this."

"Got any suggestions?"

Angela picked up her fork, broke off a piece of the cake and chewed it slowly, thoughtfully. "I suppose you want to stay on here?"

Joyce's look was frank. "Wouldn't you?"

Angela didn't reply, but her eyes were full of

understanding and sympathy for her friend's dilemma.

"Angie, I've spent seven *years* working for the position I have now. I'm proud of what I've accomplished."

"And you should be. Jonathon should be proud for you."

"He's too caught up in his own feelings of rejection." Joyce laughed shortly. "I swear, Angela, I have no idea what's going to happen."

Angela looked down at the counter top, then back up at her friend. "I just.... I don't know, it's so hard to picture you two with any problem serious enough to keep you apart. But this one is serious. I don't know what to tell you."

"Just tell me Jonathon will keep his head on straight and not do anything rash."

"Joyce, he will. I know he will. He's still the same old Jonathon."

Joyce's expression remained tense with apprehension. "The bottom line is this, Angela. I don't think I could handle a long-distance marriage."

"Aren't you putting the cart before the horse?"

"It might come to that," Joyce answered somberly. "It very well might." She looked away, her gaze focused somewhere beyond Angela's shoulder. "And if Jonathon won't talk, there's nothing I can do to influence him one way or the other."

The sound of the front door opening and closing brought Joyce's head up sharply, and Angela noticed with a pang the almost desperate sparkle of hope in her friend's eyes.

"Honey, is that you?" Joyce called out, her voice high and strained.

There was no answer, but a few moments later Jonathon walked into the kitchen. "Hello. Oh, hi, there, Angela. How's it going?" There was no expression in either his face or his tone, and Angela was alarmed by his overall appearance. He had lost weight, which on his tall lanky frame was quite noticeable. A distinct puffiness beneath his eyes added years to his face, and he was uncharacteristically disheveled. He barely glanced at Joyce as he passed both women to pour himself a cup of coffee.

"Just fine," Angela answered the rhetorical greeting, knowing he didn't even hear her.

"I wasn't expecting you home so early," Joyce said as cheerfully as possible. "Why don't you join Angela and me? I'll cut you a piece of lemon cake."

"It's really delicious," Angela added.

Jonathon shook his head, picked up the mug of coffee and started for the door. "No, thanks. I've got some things I need to get right on." He paused at the door and turned to Angela. "See you later, kiddo."

Angela said, "Sure," then looked back at Joyce. Her blond head was turned slightly away, and the hurt and defeat in her expression really got to Angela. She was at a loss for words. Jonathon's abrupt, almost rude behavior was at odds with his friendly, outgoing nature. Angela had to admit Joyce was right; something was very wrong with her husband, and possibly their marriage.

After a moment of strained silence, Angela stood up and brought her mug and empty plate to the sink. Gathering her coat and purse from the chair, she said, "Well, I really have to be getting home, Joyce. Thanks for the coffee and cake."

Joyce looked up and managed a smile that didn't reach her eyes. She nodded, biting the inside of her lower lip, and Angela could tell she was having a hard time pulling herself together.

"Well. . .I'll give you a call later, okay?"

"Yeah. Bye, Ange."

Angela left quickly, anxious to be away from the oppressive atmosphere that hung over the Colliers' like some ominous cloud.

But her friends' situation continued to haunt her all that evening. The equal stature Joyce and Jonathon had shared and nurtured for so many years was now the very thing that threatened, in a serious way, their marriage. There had to be a solution, yet Angela couldn't say exactly how she would have handled the situation, were she the one involved. There was nothing, really, that she could do except stand by and be the supportive friend she always had been.

Though the Colliers' dilemma did provide a distraction from her own troubles, that night, like every one preceding it for the past week, was filled with painful reenactments of the accident—and Melissa. Angela awoke the next morning with a heavy sensation in her chest, and lay very still for a long while. For the first time ever she rolled onto her side to block out the lovely pastel light filtering through the curtains. When she got up she went directly to the bathroom, showered quickly, dressed for work, then left the room, never once glancing in the direction of the window.

HER THOUGHTS WERE CONCERNED with Patrick as she drove to Jacksonville that evening, and she was aware of a growing anxiety. It was silly, really, for she had nothing to be anxious about with him. *But he's different now,* the words kept repeating themselves in her mind. He'd been married, had lived with and loved another woman. But it was the fact that this had taken place more recently than she'd assumed, that really bothered her. *And so what,* another voice countered. *What about you? You're not what he expected, either.*

Things were never as simple as they seemed, or people as easy to understand as one wanted them to be; Angela realized that basic tenet of life as well as anyone. She knew she was applying a double standard by expecting more of Patrick than she was willing to give herself, yet some childish willfulness made her want to hang on to her anger and resentment.

When she drew into Patrick's driveway she could see soft lights burning in the living room, and others in the kitchen. A mixture of feelings churned around inside her. The need and desire to be with him was so powerful that she longed to fly out of the car into his arms. *Close my eyes, and I can smell him, feel him, taste him,* she thought. But another, darker emotion competed with that need for him, and she knew of no other name for it except fear. Fear that she was on the verge of exposing a vulnerable spot in herself that would threaten all she had become, had worked so hard to achieve in the past three years.

She looked down at the steering wheel, surprised to see her hands still clutching it, the engine still running. Drawing in a deep, calming breath, she switched off the engine, picked up her purse, threw her trench coat over her arm and got out of the car.

No need to overdramatize, she reminded herself firmly, walking down the driveway to the back gate. She had someone to be with again, and at the moment, that was enough.

CHAPTER SEVENTEEN

SHE WAS SPEAKING in a low voice to Rusty, petting his sleek beautiful head, when Patrick answered her ring at the back door.

"You're late," he said gruffly, but his smile was cheerful and welcoming. He looked particularly handsome just then, Angela thought, dressed in a pair of beige cord slacks and a deep hunter-green pullover.

He's still the same, the voice in the back of her head said, and she felt the anxiety begin to fade as the familiarity of his home and his nearness overcame her reticence. "No, I'm not," she said. "You said any time I wanted. Besides, we ended up closing late at the store, and I couldn't get away from the house sooner."

"I was only kidding— Okay, Rusty, that's enough. Come on in, sweetheart?"

The spicy smells emanating from the kitchen were enticing, and suddenly Angela began to feel very hungry. "Mmm, that smells divine. What are we having?"

Patrick wiggled his eyebrows. "It's a surprise.

But you only have to wait another five minutes to find out. Are you hungry?''

"Starved."

"Good. Help yourself to a drink. I'll call you when it's ready."

She started to turn and go into the living room, when she felt his hand on her shoulder. She looked up and recognized the yearning in his lambent brown eyes, a mirror of her own feelings at that moment. His arms slid around her, pulling her close to him. Their kiss was warm and urgent and deep, and not nearly long enough to quench the thirst she felt so acutely. She couldn't believe it had only been a week since they'd been together; it seemed like a year. Why hadn't she made time to see him? Everything was so confusing, so—

"What's the matter?" Patrick said, pulling away but keeping his hands on her shoulders.

Angela shrugged. "Nothing." She smiled. "Why, do I look funny?"

"You feel so tense." He hesitated and appeared to be about to say something else, but changed his mind. "Go on, get your drink. I have to check on the food."

Angela nodded and stepped down into the living room. She looked all around, feeling, as always, comfortable here, almost as relaxed as she felt in her own home. Whatever doubts she might have concerning her relationship with Patrick, she had to admit she was glad to be here again.

She poured herself a sherry and took it with her to the window, gradually becoming lost in the fog-enshrouded harbor beyond. For a few moments she played a game of counting the faintly visible harbor lights that glimmered through the fog, until Patrick announced dinner was ready and she should join him in the dining room. The main course was veal Marsala, one of her favorite dishes, and as they ate, the conversation between them flowed as smoothly and as mellowly as the rich burgundy wine they drank.

"I SAW RORY TODAY," Patrick said, tearing off an end of the half-eaten loaf of French bread.

"You did? How's he doing?"

"Fine. He hasn't had any problems at all. He's been putting the bicycle you gave him through a real workout, he told me. All within the confines of the neighborhood streets."

"I'm so happy for him. I'll have to give him a call tomorrow. I've talked to the Williamses several times, but Rory's never been around when I've called."

"I'm sure he'd love to hear from you."

After dinner they went into the living room, and Patrick poured them both liqueurs. They stood for a while at the window sipping them.

"I don't think I could ever get tired of the view from here," Angela said.

Patrick put his arm around her and drew her next to him. "Ever been sailing?"

"Nope." She shook her head. "I don't know a thing about it."

"When the weather gets warmer, I'll have to take you out. I have a feeling you'd really enjoy it."

She glanced up at him. "Do you have a boat?"

"No. A good friend of mine, a colleague, does. He's taught me the basic skills. Several times he's offered to put the sloop at my disposal if I ever feel the urge to break loose."

"Well, it sounds like fun."

"Good, we'll put sailing on our itinerary."

Obviously Patrick was in a cheerful mood, judging by the frequent smile on his face and the tone of his voice, and after a couple of hours in his company much of his good humor did rub off on Angela. She sensed, as Patrick did, the growing physical awareness between them, a recognition of mutual needs and desires that couldn't be ignored or delayed much longer. Silently they moved away from the window and sat down on the couch. Patrick said nothing as he leaned closer to Angela, gently cupping her chin in his hand, his gaze heavy with longing as he pressed his lips to hers. Their tongues met with eagerness, thrusting and challenging, and when his hand slid down her back, his thumb tracing the column of her spine, Angela moaned softly. Patrick leaned back, then stood up to take her by the hand, pulling her to her feet.

"I've missed you, you know," he murmured, kneading her upper arms with his hands, his touch alone enough to ignite the flame òf passion within her.

"Me, too," she whispered, her own hands gliding across his back, her fingers pulling at the woolen material of his sweater. It was the truth; she had missed him, terribly so, and the feel of his body against hers now filled a deep, gaping hole within her that she had deliberately ignored for the past week.

Patrick's mouth grazed the top of her head. "You don't want to stay in here, do you?"

Angela shook her head slowly, and Patrick stepped away from her. He held on to her hand as he turned out the lights in the living room. Quietly he led her through the darkness, down the hall toward the master bedroom.

They undressed in silence, Angela finishing first. She shivered as her flesh made contact with the cool sheets, and she immediately drew her knees up into a tuck position until Patrick joined her.

"You're shivering," he said, sliding into bed.

"It's c-cold," she complained, and snuggled up next to him, eagerly absorbing some of the heat of his body. "Mmm, you feel good," she murmured. Her lips trailed over his collarbone. "Better than a blanket."

"Oh, yeah, sweetheart, *much* better than a blanket."

Within seconds she forgot all about being cold as Patrick's hands slowly caressed her entire body, moving from her backbone to the small sensitive depression just above her buttocks, pressing into her hips, skimming the flesh of her upper thighs and brushing the backs of her knees, then traveling oh so slowly back up her legs, his fingers whisper soft between her thighs, firmly separating them.

He rolled her over onto her back, and Angela gasped as his mouth moved across her abdomen, his tongue trailing wetly in an exploration that left her panting with tortured anticipation. His mouth dipped lower, finding the center of her passion, his lips circling and probing her tender flesh unceasingly. The flame of sensation burned, leaped out of control, finally exploding into the sweetest, most exquisite climax she had ever experienced. Her fingers pulled at his shoulders, and she saw the satisfied expression on Patrick's face as he raised his body and slid into her. He drove into her deeply, his thrusts quick and urgent until at last he filled her with the liquid sensation of his own fulfillment.

THEIR BODIES WERE SLICK with perspiration, the heat of their lovemaking defying the chill of the room, lingering about them in a protective aura.

"You're wonderful, you know that?" Patrick said into her hair.

"You think so, huh?"

"Sure do. In fact, I'm not too bad myself, come to think of it."

Angela laughed softly. "You're not deficient in the self-esteem department, are you?"

"With you to keep building it up, nope, I guess I'm not." He raised up a bit and said, "I've missed you, sweetheart, I really have."

He kissed the crown of her head, and she closed her eyes, her sigh of satisfaction explanation enough of her own heartfelt joy at being with him. But Patrick didn't need to hear any words from her, merely held her in his arms until at last they both drifted off into a restful, restorative sleep.

HE ROLLED OVER ONTO HIS SIDE and came awake for a moment, his narrowed gaze focusing on the amber numbers on the clock radio. It was a quarter to six. For an instant he felt disappointed, because he was still very sleepy and the last thing he wanted to do was get out of bed. Then he remembered that it was Saturday, and the office was closed. Though he did have rounds to make at the hospital, he didn't have to go in until later on that morning.

He turned onto his other side carefully, so as not to awaken Angela, frowning slightly as he saw that she wasn't in the bed. He raised up on one elbow, looking across the still-darkened room toward the bathroom; there was no light coming from beneath the door. "Angela?" he called out.

No answer. He swung his feet to the floor and reached for the thick, terry-cloth robe lying across the top of the dresser. He slid his arms in and tied the sash, pausing to shove his hair back out of his face. Drowsiness clung to him. As he crossed the room he noticed her clothes were still on the bureau.

"Angela?" he called out again. When he reached the end of the hallway he saw the light reflected off the dining-room wall. His footsteps slowed as he approached the kitchen door and saw her sitting at the table in the breakfast nook, dressed in his extra robe, which hung down around her ankles and over her wrists. Her auburn head was bowed; her hands cupped a half-filled mug of coffee.

She was unaware of his presence, and he spoke softly so as not to startle her. "Hey, what's going on here? You're up and about, and it's not even six o'clock yet."

Angela looked up at him, exposing the dark circles beneath her eyes, the light in them distant and feverish. He pulled out a chair across from hers. "Angie, what is it, sweetheart? Are you sick?"

She shook her head, picked up the mug and brought it to her lips. "No, I'm fine," she answered, her voice low and scratchy.

Patrick frowned, watching her drinking the coffee, and the sinking realization came to him that the wonderful, beautiful hours they had shared last night were over.

"You look awful," he said bluntly.

Her gaze remained fixed on the refrigerator door across the room. "Thanks a lot." There was no humor in her tone, only a flat, emotionless quality that scared the hell out of him.

"You're welcome. Angie, look at me for a second." Slowly she lifted her eyes and met his gaze, the distant, haunted look reminding him of one he'd seen before. Oh, yes, he had seen it before. "Did you have another nightmare?"

The question seemed to penetrate, for suddenly she frowned and brought the cup to her lips once more. "Why do you ask? Did I wake you up?"

"No. I only woke up a few minutes ago. How long have you been sitting here?"

Angela shrugged. "I don't know. Forty-five minutes, an hour. It doesn't matter." Her words ran together almost incoherently, and Patrick waited a moment for her to say something else. She didn't.

What shallow-minded optimism to have hoped last night could have made everything all right between them. He rubbed one hand against his jaw, the stubble scratchy on his palm. He had to do something; he couldn't bear to see her this way, tormented and hurting each and every time they were together lately. Even as he realized he was too close to the situation, he felt he had to try, had to do *something*.

He looked across the room, saw that the coffee maker light was still on. His body was still begging for more sleep. He needed something to cut through the fog in his brain.

Angela eyed his back as he stood at the counter,

mixing cream and sugar into his cup. His shoulders were slumped, his hair uncombed, his movements cumbersome. She was sorry he'd awakened; this wasn't his problem, and she hated seeing him so worried. She looked down into her almost empty cup, thinking how little the caffeine had done except make her jittery and somewhat nauseated. Coffee had never sat well with her on an empty stomach first thing in the morning; something to eat would help. But the thought of food was even more intolerable just then.

It hadn't been an exaggeration, her telling Patrick she didn't know how long she'd been sitting here in this position, her brain and body numb with fatigue, yet incapable of surrendering to sleep. She was so sick of this happening to her—couldn't understand why she was relentlessly tortured by the dreams, especially the one earlier that morning.

After she and Patrick had made love last night, Angela had felt so good, absolutely at peace. The last thought she'd had before going to sleep had been of Patrick, how very much she wanted him, needed him, loved him. It didn't matter about his past, or hers, for he *was* exactly what he seemed, a deeply sensitive, caring man, who loved her more than she'd ever been loved in her life. She had drifted off into a contented, easy sleep, all the more precious because she'd been deprived of it during the past week.

But the dreams had returned in the early-morning hours, as they always did. Once awake she hadn't been able to go back to sleep, disturbed by their shocking realism. She rested her forehead in the palm of her hand. *God, what is wrong with me? Why now, after three years? Three years of living alone, with no one to hold my hand or support me.* It was as though she'd completely lost control, the memories and nightmares plaguing her unceasingly. To be affected this way now just didn't make sense, but worse, she was beginning to fear there was no solution, no relief in sight.

Patrick sat down across from her, and his spoon clinked against the ceramic mug when he stirred his coffee. "Angie? Honey, look at me."

She took a long time in doing so, and when she finally lifted her eyes to his, he felt something melt inside him. A sense of déjà vu swept over him; they had played this scene before, only a different version of it, last week.

"Angie," he went on, "it was about Melissa, wasn't it? The dream."

She winced, looking away quickly. "Angela... don't you think it would help if you could tell me about the dream? You're suffering, honey, it's obvious. And I hate seeing you this way."

"My dreams aren't your problem," she said, her face tensing. The last thing she wanted was to go through any more soul searching with him.

"I don't happen to agree with you."

"It doesn't really matter. It's true."

"Goddamn, Angela. You're sitting in my kitchen, aren't you? You've shared my bed, haven't you? I think that makes me more than a little involved."

"I told you I'm sorry. It won't happen again."

"Won't it? Can't you see something is wrong, very wrong? How can you ask me to ignore how you feel? You're facing a big problem, and it damn well is interfering with us—our relationship. Let me tell you something. I spent the good part of nine years with a woman talking about everything in the world except the things that really mattered, and I'm sure as hell not going to go through that again."

Angela cast him a scornful look. "Sorry I remind you of your wife."

"Don't be melodramatic. You know very well you don't remind me of her."

"Oh, really? How can I know that, since I don't know anything about her?"

Patrick leaned forward, his cup clinking on the table top as he sat it down, hard. "You can rest assured, my dear, there's precious little to tell about Lucille. How do you describe a selfish, egotistical bore, except to use those very adjectives. But you name it, and I'll tell you anything you want to know about her." He paused, then said, "That's not the issue we're discussing here. The fact is, you've been sitting all alone in this kitchen for the past hour or so, all because of a nightmare that has apparently tormented you on more than one occasion. We need to discuss it, Angela."

She didn't move, didn't even blink, just sat staring at him blankly. His words made no impression on her whatsoever.

"All right. You don't want to talk. Fine, but tell me one thing. What are you going to do about it?"

"About what?"

"God—" Patrick sighed in vexation, running a hand through his hair "—you're stubborn about this ghost you're living with! Your memories are eating away at you, Angela, driving a wedge between us...."

He became aware of a subtle change in her coloring, a blanching of her already waxen complexion. Her eyelids narrowed; her nostrils flared slightly. Abruptly she shot up out of the chair, flinging it out behind her and stalking out of the kitchen.

Patrick was stunned by the action. Quickly he followed her down the hall into the bedroom, where she shed the robe, letting it drop in a heap at her feet, and began pulling on her underwear and clothes. Her movements were swift, precise, and she averted her eyes from his, even when he moved directly in front of her.

"What are you doing? Why are you getting dressed? It's only six o'clock in the morning."

She said nothing, still not looking at him as she buttoned the sleeves of her oxford shirt, then pulled her sweater over her head. She tossed her auburn hair back, making it swing away from her face, then stepped into her shoes. Patrick grabbed her by the arm, but she twisted away viciously, crossing the room to pick up her purse before starting for the hallway. Patrick stood in the doorway, blocking her exit.

"Angela, wait. Look, I'm sorry. I didn't mean to come on so strong. Let's just be rational about this, all right? You're not solving anything by getting in a huff and stomping out."

She stood mute, staring at the floor, her expression, her entire posture rigid.

"Say something, dammit!" he yelled at her.

She lifted her gaze slowly, and her eyes were bits of ice, distant and devoid of feeling. "What do you want me to say?"

"I want you to tell me why the hell you're walking out of here! Angela, let's be adults. This is ludicrous. Last night was beautiful, wonderful—don't you remember? Whatever it is that's bothering you—we can work it out."

"Please move, Patrick," she said quietly.

He rubbed the back of his neck, sighed heavily, then shifted reluctantly out of her way. She walked toward the front door and started to open it, but couldn't figure out the confusing system of locks. When he came up behind her she spoke to the door.

"Please open it."

"Not until you tell me what I said to make you freak out."

"I did not freak out," she said in a monotone. "Please open the door."

Patrick laid a hand against the wood, turning her by the shoulder to face him. His tone was pleading. "Angie, listen to me. I've said this before—a thousand times, probably. Don't let what happened to you come between us."

Angela shook her head slowly. "You really *don't* know what it is you said, do you? And you have the nerve to ask me to listen to you. All that tells me, Patrick, is how far apart we really are. At least on this one thing. And unfortunately, it's a very important thing to me. Now—" the brief fire in her eyes was extinguished "—please let me out. I'm really tired, and I'd like to go home and try to get at least a few hours' sleep."

Patrick swallowed deeply, letting his hand drop to his side. He unlocked the door and opened it for her, watching as she walked down the narrow sidewalk to the driveway. She didn't look back, but he waited until the Audi had reversed out onto the street before he shut the door, repeating the tedious locking procedure.

Patrick massaged his nape and sighed deeply, defeatedly, then walked back to the kitchen. He poured himself another cup of coffee, not bothering with cream and sugar, and took it into the living room. Standing near the window, gazing out unseeingly, he thought over every detail of their conversation in the kitchen. What had made her snap as she had, he kept asking himself. The subject of Melissa was enough on its own to upset her, he knew that, but this time the conversation had gone too far. He had said something that had—

Suddenly he knew. "Damn," he muttered, unable to believe he'd been so unfeeling, so stupid and cruel in his choice of words: *God, you're stubborn about this ghost you're living with. . . .* What could have possessed him to say such a thing! No wonder she'd reacted the way she had. He had chosen his words carelessly in his desperation to get a reaction out of her.

He had finally said the one thing to push her over the edge. There was no possibility that he could get through to her now. The next move would have to be hers, but he could still try to reach her. He loved her too much not to.

ANGELA HAD BEEN HOME TEN MINUTES when the telephone rang. She picked it up, hoping it wasn't Regi with a problem at the store. It was his Saturday on duty, and she wasn't in the mood to deal with anything or anyone at the moment. She almost decided to just let the phone ring. But it might be something important, a call from Joyce or her parents, so she picked up the receiver on the seventh ring.

"Don't hang up on me, Angela." It was Patrick. His voice was forceful, urgent. She said nothing.

"Are you there?"

"Yes."

"Good. Just listen to what I have to say, then I'll leave you alone. I just want you to know that I think I understand why you became so upset, and I'm truly sorry if I offended you. I didn't mean to. I've also decided I have to tell you something you really need to hear. I'm sure you're not going to like it, you may even get mad. But hell, you're already mad, so it doesn't make any difference, anyway." He paused, then plowed on. "Lorena Mayfield. I want you to remember her name. She's a psychologist, a highly respected one in the area, and—"

"What the hell are you talking about?"

There was anger in her tone, a tremendous amount of it, but Patrick didn't back off. "I think you need help, Angela. God knows, you're one of the most intelligent, admirable women I've ever known, quite apart from the fact that I've fallen in love with you, but you've got a problem. You've admitted as much yourself. And you were right when you said it's not my problem, at least not to the extent that I can do anything concrete to help you." He waited a moment. There was dead silence on the other end of the line. "Hello? Angela? Are you still there?"

Her "yes" was barely audible, and he could visualize the coldness of her expression. But at least she hadn't hung up on him yet. "I can tell you're really angry about this, but I think it's extremely important that you talk to someone, Angela. You should get professional help, and Dr. Mayfield is one of the best counselors I know of. I just want you to remember that."

He waited for her to respond. When she didn't he said, "Well?"

"Are you finished?"

"As far as that subject goes, yes. As far as you're concerned, no. I'm in love with you, Angela, and I want us to get past this. I know we can make it work. I know it."

There was silence again for a moment before Angela said, very quietly, "Goodbye, Patrick."

The telephone clicked in his ear, and Patrick slowly replaced the receiver. He heard Rusty bumping against the back door, the dog's not-so-subtle reminder that he knew his master was up and about and he was ready for some attention. Patrick opened the back door to let the dog in. Rusty's hard nails clicked and clacked as he scampered across the high-gloss linoleum floor. His tail wagged contentedly when Patrick sat down in a chair and began to gently stroke his ears. Patrick remembered the day at the beach, the night at Angela's house when Rusty had stayed outside on her patio. One memory led to another until his mind was saturated with them and he was seized by an aching for her, a sorrow that their relationship had finally come to this.

The thought of not seeing her again, at least not for a period of time, was excruciating, but he knew there was no other way. He'd done all he could for her at this point. The only thing left was for him to back off, to give her space in which to decide on her own whether or not to deal with the memories and lingering grief. He would simply have to wait for her, hoping and praying she would get the help she needed.

ANGELA WENT STRAIGHT UPSTAIRS after hanging up the telephone, took off her clothes without being aware of her movements and crawled under the sheets and coverlet. The telephone rang again, but this time she ignored it, turning onto her side and assuming the tuck position. If only she could get rid of this pain inside her chest, the gnawing, acid-ridden pain she hadn't felt in a long time, the kind for which there was no medication, no relief.

She thought about Patrick's words, but they meant nothing to her, none of them, for she knew only too well what problem she was dealing with, and how she had to handle it. That would be harder this time, much harder, but there was only one way to be free of the pain—the way that had worked before. And God willing, in the end it would work again.

CHAPTER EIGHTEEN

ANGELA LIVED THROUGH the following three weeks in a mental blur. She put in as many hours at work as possible, insisting on opening and closing the store despite Regi's protests. She needed the work, submerged herself in it, even created it when necessary to fill in the few moments when she was alone with her thoughts.

Her nights remained the same, filled with a montage of memories of her marriage, her other life, and of course the accident that had taken her husband's and daughter's lives. And as day followed day, the remembrances seemed to resurrect the people themselves. Memories of Melissa—her "ghost," as Patrick had termed it—were always with her now. In bits and pieces, Angela experienced the child's entire life—the day she was born, the sheer, inexplicable joy of simply looking into the baby's face and seeing an absolute miracle that had come from her own body.

A part of Angela kept insisting it was wrong of her to give in, to let herself remember such things, but another part of her cherished the past, wanted to believe it existed. And so she went on, letting the memories grow and grow until everything and everyone else were mere images on the periphery. There were times, a few, when Angela thought of what she had given up, and a wrenching sadness and regret would descend on her like a heavy, smothering blanket. She would never meet another man like Patrick, of that she was certain, yet there just wasn't enough room in her mind and in her heart for him to enter again. She had always lived alone with the past, never sharing it with anyone before him. She couldn't change now. Could she?

In those shaky moments when she lost conviction, she felt an almost overwhelming urge to call him, to go to him, to feel the comfort of his body next to hers. But ultimately the pull of that other life was too strong.

Tears, there were plenty of tears, buried somewhere in her chest. Incredible that she had found it relatively easy to cry with Patrick, but now, ironically, she was incapable of doing so. And oh, how she longed to cry, to know such emotional release.

There was a time when her good friends, the Colliers, would have been of some comfort, if not in the actual sharing of these feelings, in the mere comfort their nearness provided. But they couldn't comfort her now, for that relationship, too, had changed. Angela had been able to hide, or so she hoped, what was wrong in her own life from Joyce, who was beside herself with worry and despair. Jonathon's quitting his position at the college the week before had been a radical move by any standards, but especially so because he still had no other position to replace it.

He had handed his classes over to a graduate student, then left St. Augustine for a series of interviews at several out-of-state colleges, set up with the help of his colleague in New Hampshire. Joyce had no idea what was going to happen next, since any position he might secure would necessitate a move.

"Ange, I don't think I've ever been so miserable," she said one evening as the two of them shared a pizza at Angela's place. Joyce did look miserable and bereft, making Angela realize it had been a long time since she'd seen a smile on her friend's face.

"Has he called?" Angela asked.

"Oh, yeah, sure, a couple of times. He puts on this big act, you know, as if he and Jeremy are having a great old time, and that there are all sorts of openings waiting for him. It's ridiculous, Angela, because I'm positive he's just pretending, fooling himself. I know too much about the academic field. There are very few opportunities out there, at least of the kind he could accept. His ego is just shattered." She gave a short, ironic laugh. "Boy, we've come a long way, haven't we? All the talk of equal opportunity, of progress for women, and what happens in a situation like this? The precious male ego, it still takes precedence."

"But wouldn't you have felt the same, Joyce? I mean, what if the opposite had happened. What if Jonathon had gotten tenure and your position was the one to go?"

"I sure as hell wouldn't have left him!" Joyce was livid with resentment, then in the next instant, resigned and sad. "I just love him so much Angela.... I can't stand being apart from him."

Joyce's words struck Angela more deeply than she would have suspected; she had to look away for a moment and collect her thoughts. A moment later she spoke comfortingly to her friend. "You're forgetting, Joyce, that Jonathon loves you, too. As drastic as his actions may seem, I think he probably has to do this right now. He doesn't mean to hurt you. You think he's having a jolly old time of it? Believe me, he's missing you at least as much as you're missing him. I don't know what he's going to do, but I'll tell you this. If push comes to shove, he'll choose you. And if he doesn't, well, what can I say? He'd have to be certified insane."

Joyce reached across the table and took one of Angela's hands in her own, squeezing it tightly, then roughly wiping away a tear on her cheek. "I sure needed to hear that, Angela. You're one heck of a friend."

Angela smiled gently. "Thanks. You know I think the same of you. More coffee?"

Joyce nodded. "Yeah, why not? I've hardly touched this pizza. I guess I'm not really in the mood for it."

"How about a piece of delicious carrot cake, instead?"

"Sure, okay. Is it your recipe?"

"Are you kidding? It's fresh out of the frozen-food section."

"I take it you haven't been cooking lately."

"Nope. I'm into fast-food specialities myself nowadays."

Joyce watched Angela cut the oblong iced cake, then pour fresh cups of coffee for both of them. "I haven't been the most attentive friend in the world, I'll admit that," she said, "but I have noticed you haven't said much about Patrick lately. What's going on with you two?"

Angela was taken off guard by Joyce's innocent question. She brought the plates and cups to the table and took her seat, busying herself by stirring creamer into her coffee.

"Actually . . . not much."

Joyce raised her eyebrows. "Why not?"

"Oh, it's a long story."

"I've got nothing better to do than listen."

"Well, it's not that I don't want to tell you. . . . It's just that it's a little hard to explain."

"Try me."

Angela stirred her coffee, then looked directly up at her friend. "It has something to do with you."

"Me?" Joyce sat back a little. "Lord, I didn't think I had that much influence around here."

Angela stopped stirring and set the spoon down

in the saucer. "I suppose it's silly of me to beat around the bush. What I'm referring to is the fact that I never told Patrick about the accident. At least not everything. . . ."

Joyce actually groaned. "What?" Angela said.

Joyce closed her eyes and sighed. "Me and my big mouth. I know what you're getting at—the conversation I had with Patrick on Christmas Day. Ange, I'm sorry. It wasn't my place to say anything, which I soon realized at the time. I just thought he knew about Melissa, and when he told me you were crying—"

"I wasn't crying. I got a little misty-eyed, that's all. Anyway, that doesn't matter, Joyce. Patrick and I have gone far beyond that. We've had a couple of scenes because I don't care to get into any heavy discussions about something that happened three years ago. And. . . well, we just don't agree on things."

"I don't follow you."

"As I said, it's a little complicated. Patrick happens to think it's his problem. I happen to think it's mine."

Joyce took a bite of cake and chewed thoughtfully. "This is the first time I've heard you admit there was any sort of problem."

"Well, there's not. Not really."

Joyce looked questioningly at her friend.

"It—it's a matter of semantics," Angela said, stumbling over her words. "Patrick thinks we have an obstacle to overcome. I happen to think of it as a temporary relapse that I have to deal with alone.''

Joyce put her fork down. ''But why alone? I have to admit, Angela, I side with Patrick. I certainly don't understand how this arguing could mean you aren't seeing him anymore. Don't you miss him?''

Angela chewed her lower lip as she looked away. ''Yes. I really do.''

Joyce sighed. ''I know this isn't any of my business, so if you don't want to say anything, I understand. But...has he told you he loves you?''

Angela nodded.

''And do you love him?''

Again she nodded, and Joyce shook her head. ''Boy, what a couple of sad cases we are. You're no better off than I am. And you've been listening to nothing but my complaints for the past ten days.''

''It's not the same thing.''

''The hell it isn't. Let me tell you something, Angela, that man is one gem. You're my friend, so I can say what I mean and believe me, I mean this. You're nothing short of a fool if you let him go.''

Joyce's words dealt Angela a direct blow; she felt the impact in the pit of her stomach. ''What is it that's really keeping you apart?'' Joyce said.

''I don't know— Oh, all right. I...I've had these nightmares lately. Ever since Rory's accident, really. Some of them are pretty bad—about the accident and all. To make a long story short, Patrick thinks I need help—professional help."

"Aha.... And his saying so made you angry."

"Well, not just that. I think he meant well, but...dammit, I don't need help. I'm determined to see this through myself."

"Ange, I think you're being unreasonable." Joyce hesitated, looked at her friend thoughtfully for a moment and said, "I might suffer the same fate as Patrick, but this is something I have to say: he might be right. It might be the best thing you could do to get professional help. Jonathon and I have never said anything outright...but we considered it more than a little odd at times, the way you've completely shut off the part of your life involving Gordon and Melissa. I have tremendous admiration for you, Ange, as a person, a friend, a successful businesswoman. You have a courage and strength that are absolutely amazing. Yet in this one area of your life— Well, you just haven't handled it right. You haven't handled it at all."

Angela sat with her head bowed as she listened to Joyce's heartfelt monologue. Never had they had such a serious discussion, and Angela knew her friend well enough to realize she wouldn't have said anything unless she felt strongly about the subject.

"Do you have anything against psychiatry or counseling?" Joyce asked.

"No."

"Then what can you lose by giving it a try? At

least you could make one appointment. There's always the possibility that an outsider might help you." Joyce looked directly into her friend's eyes. "Hon, I'm going to tell you something. Counseling is worth it, worth a million dollars—even more—if it means you can learn to be happy again, really happy. And if therapy helps you and Patrick get back together, that would be the best kind of bonus. Believe me, I wish my alternatives were as clear-cut."

Angela said nothing, just picked up her coffee and sipped at it. Then she set the cup down and smiled vaguely, drawing in a deep breath and letting it out slowly. "I'll think about it, Joyce. Is that good enough?"

"No. But it's better than nothing." Joyce finished up the last of her cake, picked up the crumbs with the tines of her fork and drained her cup. "That was delicious." Standing up, she took her dishes to the kitchen sink. "And I need to get home now. I've taken up too much of your time already."

"You have not, and you know it."

"Well, I do have a slew of papers to go over before bedtime." She glanced at the wall clock. "Also.... I don't want to be gone if Jonathon should call."

"He's calling tonight?"

"I hope so. He said tonight or tomorrow."

"I see. At least the lines of communication are still open."

"Somewhat," Joyce said dismally.

Angela walked with Joyce to the front door. "Ten to one he'll be home in the next few days."

Joyce shook her head. "I'd give anything if you were right about that."

"Well, don't sell him short. Just remember, he loves you, Joyce. He loves you one hell of a lot."

Joyce sighed. "Yeah, that's all I've got to bank on." She stepped out onto the patio, and as she opened the wooden gate Angela said, "Call me when you hear from him."

"I will. Good night, Ange."

"See ya."

As she undressed for bed later that night, Angela thought over her conversation with Joyce, perhaps the most significant one the two of them had ever shared. Gradually Angela became aware of a subtle change in her perception of her situation. She lay awake for a long time that night, letting her thoughts meander, until strangely the numbness of the past few weeks began to wear off. She felt the first stirrings of a need to move forward, to emerge from this phase of her life and try to regain the direction and purpose she had somehow lost.

ANGELA'S DECISION to seek professional help wasn't a particularly momentous one. It was the result of a natural progression in her thinking. On the Wednesday afternoon following her discussion with Joyce, she drove home and went straight to

the telephone directory. Mayfield. Lorena Mayfield. Odd how the name had stuck with her all
this time. She found it easily enough in the yellow
pages under Psychiatric Counseling.

Without hesitation she dialed the number and
set up an appointment for the next afternoon. She
would have to arrange to take off early from the
store, but she knew Regi wouldn't object. Surprisingly, the very act of setting up the appointment
had a soothing, reassuring effect on her, and she
went to bed early that night, sleeping better than
she had in a long while.

DR. MAYFIELD'S OFFICE was located in an office
complex on the outskirts of Jacksonville. Angela
found the suite on the third floor easily. There was
no secretary or receptionist, so that the office had
a less formal air. As Angela waited, alone in the
room, she felt the tension that had been steadily
building all day ease somewhat.

The room was comfortably furnished with one
couch, several tweed-upholstered occasional
chairs and a mahogany coffee table scattered with
magazines. Three of the walls were painted a
restful antique yellow, while the fourth was completely covered by a photographed mural depict-
ing a leaf-strewn pathway through an autumn
forest. The three-dimensional effect drew her
gaze; it was curiously calming. Angela could
readily imagine herself stepping into the scene and
onto the path, hearing the snap and crunch of

layer upon layer of fallen leaves and pine
needles—

A door opened, and Angela snapped out of her
reverie. A middle-aged, attractive woman stepped
into the waiting room, a warm, friendly smile on
her face.

"Hello, there. Angela?"

Angela nodded, standing up.

"Come on in," Dr. Mayfield said brightly, and
Angela returned the magazine she'd picked up, to
the table.

The interior office was large, and as in the waiting room, attractively yet practically furnished in
a contemporary style. A small couch stood along
one wall, with a desk in the corner near the window and four midnight-blue side chairs positioned
around an Oriental rug in the middle of the room.

"Take your pick," Lorena said, indicating the
chairs, then sitting down opposite Angela. She
folded her hands in her lap and smiled once more.

"So, Angela, why don't we just start by telling
me a little about yourself."

Angela swallowed, drew in a deep breath and
produced a nervous smile. She was conscious of
her entire body, the way she was sitting, the way
her fingers stroked the nubbed fabric of the chair
arms. This was a foreign experience for her; she
wasn't sure how to begin. Finally she dived right
in and began to recite her vital statistics—where
she lived, her profession, how long she'd been in
St. Augustine, where she was from. She seemed to

go on and on, including all sorts of inconsequential details, until Lorena interrupted at one point to ask a pointed question, one aimed, Angela understood, at getting to the heart of the matter, her reason for coming.

"I guess I've come today... because I've reached a point in my life where I don't know what to do—about a certain problem, that is. I guess you could say I have a mental block about it."

"How so?"

"Well...I keep having dreams. Nightmares, sometimes. I don't seem to have any control over them anymore. They...they've begun to interfere with my normal life."

"What are the dreams about?"

Lorena's casual tone created the impression that the two of them were having a normal everyday conversation. Angela continued without hesitation.

"They're about something that happened to me three years ago. I was married then. And I had a daughter."

She paused. Lorena prompted her. "Had?"

"Both my husband and my daughter were killed in an automobile accident. I was the only survivor."

Lorena gave a single nod of her head. Her gaze was steady and unwavering as she said quietly, "The nightmares have to do with the accident."

Angela said nothing, but without warning her face seemed to crumple. Tears streamed down her

cheeks; her breath came in gasps. Placing her fingers over her mouth, she shook her head. "I...
I'm sorry. I didn't mean—"

"Go on. Don't feel as if you shouldn't cry.
There's a purpose for it."

Angela looked at Lorena through the blur of
her tears and saw the other woman's encouraging
nod, and in that moment she realized Lorena
Mayfield did understand. Despite the fact that
she'd only just met the woman, a bond of trust
was established, shattering the wall of inhibitions
Angela had been hiding behind. She cried for a
few minutes longer, and when at last the tears
abated, she reached for the tissue box on the coffee table, grabbing a bunch. After several rather
loud blows she managed an apologetic smile and a
half laugh.

"Your bill for miscellaneous must be outrageous."

Lorena smiled and tilted her head to one side.
"All part of the overhead." She waited while Angela blew her nose again, then said, "I want you to
do something, Angela." Angela looked at her
curiously. "First of all, I want you to get really
comfortable—tilt your head back against the
headrest.... Good. Now just take in a long, deep
breath. Hold it. Let it out. Good. One more
time."

She had Angela repeat the breathing exercise
several times, until gradually Angela could feel
her whole body responding, relaxation spreading

from her head to her toes. When finally she opened her eyes, Angela felt a peace within her that she hadn't known in years. Nothing else mattered except what was happening between the four walls of this room. Once she had accepted that, everything else, all other responsibilities of her day-to-day life were put on hold, to be dealt with some other time.

After a while Angela began talking without any prompting from Lorena, pouring out the events of the past few months in stream of consciousness, describing the accident with Rory, her belief that it had provoked an unwanted onslaught of memories and dreams. Then she went into her relationship with Patrick, how it had begun, how it had progressed so quickly, how they were no longer seeing each other because of her refusal to talk about that other part of her life.

"Are you in love with him?" was Lorena's first question.

Angela nodded. "Yes. And he says he's in love with me."

"Then what exactly is keeping the two of you apart?"

"Me, I suppose. He happens to be the one who recommended I come and see you."

Lorena's expression was expectant as she waited for Angela to go on.

"His view of dealing with the situation and mine don't quite coincide."

"Why don't we go into that."

Angela only stared at the woman for a moment; she was momentarily stymied, for there was no avoiding the truth—her way of dealing with the situation had failed so far. Certainly it hadn't worked as it had before. She said as much to Lorena.

"Tell me how you've failed," Lorena said.

Angela's fingers moved in small circles over the fabric of the chair. "Well. . . I've always been able to keep the. . . memories, you know, under control. I haven't let them be a burden on those around me—my friends, my family, the people I work with. But as I said, after the accident with Rory, things started to get a little out of hand. More than a little, at times. Rory had a setback one day at the hospital when I went to see him, and. . . ." She paused, swallowed, then said, "And I freaked out. Patrick was with me at the time. There were a few other incidents, as well, when I woke up crying, shaking. I don't know. . . it was bad."

"Patrick was with you then also."

Angela nodded.

"And he tried to get you to talk about what was bothering you."

"How did you know that?"

Lorena shrugged. "I happen to know him. Professionally speaking. His intuition was on target. He was trying to get you to do the right thing."

"Well," Angela said, "we did talk about the accident. . . Melissa. . . once. In my opinion that was enough. More than enough."

"Why?"

Angela's eyes opened wide. "I would think it would be obvious. That part of my life is too painful to open up for general discussion. I don't see the point in inflicting that pain on someone else."

"Even someone who's willing to share it with you, to help you with it?"

"I'm dealing with the situation."

Lorena smiled. "I thought that's why you came here—because you weren't able to deal with it anymore."

"True," Angela said rather sheepishly.

"You *can* learn to deal with traumatic memories, Angela, but first of all, let me ask you something. Are the memories of your daughter and husband something you're willing to put to rest, to leave as part of the past so you can go on with the rest of your life?"

Angela frowned. "What do you think I've been telling you? I *have* put them to rest. Or at least, I had until now." The frown deepened as she grew more confused. She wasn't making sense.

"I have no quarrel with your intentions, Angela, but it's obvious the methods you've employed haven't worked. You've done admirably well in putting your life back together; losing those you love, especially a child, can be devastating. The number of people who aren't able to function, let alone make their lives better after such a tragedy, are far greater than one would expect. Your mistake, Angela, was in assuming you were going to be able to cut that part of your life out, to pretend it never existed.

"The brain simply doesn't work that way. Whatever it is you internalize and refuse to give adequate attention remains there, inside your head. Especially something unpleasant or hard to deal with." As Lorena talked, her voice remained at the same even level, but her gestures became more animated. Angela was unaware of the subtle change in her own body's position; unconsciously she had leaned slightly forward, her eyes narrowed in concentration as she listened to what the counselor was saying.

"No, whatever is in here—" Lorena tapped a finger to her temple "—doesn't just vanish. It festers, continues to eat away like an ulcer in the stomach, until you decide to treat it. What you've done, Angela, and I might add, very successfully for a surprising length of time, is repress all the suffering and grief that are normal consequences of such a tragedy." Lorena shook her head and smiled ruefully. "It was inevitable that you would have to face your feelings someday. You were correct in thinking the accident with Rory was the key that unlocked everything, brought it to the forefront of your conscious mind."

Angela propped her elbow on the armrest, her chin in the palm of her hand. She waited, watching as Lorena shifted her position, crossing one leg over the other.

"I want to tell you something else about the way

the mind works, Angela. When the human brain is exposed to a traumatic situation such as the one you went through when your husband and daughter were killed, there are several ways in which it reacts self-protectively. Very often it uses denial, a simple blocking out of everything that has happened. This in itself is an acceptable method of coping, provided one thing: that one eventually comes out of this phase and faces reality. There is no escape in the end from trauma and its effects on us, our lives and those around us.

"From what you've told me about yourself, Angela, you avoided a very painful reality by refusing to experience the grieving process —which in itself is a healing process. You left for Florida very soon after the loss of your husband and daughter and proceeded to start a completely new life. A very commendable move in many respects, but as you discovered, we cannot run from the problems in our lives. There is no place to run *to*, for the problems are within ourselves. In essence, this is what your dreams and your 'freaking out' are all about. Your brain is dealing with the grief you've ignored for so long, whether or not you like it."

Angela nodded several times, the glimmer of understanding growing and expanding. It was as if a light had come on in her mind, soft and luminous, once more defining the direction of the path she had abandoned and now must meet and travel again. "It does make sense," she said softly, looking at Lorena. "This isn't at all what I expected from coming here."

Lorena smiled and raised her eyebrows questioningly.

"I thought—I don't know—that you would just ask me a lot of questions. Make me figure out everything myself."

"You *will* figure it all out for yourself. You're the only one who can."

"I guess I've known all along—deep down—everything you've said. About denial and all that. But what you said about letting the memories become a part of the past...." Angela's voice trailed off.

Lorena leaned forward and spread out one hand, palm upward. "When I asked you if you were willing to let go of the memories, I also meant, are you willing to come to terms with your grief, to live it through, the way it should have been lived through three years ago."

Angela looked away, staring unseeingly out the window. "That's kind of a tough question," she said in a small voice.

"I know it is. But one you must answer."

After a few moments Angela's eyes returned to Lorena. "There's a lot of guilt involved that I haven't mentioned."

"That's not unusual. That, too, has to be dealt with. All of it does, Angela, before you can truly go on with your life."

Lorena glanced at the hexagonal clock prominently displayed on the wall next to her desk, and Angela said, "Have I run over the time limit?"

"No, we've got a couple of minutes left."

Angela drew in a lungful of air, expelling it slowly. "There's so much more I need to talk about."

"Then why don't we set up another appointment?" Lorena got up, walking toward her desk. She slid a large appointment book toward her.

"I kind of thought—" Angela laughed lightly "—that you were going to tell me you thought I needed to come in three times a week for the next year and a half."

Lorena smiled. "Hardly. The very fact that you're doing something about your problem is at least seventy-five percent of the solution."

The words were like magic to Angela, filling her with a reassurance and comfort she sorely needed. "How about next Tuesday afternoon? I can manage to take off early then."

"Three o'clock?"

"Yes. That's fine."

Lorena made the notation in the appointment book, then walked around the desk to accompany Angela to the door. When she opened it, she said with a warm, genuine smile, "I've really enjoyed meeting you, Angela."

Angela grinned back. "Well, I can certainly say the same. I had no idea this meeting—it was nothing like I expected. You know, I have this strong suspicion I might have a perfect night's sleep tonight."

"Good! But if you don't, just remember it's part of the healing process. In time you *will* get past the pain. Believe me."

"Thanks. I want to believe that, I really do." Angela stepped into the waiting room. "Goodbye, Dr. Mayfield."

"Lorena. I'm partial to the informal."

"All right. Lorena, then. See you next time."

Angela's footsteps were light, almost bouncy as she made her way to the parking lot. Swiftly moving dark gray clouds had passed across the sky, and she felt the first few drops of rain on her nose just before she reached the car. As she pulled out of the parking lot, the sky seemed to open up; the rain poured down. If it kept up, Angela knew it would slow her trip back to St. Augustine considerably.

But the possibility didn't bother her in the least. Contentment brightened her formerly tense expression as she realized that nothing as insignificant as a torrential downpour could destroy this newfound, wonderfully satisfying feeling of accomplishment. Because she *had* accomplished something that day—more than she would ever have thought possible.

CHAPTER NINETEEN

SLEEP DID COME EASILY that night, as Angela had hoped, but in the early-morning hours the dreams returned, and she awakened with tears on her face and an aching space within her chest. But she didn't fight her feelings this time, simply turned onto her side and sobbed her heart out for several minutes. As the tears abated her eyes slowly took in the shadowy details of the moonlit room.

Peace enveloped her, replacing the sorrow and remorse with a calmness and acceptance. She thought of the session yesterday with Lorena; she was amazed, gratefully so, by the almost immediate trust she'd developed in the therapist. She hadn't expected to feel that so quickly, and the experience had changed her previous views of what psychology and its applications were all about. Perhaps her bias had prevented her from seeking professional help earlier; she had always balked at the idea of paying someone to simply listen or ask rhetorical, meaningless questions for a fifty-minute hour. Some therapists operated that way, but Lorena wasn't one of them. She had verbally taken Angela by the shoulders, turned her gently in another direction and said, "Okay. That way, Angela. That's the road you need to take." Angela understood it was a road she would travel alone, for only she could come to terms with the past and the grief, face them with courage and determination, as she should have done a long time ago.

And now she knew she could. She would reach for the pain, hang on to it and work it through her system until it released her completely. If she faltered, there would be someone who could tell her, "It's all right. Just keep going." Lorena would fulfill that role, and as much as Angela had insisted before on dealing with her problem alone, she was now convinced that getting professional counseling had been the right decision.

And then there was Patrick. Ah, how she had thought of him, dreamed of him—missed him. On the drive home from Lorena's office yesterday, she had thought about him incessantly, possessed by a longing so intense it was hard to believe she had suppressed it for three entire weeks. The counseling session had brought her out of that anesthetized numbness of body and spirit, catapulting her into a state of agitation and impatience that was almost too much to bear.

Where was he, she had agonized—what was he doing? The questions had played havoc with her imagination, rousing a fear that Patrick had decided to end their relationship, that he'd given enough of himself already. Yet he had told her he loved her, and she hung on desperately to the memory of those words. Her anxiety had intensified later on the previous evening when she had called his house and there was no answer. That wasn't unusual, of course; he could still have been working. She had considered calling his answering service to leave a message, but that was out of the question. It was *her* responsibility to get in touch with him, and she would have it no other way. Just before going to bed Angela had called him again, but again there was no answer, so she had decided to wait until morning.

Now as she lay in bed mulling over her and Patrick, the curtains were gradually backlit in pale peach as the morning's first feeble rays filtered through the window. Angela glanced at the clock on the nightstand. It was almost five-thirty.

Abruptly she threw back the covers and got out of bed. Minutes later, dressed in a lavender cotton warm-up suit, she sat down on the floor to tie the laces of her jogging shoes. Downstairs in the kitchen she drank half a glass of orange juice and a full glass of water, then left by the back door.

The bottom edge of the horizon glowed with a golden-rose tinge, and the early February air was chilled and dry. Angela's footsteps made no sound on the pavement as she strode along the familiar alleyways and sidewalks that eventually branched off in various paths to the beach. She passed the

Colliers' home. She'd been so caught up in her own problems that she hadn't given a thought to what was going on with her good friends. But Joyce hadn't called, which she'd promised to do if anything developed as far as Jonathon was concerned. *Well,* Angela decided, *if there's still enough time later, I'll drop by before she leaves for school.*

A strong breeze was blowing as Angela headed off along the shore, jogging in a steady, sure rhythm toward the distant landmark she had often used before. She looked up, her attention captured by the graceful, fluid motion of a lone sea gull, rising effortlessly on a current of air, tilting its body to one side, then the other, then plummeting toward the earth, buoyed up by the wind at the last moment. What a wonderful creature to come back as, she mused, granted, of course, that one believed in reincarnation. Such freedom, such precious, unbridled freedom, knowing no such thing as pain, or tears, or memories.

The thought drifted away with a gust of wind, and she continued on her steady path, the run having its usual calming effect. All analytical thought was suspended. Her brain became an empty stage on which images and memories danced and darted about freely, and for once, painlessly. . . .

Rusty, dashing and tumbling across the sand, jumping and dodging the waves in tireless enthusiasm. Patrick, holding her, pressing his body against hers, covering her eyes, her cheeks and mouth with the salty taste of his kisses, the wind and sand and scurrying clouds dissolving into the sultry brown of his eyes. . . .

A beach scene, some six or seven months after Angela had first moved here; she had already met the Colliers, and their relationship had solidified into unquestionable friendship. Having already launched their ceaseless campaign to rectify Angela's social life, they had invited her to a party they and some of the other condo owners were hosting. Food and drink were plenteous, and the air was filled with the shouts and laughter of the group, their voices competing with the crashing surf and the squawking sea gulls.

Angela had joined in a volleyball game, getting caught up in the surprisingly fierce competition, and afterward was voted the most valuable rookie addition to the team. That day had been great fun. She had laughed her share at the jokes, the raucous teasing. Yet there had been a superficiality to her enjoyment, for always at the edge of her consciousness the remembrance of another beach, another day of sunshine and laughter had lingered.

The landmark, a large, flat-faced rock near a crop of tall, undulating weeds, was looming larger. Angela began to slow her pace, letting the memory wash over her without resistance. Melissa had been five years old then, wearing a two-piece bathing suit Angela's mother had bought for her. It was her first time at the beach, since Angela and

Gordon lived hundreds of miles inland and trips to the ocean were inconvenient.

Enthralled as Melissa had been with the unfamiliar environment, it had taken a great deal of resolve on Angela's part to see that her daughter didn't overdo it and get too much sun. Melissa had been tireless, though, loving everything about the ocean and beach: the sand castles and seashells and disappearing sand crabs, the sights and sounds of others enjoying the glorious summer day.

But she had paid a heavy price for her fun in the sun, had cried most of the evening and into the night from the ferocious burn her delicate skin had suffered. Her mother had bathed her in a cool bath, then slathered her from head to toe with a soothing medicated cream. She had been racked with guilt that she hadn't prevented the child from coming down with such a terrible case of sunburn. *This is what motherhood is all about,* Angela remembered thinking at the time. Worry, guilt, and more worry and guilt. Yet she wouldn't have traded places with any other woman for the world, because she also knew a joy that was unique and irreplaceable....

Angela stopped as she reached the rock landmark, her breathing heavy and loud, her lungs burning from the exertion of the run. Normally she wouldn't have broken stride, would have made a wide loop and started back. But she just stood there, facing the east, amazed anew by the spectacle of yet another daybreak. And while she stood watching, there arose in her mind's eye another image of her daughter.

It's time now, Angela. Time to let go. The words came to her as clearly as if spoken aloud; Angela's eyes narrowed when the truth of them hit her fully. In that moment, she knew something inside her had changed irrevocably. "Oh, baby," she whispered into the cool morning air, kissed with the salty spray of ocean mist. "I love you. I'll always love you." She closed her eyes, and the image of her small daughter, who had blessed her life for seven unforgettable years, began to recede, embraced and enveloped by the morning light, leaving behind the precious shadow of her memory, which would live forever.

When at last Angela opened her eyes, the sun had become even brighter, the reflection shimmering across the deep-green body of water. The brilliant rays danced on the whitecaps as they rolled endlessly toward the shore, and Angela, too, was blessed by that promise of warmth and hope and renewal.

NEARING THE STARTING POINT of her run she glanced at her watch; it was still early enough to stop by to see Joyce before she left for her morning classes. She was perspiring and winded, but as she walked down the familiar sidewalks, her breathing began to slow to normal.

Joyce came to the door as soon as Angela rang. She was dressed for work, holding a cup of steaming coffee. The seductive aroma of bacon wafted out onto the morning air.

"Hi!" Joyce greeted her cheerily, pulling the door wide open. "Fancy finding you on my doorstep at this hour."

"I went for a run and decided I had enough time to stop by before I go home and get ready for work myself. Mmm, smells delicious in there."

"Come on in. Have some breakfast."

Angela stepped inside but shook her head. "Oh, no. I don't have that much time. We haven't talked in a couple of days, and curiosity got the better of me. I was just wondering how things are going with—" There was a loud thumping on the staircase behind her, and Angela turned to see Jonathon, dressed in pajamas and bathrobe, taking the stairs in his usual two-at-a-time fashion.

Stunned, Angela opened and closed her mouth twice before anything came out. By that time Jonathon was standing in the foyer next to Joyce.

"Hi, Jonathon," Angela said in a feeble voice.

"Hi, Angie. You're looking the picture of health this morning."

"Uh...thanks." Angela glanced helplessly at Joyce, her eyes begging for an explanation.

Joyce kissed her husband on the cheek, smiling as he slid his arm around her waist. "Isn't it wonderful? He's back. All six feet, three inches of him. My Incredible Hulk."

Angela moved her head slowly from side to side. "Would someone mind telling me what's going on around here?" She glanced at her watch. "And you've got approximately two minutes in which to do so, because I have to get going. No, wait a minute. Just answer two questions, Jonathon. First, when did you get back, and second, are you going to stay."

Jonathon grinned easily. "Well, let's see, I got back at approximately eleven o'clock last night—"

"One-thirty," Joyce countered.

"Make it twelve forty-five, something like that. And yes, I'm here to stay."

Angela's face lit up in a broad smile as she looked at the obviously elated couple. "That's fantastic, Jonathon. But, well, I thought— Never mind, that's none of my business."

But Joyce started to explain. "He's still going to sit out this semester, and—"

"And I'm going to put my nose to the grindstone and get started on my book," Jonathon finished for his wife.

"Your novel?" Angela asked.

"Yes. I've put it off too long already. I've had all the positive feedback one could want, and I finally decided, what the hell, my not obtaining tenure was probably the best blessing in disguise I'll ever get in this life."

Angela knew well enough that even though Jonathon had acquired many nonfiction publishing credits over the years, his real dream was to write a contemporary novel, a goal he'd been pushing aside for later. And later was finally here.

"This is absolutely wonderful news, Jonathon!" Angela told him, noticing the proud expression on Joyce's face.

"We can make it on what Joyce will be earning now," Jonathon went on, "and if I get the urge to, I can always teach a few free-lance courses on a part-time basis." He gave Joyce a hug and winked at her. "Whatever happens, we'll work it out."

"Gosh," Angela said softly, "this just knocks me right off my feet. You two are going to make me cry."

"Nah, it's not that much to get worked up over," Jonathon said.

But it is, Angela thought. *It's the most important decision in your lives, not letting go of the love you've shared and cherished for so long.*

"Please, are you sure you don't have time to stay?" Joyce asked.

"No, I really don't." Angela placed a hand on the doorknob. "I'll give you a call later, though."

"All right."

"And Jonathon," Angela said as she opened the door, "I think you made a terrific decision."

"Yeah, me, too."

Angela hurried back to her house, thinking how wonderfully things had turned out for her friends. Such an ending to a potentially disastrous situation! The test they had undergone had been the "proof of the pudding," so to speak, a demonstration of the real strength of the love that bound their marriage.

Angela wondered if she and Patrick could have withstood such pressures concerning their own careers. The thought made her slow down. What was she thinking? She hadn't even seen or spoken to Patrick in three weeks. The realization sent a shiver of alarm through her, and as she walked in her back door, the happiness she felt for Joyce and Jonathon began to dissipate, overshadowed by a growing sense of dread—perhaps it was too late for her and Patrick. *Please, God, don't let that be true.*

She hesitated inside the door for a mere fraction of a second, then went directly to the telephone. She would call him and call him until he answered, and if that didn't— He answered on the second ring, so that Angela was momentarily taken aback.

"It's me," she blurted out, "Angela."

There was the briefest hesitation, and Angela cringed as it occurred to her that he might not want to talk to her, to ever see her again. "How are you?" he said finally, his tone as pleasant as always.

"Ah...fine I suppose. Look, I know this is really odd, to be calling so early in the morning. I hope you weren't on your way out the door."

"No, as a matter of fact, I'm not going in to the office today."

"You're not?"

"No. It's Thursday. I don't have office patients on Thursday."

"Oh. Yes, that's right."

"I have to make rounds at the hospital, of course, but not until this afternoon."

He was talking to her as if they'd spoken yesterday, as if nothing at all had happened to threaten their relationship. Yet she could hear—or did she just imagine it—wariness in his tone.

"I just called to...." Her voice trailed off uncertainly.

"Yes?"

She drew in a deep breath and let it out with the words, "I had an appointment with Lorena Mayfield."

"I'm glad. Did you like her?"

"Oh, yes, very much. She— Listen, Patrick, is there any way we could talk about this... together?"

She had no inkling of the effect of this conversation on Patrick. His heart soared as she said the very words he'd almost abandoned hope of hearing.

"Of course. Would you like me to come over?"

Angela's mind scrambled for a moment. She wanted to see him this instant—waiting all day would be intolerable. The decision was made in the next instant; she would call Regi and tell him she needed the day off. He could handle the store alone, and after all, she owed this one to herself. In fact, she was long overdue! But still she would be too agitated to sit around and wait for Patrick to drive over here.

"No," she said. "I'll go to your place. I can be there in about an hour and a half."

"Sounds great. See you then."

As she hung up, Angela was seized by a frantic need to get moving. She raced up the stairs, stripping out of her clothes as she got to the bedroom, letting them drop on the floor behind her. She showered thoroughly yet quickly, her flesh tingling beneath the sting of the water. After blow-drying her hair, she curled it lightly, put on a bit of makeup and dressed in khaki slacks and a long-sleeved knit top.

She remembered that she hadn't called Regi yet. He sounded surprised—Angela was rarely impulsive—but said her taking the day off would be all right; he could handle things well enough.

The morning air had lost its crisp edge by the time Angela entered the feeder lane to the freeway. She found it required a conscious effort to ease up on the accelerator. Her spirits soared as she flew down the highway with the window down and the wind rushing through her hair. Music from the stereo was snatched and scattered by the rush of wind. Butterflies fluttered around in her stomach, anxiety and nervousness competing with hope and anticipation. Patrick had sounded willing to see her, but three weeks were three weeks. Things could change in that length of time—a lot of things. Her foot pressed a little more heavily on the gas pedal, and the speedometer crept farther and farther to the right.

HE WAS IN THE GARAGE when she arrived, bent over the engine of the Bronco. Rusty, who was curled up on the garage floor not far from Patrick, barked several times until Angela shut off the engine and opened the car door. When she stepped out of the car the dog trotted over to her, his head bowed a little to accept the familiar stroke between his ears.

"Hi, fella," Angela said affectionately, surprised by the depth of emotion that simple gesture evoked. She knelt down and hugged the dog close to her, unaware that Patrick, who was wiping his oil-stained hands on an old rag, was watching her from the garage.

When she straightened and looked up, her stomach seemed to turn over. She stood rooted to the spot. Patrick, in an old pair of jeans, sneakers and a faded blue tank top, was more captivating than she'd ever seen him in, even in formal clothing.

"Come on inside," Patrick called out to her, tossing the rag down next to several empty cans on the cement.

"Hi," Angela greeted him as she walked into

the garage. She glanced at the opened hood of the Bronco, at the various cans and pans and rags lying around. "What are you doing?"

"Oil change. I just finished."

"You're kidding. You did it all by yourself?"

Patrick gave her a wry look. "Yeah, believe it or not, I did. Are you so amazed that I would be able to handle such a challenging chore?" He wasn't serious; she could hear the gentle teasing in his tone.

Nevertheless she answered somewhat defensively, "No. I just thought you wouldn't have chosen your spare time to work on a car."

He shut the hood of the Bronco and started to clean up. "Actually, there are quite a few weird things I like to do in my spare time. And a lot of them get you dirty."

Wiping his hands on a clean towel lying on the worktable, he turned to her, placing his fists at his waist and letting his gaze run slowly down, then back up the length of her body.

"You look good," he said, the tiniest smile tugging at the corners of his mouth.

No gallantly stated compliment could have produced such an intense reaction. Angela sucked in a small breath of air and smiled tremulously at Patrick. Just standing there in the middle of his garage, she was seized with a longing and desire for him like none she'd ever known before. She wanted to dash across the few feet separating them and throw her arms around him, to feel her cheek against his chest, the tickle of his chest hairs. . . .

Her gaze flickered lower, to his grease-spattered shirt, his tight grubby jeans, and Patrick's own eyes followed. He lifted the cloth away from his chest, which was damp from warmth, humidity and exertion. "Kind of yucky, huh?"

Angela smiled and averted her gaze.

"Tell you what," Patrick said. "I haven't had breakfast yet, and I was going to start a pot of coffee. Are you hungry?"

Angela nodded. "Actually, now that you mention it, I'm starved. I've only had a glass of orange juice, and that was over two hours ago."

"Good. I'll make us both breakfast, then. It's a great day to eat outside."

"Sure is," Angela said as they started for the back door of the house.

She went inside ahead of Patrick, and was surprised when he suddenly took one of her hands in his. She turned, a curious, expectant expression on her face.

"My hands are clean," he said, adding in a lower tone, "and there's not a thing wrong with my mouth."

Angela swallowed. Her eyes remained open as he lowered his head slowly and carefully to hers, his brown eyes warm with welcome and longing. Their kiss was brief yet thorough, and Angela wouldn't have cared one bit if he'd just finished replacing the engine and was covered from head to toe with oil and grease and grime. She wanted him so badly at that moment, she was tempted to grab hold of his shirt and pull him to her. But he took a step back just then, and she closed her eyes briefly and bit her lower lip. Turning, she walked into the kitchen with a lightness of step that belied the nervous tension gripping her.

"Why don't you start the coffee while I make myself a little more decent," Patrick suggested, bending over to untie his sneakers.

Angela nodded. "Sure. I'll look around and see what you have in the fridge and get started on breakfast."

"All right. I won't be long." Once Patrick had left, Angela looked around for a moment, thinking how odd everything here seemed. Odd in the way a place does when you haven't seen it for a while. Yet the room also felt familiar and welcoming and oh so comforting. Like Patrick. He still acted as though they'd seen each other only yesterday. Angela pressed her palm to her chest, just above her breast, and could feel the rapid beat of her heart. *Please,* she prayed silently. *Please let this all be for real. Please let him not have given up on me. Please let me matter to him. As he does to me.*

The sound of the water heater and the faint creaking of the pipes told her Patrick had started his shower, and Angela steeled herself against another onslaught of emotion by opening the refrigerator door and scanning its contents. The rule of this game was one thing at a time.

RUSTY LAY NEAR ANGELA'S FEET as they sat outside on the patio, the breakfast dishes cleared away except for the coffee mugs. Patrick had picked up the paper from the driveway, and they sat browsing through the various sections, occasionally sharing a comment or two about what they were reading.

Angela found it amazing that they were sitting there at all, enjoying each other's company over breakfast as if it were a perfectly normal, everyday routine for them. Neither she nor Patrick had mentioned their separation. He acted as he always had with her—attentive, open...loving. Angela realized it was up to her to make the first move.

She folded the editorial section she'd been pretending to read and set it down on the redwood table. Patrick was engrossed in the sports section, so she waited until he began to turn the next page. When he did she placed her fingers at the top of the page, and he lowered the paper, his expression quizzical.

"Don't tell me you want this section," he teased. "Since when did you become a sports buff?"

Angela grinned at him and leaned back in her chair. "Don't worry, I haven't. I'd like to talk to you."

Patrick's eyes were serious now. "I'm glad. I've wanted us to talk for a long time."

Angela pressed her fingertips together for a second or two, then looked away, fingering the breeze-tossed auburn strands at the side of her neck. "As I told you, I had an appointment with Dr. Mayfield."

Patrick nodded, the newspaper rustling in his lap as he adjusted his position slightly.

Angela cleared her throat and looked at him. "I really liked her. Thank you for the recommendation."

"You're welcome."

"I'm going back to see her next Tuesday. And as many times after that as I feel necessary. The schedule is up to me, she said."

It was hard for Patrick to contain the expression of sheer relief, but he didn't interrupt.

"Anyway," Angela said, clearing her throat a second time, "I just want you to know that I know now you were right and I was wrong."

"Angie, it wasn't a matter of right and wrong," Patrick protested.

"No, you misunderstand me. All I mean is that you were right when you said I needed someone else—someone outside—to help me. And I was wrong to continue to tell myself I could handle the memories alone. Obviously I couldn't."

She stared off into the distance for several moments, finally saying in a very soft tone, "I want to tell you about her, Patrick. About Melissa. I want you to know who she was, what she meant to me. . . ." Angela swallowed and shifted her gaze to

Patrick's. Her eyes were bright and moist, yet she sensed there would be no tears—not this time. "I want you to understand how much I loved her—how much I love her still."

"I know you do," Patrick said gently.

"I'm not. . . really ready yet," Angela said, feeling the conviction of her decision grow stronger as she spoke. "But when I am, I want to know. . . if you'll be there. That you'll be willing to listen, to share. . . ." Her voice trailed off questioningly, uncertainly.

The newspaper fell to the ground as Patrick stood up, the breeze lifting a few pages and tossing them around the patio. Rusty raised his head at the intrusive noise, then settled down again when he saw there was nothing amiss.

Patrick skirted the table and took both Angela's hands in his, urging her to stand up. Her green eyes shimmered with a new light, and as Patrick looked into them, he could see that there had truly been a change in her, a great change. Placing his hands on either side of her face, he pressed his lips to her forehead.

His voice was a mere whisper, though his words were absolutely sincere. "Don't you know how much I want to listen, Angela? Don't you know I realize how much a part of you Melissa was and will always be? Sweetheart, I'll wait forever if it takes that long, and I'll listen to *everything, anything* you want to tell me. And I will be there for you, Angela. I love you. Very, very much."

Angela nodded her understanding, and Patrick placed a gentle kiss on her lips. Then he stepped back and took her by the hand. He said nothing more, but words were no longer a necessary form of communication between them. For as their hearts spoke and understood, so did the passion that would forever be theirs to share and to nurture.

ANGELA LAY ON HER BACK in Patrick's huge bed, one arm behind her head, her gaze focused on the ficus plant at the window. Patrick lay on his side next to her, his head resting in the palm of his hand. With the fingers of his free hand he traced a line down the center of Angela's naked torso, lazily detouring to circle one breast and then the other.

"Think you'll ever get tired of me?" Angela asked suddenly.

Patrick gave a short laugh. "You're nuts, you know that? After what just happened here, how can you ask such a ridiculous question, let alone think it?"

"People get old, you know."

Patrick clucked his tongue. "Such a profound statement. And so what?"

Angela shrugged. "So they can get bored with each other. Things don't always stay the same, or remain as passionate."

"Can I ask you something?"

"What?"

"What the devil brought this on? You've been as silent and mellow as a pampered kitten for the past twenty minutes, and now you're turning all heavy on me."

Angela brought her face close to his. "*You* turned heavy on me, if I recall correctly. Or perhaps I didn't hear you right, Dr. Merrill. Did you or did you not mention the fact that you wanted to marry me?" A teasing smile played around her mouth, but Patrick noted the solemn glint in her eyes.

Slowly he nodded. "Yep."

"'Yep'! Now how serious am I supposed to think you are when you come off sounding like some tobacco-chawin' cowboy?"

Patrick lowered his head so that he could kiss the tip of her nose, and when he drew back there was no hint of teasing in his expression. "You can rest assured that I'm very, very serious, Angela Carruthers. Because I love you, very much, and if you don't know that by now...."

Angela's arm snaked around his neck; he bent over her, his chest flattening the mounds of her breasts. "And you really intend to make an honest woman out of me, huh?" she murmured, her lips nibbling at his.

"You're danged right, woman," Patrick growled.

Angela giggled. "Well, then, cowboy, it wouldn't hurt to demonstrate the seriousness of your intentions." Her arms slipped down around his waist, and Patrick moved his body above hers.

"Why, I'd be much obliged, if I could, ma'am," he drawled lustily. "Much obliged."

Dreamweaver

THE EXCITING NEW BESTSELLER BY THE STAR OF TV's ANOTHER WORLD

FELICIA GALLANT

ᵀᵀᴴ REBECCA FLANDERS

The romance queen of ytime drama has written a passionate tory of two people whose souls exist beneath shimmering images, bound together by the most elemental of all human emotions...love.

RIDE A PAINTED PONY

by BEVERLY SOMMERS
The third
HARLEQUIN AMERICAN ROMANCE
PREMIER EDITION

A prestigious New York City publishing company decides to launch a new historical romance line, led by a woman who must first define what love means.

Available in October or send your name, address and zip or postal code, along with a check or money order for $3.70 (includes 75¢ for postage and handling) payable to Harlequin Reader Service to:

Harlequin Reader Service

In the U.S.	In Canada
Box 52040	5170 Yonge Street
Phoenix, AZ	P.O. Box 2800, Postal Station A,
85072-2040	Willowdale, Ontario M2N 5T5